P9-DOE-841

THE BATTLE OF THE WEREPENGUINS

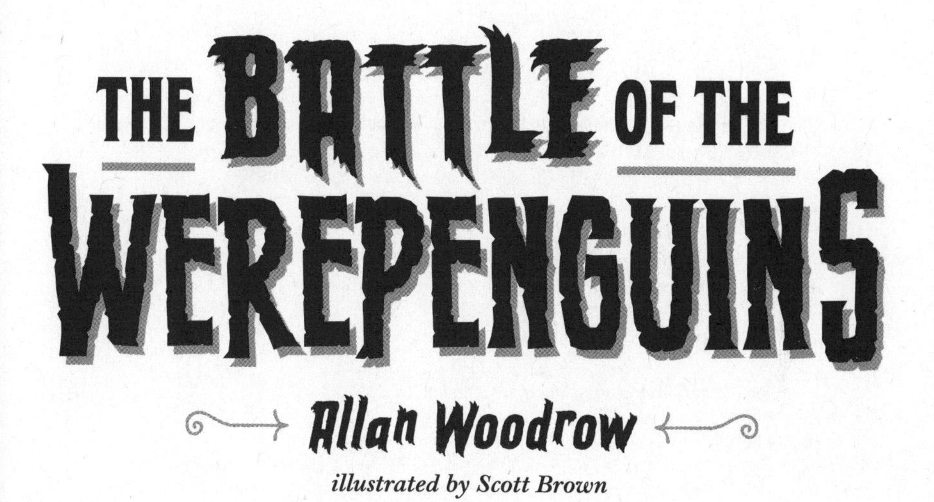
THE BATTLE OF THE
WEREPENGUINS
Allan Woodrow
illustrated by Scott Brown

VIKING

VIKING
An imprint of Penguin Random House LLC, New York

First published in the United States of America by Viking,
an imprint of Penguin Random House LLC, 2021

Visit us online at penguinrandomhouse.com.

LIBRARY OF CONGRESS CATALOGING-IN-PUBLICATION DATA
Names: Woodrow, Allan, author. | Brown, Scott (Illustrator)
Title: The battle of the werepenguins / Allan Woodrow ; illustrated by Scott Brown.
Description: New York : Viking, 2021. | Series: Werepenguin | Audience: Ages 8–12. | Audience: Grades 4–6. | Summary: After receiving a clue from Omneseus the Seer, twelve-year-old werepenguin Bolt and his friends Blackburn and Annika set off to defeat "the Stranger" and free the world's penguins from his reign.
Identifiers: LCCN 2021021649 (print) | LCCN 2021021650 (ebook) | ISBN 9780593114261 (hardcover) | ISBN 9780593114285 (ebook)
Subjects: CYAC: Penguins—Fiction. | Shapeshifting—Fiction. | Good and evil—Fiction. | Adventure and adventurers—Fiction. | Humorous stories.
Classification: LCC PZ7.W86047 Bat 2021 (print) | LCC PZ7.W86047 (ebook) | DDC [Fic]—dc23
LC record available at https://lccn.loc.gov/2021021649
LC ebook record available at https://lccn.loc.gov/2021021650

Printed in the United States of America

10 9 8 7 6 5 4 3 2 1

SKY

Set in Bell MT Std Book design by Kate Renner & Lucia Baez

To the not-so-gentle reader,

for while books are often written for "the gentle reader,"

I encourage you to read ferociously. —A.W.

For Michael McDougall,

thank you for always rooting for me, Captain. —S.B.

“Penguins, penguins! They are everywhere and oh, they are magnificent.” —Amundsen

CONTENTS

PART TWO
The Tundra

Prologue: The Docks

As the crew loaded large wooden crates and smaller iron cages onto the steamship, the misty salt water tickled my ears. Ear-tickling is very annoying, so I cursed the ocean spray. Rattling chains and hydraulic hums echoed across the pier, along with the grunting of apes, the whoops of flamingos, the roars of lions, and the shrieks of a dock-worker who forgot to close the crate of roaring lions before loading it onto the ship.

But, despite the menagerie of yips and yaps, the penguins were silent. I watched as their crate was lifted with ropes that were attached to a large crane, to be loaded onto the ship. Their crate had a window, and I could see the penguins lounging on their pillows, watching a show on the big-screen TV I had thoughtfully placed inside for their amusement. Penguins love soap operas.

"Be careful!" shouted the penguin caretaker as the crate swung from the crane. The man—short, balding, and roundish with a long, thin nose—wore a long black overcoat with a white shirt underneath. It was the same outfit he had worn every time I had seen him, an outfit that made him look, if you squinted, eerily similar to the birds he cared for.

"Relax, my friend." I clapped the man on the back, and he jumped. He was jittery. Anxious. "Your penguins will be fine," I said in my most soothing voice. "After all, penguins don't get seasick. It's the giraffes I worry about." There are few things worse, or harder to clean up after, than a seasick giraffe. "We should be at the zoo within the week. There, the animals will find happiness. I hope."

"It was kind of you to offer them a new home," said the man. He choked up; his gratefulness was genuine.

"We had a deal," I reminded him. "You tell me your tale, all of it, and I give the animals a new beginning."

"Although perhaps you wish I had never begun to tell you my story at all?"

"Perhaps." My evenings had been filled with nightmares since my first visit to this zoo. So, why was I here? Why return to hear the rest of a story that had turned my hair white, my face wrinkly, and my stomach perpetually queasy?

Because perhaps after the story ended, my nightmares would cease and my stomach would un-quease itself. I could only pray they might.

But, upon my return just the other day, I discovered the St. Aves Zoo had been torn down, a result of accidents and circumstances that involved an iceberg and a clumsy cow. I was the animal procurer for a new zoo, a great zoo, and so I struck my bargain: a home for the now homeless animals if the man told me the rest of his story.

To be honest, the zoo already had plenty of giraffes and apes and dung beetles—and really, how many dung beetles does one zoo need?—but to hear the conclusion of this man's tale, I would have accepted a thousand dung beetles. Fortunately, he only had twenty-eight of them.

But our deal was not entirely one-sided. For my zoo would also now feature the St. Aves Zoo penguins—the most celebrated penguins in the world. I pinched my arm to make sure I wasn't dreaming. "Ow!" I howled, wishing I hadn't pinched so overzealously.

I turned to my companion, who was still watching the penguin crate, which now lay quietly on the ship, snuggled between the opossum cage and possum cage, although I wasn't sure which was which. The loading of the rest of the cages and crates would take hours. As we stood on deck I figured this was a good time to collect the rest of

my payment. "Your story is not yet finished," I reminded the penguin caretaker.

"Are stories ever finished?" he asked. "For even as one story ends, another begins. The world continues to spin, lives continue to be lived, penguins continue to waddle."

"And storytellers continue to delay ending them."

The man smiled and sighed. "Very well. Where did I leave off?"

"Bolt and his companions, the bandit Annika and the fearless pirate Blackburn, had set sail for the island of Omnescia. Bolt needed to speak to the great seer Omneseus in hopes of discovering how to defeat the Stranger, the most powerful werepenguin of them all."

The man nodded, his long, thin nose flapping against the bitter winds blowing across the deck. "Yes, they were happy then, sort of. Happyish. All was well, for the moment. But Bolt and his friends would soon discover their happiness was as fleeting as a feather in the wind. As the caretaker for penguins, I know how fleeting feathers in the wind can be."

Coincidentally a feather, perhaps from an ostrich, floated under my nose. My sneeze was so loud it woke a sleeping hippo nearby, and you never want to wake a sleeping hippo. The hippo grunted, thumped its feet, and overturned the snow cone machine in its cage. A shame.

Hippos love snow cones, and I hadn't brought another machine as a backup.

The caretaker waited for the hippo grunts to quiet before continuing. "Our three heroes arrived the very next day. Bolt made the trek up the Omnescian mountains to speak to the great seer. That is where we will continue our story. That is, if you are certain you want to hear its conclusion."

"I am. I must." I wrung my hands with excited nervousness. "For once you let the cat out of the bag, it can never go back in."

"I hope you're mistaken by that," said the man as a pride of escaped lions ran across the deck below us, chasing a dozen screaming dockworkers.

PART ONE
Pingvingrad

Humboldt Wattle—although everyone simply called him Bolt—sat on the frozen ground in a dimly lit cave high up in a mountain on the island of Omnescia. Despite the cold, he wore just a simple white T-shirt and a pair of ratty gray sweatpants. Strapped across his shoulders was a unicorn-and-rainbow backpack that held two more white T-shirts and two more pairs of ratty gray sweatpants. It also held some dead fish in case Bolt got hungry.

A small campfire crackled. On the other side of the flames sat a bald man in a tunic and cheap plastic glasses. Black spirals were painted on the lenses, which made the man look strangely mysterious, or maybe mysteriously strange. This was the great seer, Omneseus.

Closing his eyes, Bolt thought back to a week earlier, when he had sat in this exact same cave. Then, the seer had told Bolt how to defeat the Earl, the ruler of the city of Sphen and a werepenguin. Bolt had to scale a mountain to get an egg so he could defeat the Earl, who was then eaten by his newborn son. You sort of had to be there.

Omneseus raised his arms, his powerful voice echoing through the bowels of the cave. "Welcome, Bolt. You are back, just like I foretold. For I see all!" He waved his fingers above his head as if casting a spell. "I see a band of bunnies about to eat dinner. I see a girl eagerly picking wax from her ears. I see a little silhouetto of a man!"

Bolt nodded. The seer did see all, but a lot of what he saw tended to be somewhat random. "I'm here to—"

The seer held up his finger to quiet Bolt. "Oh, I know why you are here. I can see it as plainly as I see the nose on your face! There!" He pointed four feet to Bolt's left.

"Um, my nose and I are over here," said Bolt, waving.

The seer blinked a few times. "Right. Sorry. I can barely see anything while wearing my strangely mysterious X-ray glasses. Or maybe they're mysteriously strange." He removed his glasses and blinked a few times. "Ah, better." He cackled.

"Can you please not cackle? It sounds evil and spooky, and there's nothing particularly funny," Bolt said.

Fortune-tellers and seers cackled all the time, which was annoying and a little scary.

Omneseus cackled one more time anyway. "I know why you are here. Yes! You are here for . . ." The man jumped up and held out his hand. "You are here for salmon-flavored corn chips!" He held up a bag of corn chips.

"Actually, I'm here for a totally different reason. But, well, I guess I'm sort of hungry." Bolt stood up and reached across the fire to grab a handful of fish-flavored snacks. They were delicious.

"You are also here to learn how to find and defeat the Stranger, aren't you? He is the mightiest of your kind. The father of all werepenguins in the world."

As the seer spoke, Bolt switched from chewing chips to chewing his lips with fright.

"You shouldn't bite your lips," said the seer. "It's a bad habit."

"Sorry," said Bolt, picking his nose.

"Tell me, Bolt. Are you up to the task of stopping the Stranger?"

Every penguin in the world had a slim coating of evilness inside them, implanted by the Stranger. That coating made them cruel and vicious. But if Bolt could stop the Stranger, he would free the penguins from that hate. The world's penguins would once again be happy,

kind creatures. “I’m ready—at least I think I am.”

“You think?” the seer demanded. “You must know! Do not doubt, or you will no doubt lose!” Bolt gulped. “The Stranger does not doubt. He lives in the South Pole under a great magical moon where he is invincible. And immortal. Unless.”

“Unless what?” Bolt was glad to hear that there was an *unless.*

“I will sing you a chant.” The seer sat back down and closed his eyes. He lifted his palms and began to softly hum.

Bolt groaned. Seers gave advice coded inside cryptic, confusing songs just as often as they cackled. Bolt had figured out the meaning of other chants he had been given, but he would have much preferred simple printed directions.

Still, he waited politely as the seer chanted, slowly and off-key:

Discover your code—and embrace it you must.
Turn away the bloodlust. It’s love you must trust.
The hunger inside, it’s so strong and so real!
Its threat you’ll repeal with the tooth of a seal.
But you won’t win unless you take this advice—
Born from love may entice, but a bite’s twice as nice.

Bolt's hair stood up in the shape of two horns, and he pulled them in frustration. "What does that mean?"

The seer shrugged. "How should I know? I'm a seer, not a translator."

Frustrated, Bolt continued pulling his hair until he accidentally yanked three strands out. He knew the chant was important. The fate of the world could be hidden inside its confusing lyrics.

"I might not know much of the chant's meaning," the seer continued, "but I can guess some of it. Have you heard of the Ilversay Oothtay Ealsay?"

"The Silver Tooth Seal?" asked Bolt, who was quite good at pig latin. He recalled a line from the chant: *Its threat you'll repeal with the tooth of a seal.*

"The beast lived high in the polar mountains long ago. It was twenty feet long and devoured penguins as if they were Pez candies from a dispenser. Speaking of which—" He pulled a small Pez dispenser from his tunic. The dispenser was the shape of a moose. "Want a candy?"

"No thanks."

"Good call. I've had this dispenser in my pocket for decades." The seer sniffed the dispenser, winced, and then tossed it into the fire. "Anyway, what made the Ealsay especially terrible was its tooth, a single tooth made of pure silver. And as you know, werepenguins hate silver."

"They do? I don't hate silver." Bolt didn't have any feelings at all about silver or, for that matter, any metal.

"Well, most do. Maybe it's because silver clashes with their orange beaks. Anyway, the ancient scrolls say that this tooth, and this tooth alone, can slay even the mightiest werepenguin."

"How ancient are these scrolls?"

"Even older than my Pez candies. According to the

scrolls, if you stab the Stranger with the Ealsay's silver tooth, his reign will end forever."

Bolt squirmed. He didn't want to plunge a tooth into the Stranger, or anyone. All werepenguins were naturally evil, and Bolt constantly battled his own yearnings to rule and destroy things. As a result, he had vowed never to kill, no matter what. Killing might be just what it took to push him into the eternal darkness of werepenguin wickedness.

But he'd worry about that after he got the tooth. "You said the creature lived long ago?"

"Yes, but its silver tooth survives. It is guarded by a group of whale dentists. You know of PEWD?"

"Pooed?"

"No, *P-E-W-D*. The Pingvingrad Establishment of Whale Dentistry. They keep the tooth in their heavily guarded island fortress."

"You're kidding, right?"

"I'm not much of a kidder. The head of the institution is a werepenguin. Her name is Dr. Helga Walzanarz."

"Gesundheit."

Bolt bit his lips again; they were getting quite chapped. The world was depending on him, and now he had to face another werepenguin to get a tooth so he could fight another werepenguin? He groaned from the weight of it all.

"Do not groan!" said the seer. "I see darkness, but I also see hope. I see cities filled with laughter. I see dogs

hugging cats. I see the entire world holding hands and singing with joy."

"Do you really see those things?"

Omneseus shrugged. "Maybe I embellish a little." The seer stood up, stepped around the fire, and rested his hand on Bolt's shoulder. "Have faith, Bolt. I see a light at the end of your dark tunnel."

Bolt perked up, a smile threatening to spread onto his lips. "So, you're saying I'll win?"

"No, I said you will walk through a dark tunnel. Pay attention." Bolt no longer felt like smiling. "But let me ask you a question. Does the Stranger talk to you?"

"I've never even met him."

"Yes, but does his voice echo in your head? Do you feel his voice crawling inside you, whispering, cajoling, enticing you to join him in his evilness?"

"Of course not," said Bolt.

"Good," said the seer. "Let us hope it never does. That would make fighting him much more difficult. Now, go. You have the power of a werepenguin in your blood, Bolt. It is what connects you to the universal power of the penguin-verse. You must learn how to use it. It is your only chance!"

"Back up a second. The penguin-verse?"

"Yes! The penguin-verse is what binds you to all penguins! To win, you must harness its infinite strength!"

"How do I do that?"

The seer patted Bolt on his head. "I've got no idea. But you'll figure it out, at least I hope so, or everyone in the world is doomed."

The seer snapped his fingers, and a cloud of smoke enveloped him. The smoke cleared, and the seer had vanished. It was a very cool way to exit a room.

"Great. No pressure," Bolt mumbled to himself.

As Bolt turned to walk out of the cave, the seer's words lingered in his head, filling it with worry, dread, and a million other emotions, all bad. The penguin-verse? Another dangerous quest? But one thought loomed larger than the rest: *Does the Stranger talk to you?*

Bolt had said the Stranger didn't. He wasn't sure why he had lied about that.

2. Happyish Together

It had been midmorning when Bolt first climbed the mountain to visit the seer, and it was early evening by the time he climbed back down. Quad, one of the seer's disciples, was there to greet him. Like all the Omnescians, Quad was bald and wore a white tunic. But he was fairly easy to spot because he stood on stilts.

The disciple peered down at Bolt. "Welcome back. Did the seer give you what you came for?" Bolt nodded. "I think I can guess what you discussed." Quad closed his eyes and rested his long fingers on Bolt's head, softly rubbing up and down. The man was studying to become a seer himself one day, although his predictions were never accurate. "Ah, yes. I see a banjo and a glass of milk." He pressed his fingers harder on Bolt's head, digging in with more force. It was quite uncomfortable, really. "Ah! Ah! You wish to strum! And, and . . . sing songs about skim milk." He opened his eyes and smiled excitedly. "How did I do?"

"You weren't even close."

The man kicked the dirt with one of his stilts. "Drat. I also saw something about a whale dentist, but the banjo thing seemed much more likely."

"Well, keep trying," said Bolt encouragingly. He waved goodbye and then continued walking until he reached the sandy beaches of Omnescia. There, he saw his friends engaged in a duel on the shore. Blackburn swung his swordfish, a mighty serrated blade. It whistled in the wind. Annika held only a tree branch, and while she lacked both the weaponry and the sword skills of her older, more experienced adversary, she made up for it with speed and quickness. She leapt over the pirate's swing, ducked under a thrust, and rolled under a jab. She then popped up and poked him in the gut with the end of her stick.

"Bah. Yer a difficult one to fight, missy," said the pirate, scowling. "Who can keep up with all that leapin', duckin', and rollin'? Borscht!" Blackburn often cried out *Borscht!* It was his calling card, as were the thick, plush sideburns that covered half his cheeks. "Stay still, missy!" the pirate bellowed.

He swung his swordfish again, but Annika had already

leapt, ducked, and rolled away, the bobby pins in her long blonde hair clattering together. "If I stay still, you'll hit me," she pointed out. "And. Don't. Call. Me. Missy." She knocked the tricorn hat off Blackburn's head with a quick swing of her branch. Bolt was impressed. She had learned a lot about dueling in a very short time.

The pirate sputtered curses as he picked up his hat. As he did, Annika noticed Bolt watching them. "You're back!" She dropped her branch and hurried over to her friend. "So? Did the seer give you a secret weapon? Did he tell you how to find the Stranger? Or did he just sing a confusing chant?"

"He sang a confusing chant," said Bolt, frowning. "And we have a mission. We have to steal a silver seal tooth from a bunch of dentists."

"Wait. Really?" Annika studied Bolt, as if waiting for the punch line.

"Borscht!" said the pirate, joining them. "That sounds like the tooth of the Ilversay Oothtay Ealsay." When Bolt shot the pirate a surprised glance, Blackburn added, "All pirates know of the Ealsay. But I thought the creature was a myth, like goblins and witches and were-creatures." Bolt cleared his throat and pointed to himself. "Sorry, matey. I mean like goblins and witches and *unlike* were-creatures."

Bolt explained the entire mission to his friends, including the part about the werepenguin.

"Another one? How many werepenguins are there in the world, anyway?" Annika asked.

"To become a werepenguin you need to be born with a penguin-shaped birthmark like mine," said Bolt, "and be bitten by another werepenguin under a full moon after midnight, so probably not many." Bolt could tell from the shocked looks on his friends' faces, they were as unhappy about the whole task as he was.

"We've defeated werepenguins before. We'll just have to do it again," said Annika bravely. Bolt appreciated her confidence. It almost made him feel brave himself. "Right, Blackburn?"

The pirate said nothing.

"I said *right*?" Annika repeated.

Blackburn squirmed.

"Um, you're squirming," Annika pointed out.

"Aye," agreed the pirate, who continued to squirm. "It's just that, well, ye know, I'm a pirate. We fight for profit. But where's the profit in fightin' another werepenguin?"

"This isn't about treasure. It's about saving the world," said Bolt.

Blackburn shrugged. "What do I care about savin' the anything?"

"Stop it," said Annika, waving her hand away as if his arguments were as silly as giving a snow cone machine to a hippopotamus. "You can't be serious."

"Do I look serious?" asked Blackburn.

The pirate narrowed his eyes and puckered his lips. Bolt had to admit, he looked quite serious.

The pirate removed a small handbook from his breast pocket and waved it in the air. A knife hole remained in the leather cover from where it had been stabbed a few weeks earlier, saving his life but marring the book. "This is me Pirate Handbook, as ye know. We pirates live by this book. And there is nothin' in here about savin' the world."

"As you know, I also have my own handbook: The Code of the Bandit," said Annika, removing a thick book from a pocket in her shirt. It didn't have a knife hole, but otherwise it was in way worse shape than Blackburn's book, frayed at the edges and covered with creases. "But I've learned you can't live your life following a code someone else wrote. You have to make your own path. Write your own book. And sometimes that book says to fight for your friends and the world, even if there's no treasure in it." She flashed Bolt a smile, and Bolt smiled right back.

"Bah," said Blackburn, who did not join their smiling. "Pirates seek adventure for gold. Rubies. The latest video games."

"But what about fighting for friendship?" Annika asked.

"That's not good enough, I'm afraid. Ye can't spend treasure if ye are some werepenguin's dinner. Borscht!"

Annika looked angry, her face turning red, but Bolt merely sighed. When she and Bolt first met Blackburn, back in Sphen, the pirate said he would only help them if he received treasure in return. Bolt thought Blackburn had changed. Maybe not.

Annika put her hands on her hips, but she looked more sad than angry. Her eyes misted. Bolt knew she had grown close to Blackburn; his reluctance to fight with them obviously hurt her. "Fine. If it's treasure you want, it's treasure you'll get," she said, spitting. "Fight with us, and I'll get you a chest of diamonds and another chest of video games. I promise. And a bandit always keeps her word, at least usually."

"Where will ye get a treasure chest?" the pirate asked.

"Last time we fought together I got you your ship back, didn't I? You'll just have to trust that I can get your treasure."

Bolt shook his head. After they had defeated the Earl of Sphen, Blackburn had gotten his old pirate ship back, that was true. But Annika didn't have any chests of treasure to give away, and Bolt doubted she could get any. Still, Blackburn stared at Annika and appeared to be mulling over his options. He could decline to join them. If he did, it would be the same as calling Annika a liar. Or he could agree to go on the adventure even if he knew Annika *was* lying. Sure, bandits kept their word, usually—just as

Annika had said. But *usually* was not the same as *always.*

"Very well," said the pirate. "I will help ye. But I won't promise me help beyond gettin' this tooth. And when we get that tooth, I get me treasure chests. Deal, missy?"

"As long as you don't call me *missy*"—Annika put her hand out, and Blackburn gave it a firm shake—"we have a deal." After everything was settled, they all headed toward the pirate ship, the *Bobbing Borscht.*

As he walked, Bolt was relieved. Their chances of getting the tooth were much higher with Blackburn's help. And then, after they succeeded, perhaps Blackburn would change his mind and accompany them to the South Pole. They needed him, although Bolt couldn't really blame the pirate for his reluctance—he was right: you can't spend treasure if you're a werepenguin's meal.

Bolt hoped they weren't walking straight onto a dinner plate.

The *Bobbing Borscht* sliced through the calm sea. It was a beautiful craft, from its tall, billowing sails to the mahogany wood lining the deck. The ship barely rocked, which was fortunate for Annika, as she was prone to getting seasick.

Blackburn was an expert navigator. "Follow the stars and the constellations," he said. "The Big Dipper leads to the North Star. The constellation Orion the Hunter sets in the west and rises in the east. And the mighty wing of Pepe the Penguin points to the south, and that is the direction of Pingvingrad, according to me pirate maps. The maps are old, mind ye, but accurate."

"How old are they?" asked Annika.

"As old as these candies I have in me pocket," answered

the pirate, removing a moose-shaped Pez dispenser from his breeches.

"But it's daytime," Bolt said, looking up at the sky. "If you can't see any of the constellations, how can you follow them?"

"We pirates have excellent memories for that sort of thing. We know the constellations like the backs of our hands." Blackburn held up a hand.

"That's the back of my hand," complained Annika, yanking it away from Blackburn's grasp.

"Right, sorry," mumbled the pirate. "And now that I think of it, we're heading the wrong way."

Blackburn rushed back to the wheel to steer, while Annika and Bolt went to the prow. Omneseus had instructed Bolt to embrace his penguin-ism. Use it. Bolt wasn't quite sure how to do that, but he had some ideas. Annika agreed to help him, although she was skeptical of the seer's advice. She rested her practice sword on the ground as she tied a blindfold over Bolt's eyes. "The penguin-verse?" she asked.

"Yes. Omneseus said it is all around us."

"That's sort of disturbing."

"All penguins are united with a universal energy." Bolt could feel it sometimes. If he could tap into that power, who knew what he could do? Maybe he would have extra sharp penguin senses. Maybe he could control

time and space. Or maybe he would just start waddling more.

He wouldn't know unless he tried something.

"Are you ready?" Bolt asked. In his left hand, he held a dead, limp fish.

"I guess so," said Annika. "But why did the seer tell you to fight blindfolded with a dead fish?"

"Well, that was my own idea, actually. I don't need mighty weapons—at least I don't think I do."

"The whole thing sounds like a farce to me."

"Let the farce be with you," said Bolt, bowing his head.

"I don't even know what that means."

Bolt wasn't nearly as confident as he pretended to be. Fighting Annika with a fish? But something about it seemed right to him. He couldn't explain it. It was a leap of faith, but Bolt needed all the faith he could get, and plenty of leaps. He just needed to focus and see the universal aura of penguins.

Unfortunately, the only thing Bolt saw was the blackness of a blindfold. He took a step backward. He could hear her practice sword swooshing in the air as Annika stepped toward him. This was going to hurt.

No.

Wait.

Maybe he couldn't *see* Annika, but it was like his other senses, those of hearing and smell, had awakened

from some dormant sleep. He could hear her back creak. He could smell behind Annika's ears, although he wished he couldn't. He felt the air parting as her weapon sliced through it, and he hopped backward, out of the way. Easy. He sensed her countermove, an upward thrust aimed at his shoulder. He held up his fish to block the blow.

Annika's stick banged against Bolt's knee. He fell to the ground, holding his leg, yelping. "That hurt!"

"Oh, quit complaining. I barely touched you."

Bolt slipped off his blindfold to make sure he wasn't bleeding. He wasn't. "Let's go again."

"This is silly," said Annika.

"I must learn to harness my power."

Annika took a deep breath and frowned as Bolt hobbled up on his feet. "How about if I fight you with a bobby pin instead?" She removed one of the pins from her hair. "If you can stop this, we'll try the stick next."

Bolt knew that, in general, a bobby pin made a terrible weapon. Still, maybe it would be a good place to start. Baby steps. Bolt held out his arms and bent his leg—the one that didn't hurt from being thwacked by Annika—in a sort of martial arts stance that felt fighter-like. He slipped the blindfold back into place.

The air around him churned with penguin energy. Each of Annika's movements disturbed that energy, like ripples in the water. But Bolt was powerful! He was one

with the penguin cosmos, or something like that. He sidestepped, and his foot hit the edge of the boat, but he steadied himself as Annika feinted to the left and jabbed with her right. He raised his arm to block her.

"Ow!" The bobby pin jabbed his shoulder. "I thought you were feinting to the left and jabbing with your right," Bolt complained, yanking off the blindfold.

"No, I feinted to the right and jabbed with my left. But you were close, I guess."

Bolt rubbed his shoulder and winced. "I think, for a split second, I felt some kind of penguin energy."

"The split second when I was jabbing you with a bobby pin? Or the split second when you almost tripped?" Annika tossed him her "weapon." "Why don't you take this and practice picking locks instead? I don't think you're quite ready for the penguin nurse, or whatever it is." The boat hit a large wave, and the boat rocked back and forth. Water spilled onto the deck. "While you practice your mind-stuff," said Annika, "I'm going to stand over the railing and get sick."

Which she did.

4. The Friendship Code

Late that night, Annika sat at a desk in her cabin. The ship held a few rooms belowdecks, including some large enough to hold ten men. Many years before, the *Bobbing Borscht* had sailed the seas with a full crew who explored islands, stole riches from merchant ships, and engaged in long swashbuckling battles. Annika would have loved participating in exciting feats like those, as long as they all happened on land. The sea was not for her, or her stomach.

But the sea was calm for now, thankfully.

Blackburn remained on deck, navigating. Annika could hear Bolt in the cabin next to her, moaning and shrieking. He was having another nightmare; Annika had grown used to his nighttime yelps. She worried about him. He wasn't a natural-born fighter, like Annika was. And this whole penguin-verse talk? She didn't believe in spiritual, superstitious nonsense like that.

At least the moon was merely half full in the sky, so Bolt wouldn't be turning into a werepenguin, as he did under the full moon. In some magical places, the moon was full every night. Bolt said that he suspected Pingvingrad was one of those places. Cities under magical full moons tended to attract were-creatures.

Annika held a quill and had both the Code of the Bandit and a blank piece of parchment in front of her. Annika would have preferred writing with a pencil, but all she had was this quill. She dipped it into an ink jar and then crossed out a section of the bandit code. Next, she wrote an addendum on the blank parchment paper.

THE CODE OF THE BANDIT, CHAPTER 87, SUBSECTION 14

ON FRIENDSHIP

~~No friends! A forest bandit must never make friends with anyone outside of his bandit clan. Why is this so important? First, bandits have to be mean and scary, and there's nothing mean and scary about having friends. But, most of all, it's because a bandit must only be loyal to his clan,~~

~~and friendship outside the clan could lead to complicated choices. Let's say you are supposed to rob a carriage one night, but a friend calls asking if you want to grab a pizza. You ask yourself: "What do I do?" If you didn't have a non-bandit friend, you wouldn't have to ask yourself anything. You would just rob the carriage. But because you had a friend, by the time you asked yourself what you should do, and made up your mind, the carriage would have driven away and the pizza place would have closed for the evening.~~

~~Here's another example: let's say you had a non-bandit friend who was about to be eaten by a giant bullfrog. Across the street, one of your fellow forest bandits sneezes. Should you rescue your friend, or give the bandit a handkerchief? Of course, you give the bandit your handkerchief, because you shouldn't even have a non-bandit friend. Then, get as far away as possible. I mean, really? A giant bullfrog? How would you even fight that thing? Run!~~

THE CODE OF THE BANDIT, CHAPTER 87, SUBSECTION 14

ON FRIENDSHIP—*amended by Annika Lambda*

Hey, I've got nothing against being friends with your fellow forest bandits. Of course that's important! But it's also important to have as many friends as you can, and friends come in all shapes and sizes and kinds.

I mean, my best friends are a werepenguin and a pirate. Who would have thought that would happen?

Friends, even non-bandit friends, make you feel better when you're sad, and make you happier when you are happy. They give you a hand up when you are down, a smile when you feel blue, and can make you un-lonely when you are feeling alone. I know bandits are mean and scary, and we have to be mean and scary to rob and kidnap, but we can be mean and scary and friendly, too.

I know that if your non-bandit friend really needs your help, and so does a bandit, you could be torn about who to help. But if you ask me, I'd rather have as many friends as possible and figure out the other things as I go. And I don't need to be promised a treasure to help them either, unlike some people.

Also, if a giant bullfrog attacked my friend and another bandit sneezed? The bandit can wipe his own nose, thank you very much—I'm saving my friend. Maybe we should add a section about always carrying your own handkerchief. That would make a lot more sense than telling us we should let someone be eaten by a giant bullfrog.

Annika Lambda

Annika folded the piece of parchment and slipped it into the Code of the Bandit. The spine of her book was threadbare, so she had to be careful.

She put the book under her pillow so no one else would find it. The Code of the Bandit could only be read by bandits. While she wanted to change parts of the bandit code, she didn't dare break section 14, which read:

> Never let any non-bandit read your copy of the Code of the Bandit. Cross your heart, hope to die, stick a needle in your eye—the needle penetrating the iris and into the vitreous humor, but not so far as to damage the optic nerve.

The bandit code could be very descriptive.

Annika's father didn't agree that the Code of the Bandit needed updating, just like he hadn't understood her insistence that she travel with Bolt to help him stop the

Stranger and save the world. "Your responsibility lies with us," he had said. "Why did you give your word to help that werepenguin boy anyway?"

"He's my friend, Papa."

"Bandits don't have non-bandit friends!" snapped her father.

"We should! Besides, that werepenguin boy, as you call him, has saved us. Twice. First he freed Brugaria, and then he freed you from the Earl's cage. We are in his debt. And bandits should *always* pay their debts."

Her father couldn't argue with that. Repaying debts was in the Code of the Bandit, section 44. Annika would not be rewriting that section either.

Although it was late, Annika didn't feel tired. Her writing had energized her. So she opened the door to her cabin and walked up the steps to the main deck. Outside, the half-moon failed to make much of a dent in the darkness. She looked up and tried to find the constellation Pepe, but didn't see any discernable shapes, just a random collection of stars—hundreds of them, like freckles in the sky.

"Yer up late." Blackburn sat next to the steering wheel, drinking from a large leather canteen. A brown syrupy liquid dribbled down his cheeks.

"So are you."

"Aye, and probably for the same reason ye are." Annika

raised her eyebrows. "Ye were wondering if dogs and cats are ever allergic to one another, aye?"

"Actually, I was thinking about my father and the Code of the Bandit." Annika sat down next to Blackburn. "But I have wondered about dogs and cats before. How much longer to Pingvingrad?"

Blackburn belched. "Hard to say. But we'll keep following the stars. Shouldn't be more than a day more, I reckon. Right now we're somewhere in the middle of the Blackest-Deadest Sea."

"I've heard of the Black Sea, the Dead Sea, the Blacker Sea, and the Deader Sea."

"This sea is the blackest and deadest of them all."

The ship hit a small wave, and Annika's stomach gurgled. She hated feeling so sick. She was a bandit—the greatest bandit in the world, or at least she would be someday, after a little seasoning—and bandits were tough. Being seasick wasn't tough, it was weak.

"I haven't been in these parts since I was a lad, ye know," said the pirate, yawning, stretching, and taking another sip of his brownish syrup. "Aye, those were the days! Reminds me of me youth as an up-and-comin' buccaneer. Have I ever told ye how I became a pirate, missy?"

Annika managed to spit out, "Don't call me missy," before taking in a big breath to ease her shaky stomach.

"Back then, it was me job to wax the gangplanks," continued the pirate. "The trick was to not over-wax them, or they'd be too slippery. Can ye think of anything worse than bein' forced to walk the plank and into crocodile-infested waters, but slippin' off instead?"

Annika could think of many things worse, such as having to walk the plank into crocodile-infested waters in the first place. But she was too busy feeling sick to answer.

"Then one day our ship was attacked by another pirate crew wantin' our treasures," Blackburn continued. "The invaders fired their cannons and tried to board our vessel by scamperin' over our gangplanks. But I figured that's what they'd do, so I had over-waxed the planks! The invaders slipped right off them and into the sea. They had not expected that!" Blackburn pumped his fist with glee. "The captain was so grateful he named me assistant captain on the spot, and then was so impressed with me skillful *Borscht* that he retired, and I became captain that very evening. Borscht!"

"That's a great story!" exclaimed Annika.

Blackburn smiled and nodded. "Aye. Life was simpler then, before treasures and werepenguins and such."

At the mention of *treasures* Annika bristled. "Don't worry. You'll get yours. I made a promise." She scowled. "I know it's all you care about."

"I also care about not being killed by monsters. I've

been thinkin' of settling down, ye know. I'm not the pirate I once was." He straightened his tricorn hat, which had slipped to the side. "I'm no spring chicken. I'm not even a summer chicken, for that matter. See, even me cap is saggin'." He primped up his tricorn hat.

Another large wave crashed against the boat, rocking it back and forth. Annika's stomach rocked back and forth with it. She felt the food in her stomach sloshing around.

Blackburn held out his canteen. "Here. Have some grog. It'll calm yer belly."

Annika accepted the canteen, smelled the brown murky liquid, and made a face. "It smells like turkey juice, honey, bananas, and liniment oil. What's in it?"

"Turkey juice, honey, bananas, and liniment oil. But no one drinks it for the taste. Grog makes ye groggy. It can be hard to sleep on the sea." He gave a deep yawn and rubbed his eyes.

Annika put the canteen to her lips. She chugged it, hoping that if she downed the drink quickly, it wouldn't taste as terrible as she feared.

Actually, it tasted worse. But she immediately fell asleep.

5. The Power Inside

Bolt awoke early the next morning. He had dreams—bad dreams, as he often did—although he couldn't remember much about them. He mostly remembered the voices speaking to him:

We will be together, you and I!

Werepenguins were meant to rule!

Can you roll over so your left arm doesn't fall asleep?

Some of the voices were more alarming than others.

Mostly, the voices made Bolt want to raise a penguin army, or watch penguins poke one another in the eye. And then he'd wake up, shivering at the thought of those horrible yearnings, recoiling at the evil swirling inside his brain.

Fortunately, they were just dreams. Or so he told himself.

Bolt was the first one awake on the ship; he went upstairs, and the deck was deserted. He welcomed the quiet. It would allow him the chance to hone his penguin skills.

Standing near the railing of the ship, eyes closed, Bolt focused his thoughts over the water. He tried to sense penguins, or something remotely penguin-like. Penguins have an energy about them, like radio waves, and it's all about tuning to the right station. Go too far one way and you get static. Go a little too far the opposite way and you get a commercial for fish sticks.

Yum, fish sticks.

Focus, Bolt told himself. *Focus.*

He continued to spread his mind out, over the waves. But it felt like he was doing nothing at all.

Wait.

He felt something, a damp wetness that smelled like spoiled fish. He could almost taste it, and it tasted awful. No, that was just some leftover vomit from when Annika got seasick yesterday. Ugh.

Wait, again.

Sea mist sprayed on his face, but it wasn't actual sea mist. More like a virtual sea mist. This was different from what he had felt earlier when he was fighting with Annika.

Deeper. It was as if his mind was free from his body and he was diving beneath the waves. He accidentally swallowed some not-really-there seawater and coughed.

Yes! He was the sea itself, or at least partially so, for he was still him. He could hear the seaweed waving, and that's hard to do. He could taste a family of anchovy swimming by, two hundred yards away, but then groaned because he didn't particularly like anchovies.

He wasn't sure if identifying fish two hundred yards away would be helpful when fighting werepenguins, but maybe it could help him get lunch.

This was the penguin-verse, in its infinite majesty.

He sensed penguins. A group, maybe two dozen of them, out for a swim miles away, heading in Bolt's direction. Yet, despite their distance, he could see them as plain as the nose on his face, or even plainer, since you can't see the nose on your face unless you have a mirror or an extremely large nose.

Bolt could speak to penguins, he could bury his mind into theirs; it was one of the gifts of being a werepenguin. But could he communicate with them from this far away? He let his mind float to them, bobbing within the waves. It was so easy! It felt so right!

Bolt spoke to them. *Hello, my friends. Somersault.*

And they somersaulted. He could see them as if they

were swimming next to him, somersaulting over and over again. They were quite talented, actually. But they were getting dizzy, and it made Bolt dizzy, too.

Bolt had battled werepenguins who controlled penguins as if they were their own personal servants, and Bolt now understood, a little, how gratifying it felt to make penguins obey your every whim. This was fun! They would dance for him. Twirl for him. Attack for him!

No! Bolt broke the connection, *twang!*, like a broken guitar string.

Bolt grasped the railing, his legs weak, forehead sweaty, the penguin-shaped birthmark on his neck throbbing. What had he been doing, thinking of ordering penguins to attack? That's not who Bolt was. Controlling penguins wasn't *fun.* That's what monsters did, what evil werepenguins did, and Bolt wasn't a monster!

Well, he might technically be a monster, under pretty much any definition of a monster, but he would not be an evil one if he could help it.

The seer had chanted: *Turn away the bloodlust.* Bolt knew what that meant, and had from the start. But could Bolt turn it away? Could Bolt ignore the voice inside him calling for him to destroy and spill blood?

Bolt took a deep breath, but this time, instead of reaching outside himself, he reached *inside* himself, trying

to feel his werepenguin blood stirring. It's pretty much impossible for anyone to feel their own blood, as it just sort of does its thing under the skin, and he quickly gave that up and instead dipped into his brain. He could explore the minds of penguins, but he had never explored his own. Could he traverse its narrow, winding passageways?

Maybe. He felt . . . something . . . something buried deep like an itch you can't scratch because it's right in the middle of your back, which can be really annoying. It didn't just itch, it wiggled like jelly. A wiggling itch was as annoying as it sounds. He couldn't scratch it, though. That jelly was unnatural, planted like poison ivy, but with roots that were too deep to yank out.

Somehow, Bolt knew it had been planted by the Stranger. Bolt concentrated on the weed, but it was too firm to pull.

Hello, Bolt.

A voice popped into his head. Bolt gasped, hopped, and hit his ear, although none of those things did anything to dislodge the weed.

You can't pull out the roots, Bolt. It's there. Growing.

The voice was the Stranger's. Bolt squeezed his eyelids closed. He clenched his fists. He concentrated on kicking the voice out, out, out, out.

I'm still here, you know.

Why can't you leave me alone? Bolt thought back.

Because it is your destiny to join me, Bolt. You are wasting your time fighting it.

Never! I will stop you! The world will be free of your horror!

Says you. Don't you feel the hate, Bolt? It is everywhere.

No! "Leave me alone!"

POP! Like a cork from a bottle, the voice was gone, but whether it was gone because Bolt forced it out or the voice flew away on its own, Bolt wasn't sure.

"You're awfully sweaty, Bolt," said Annika. Bolt had not heard her come up on deck. "Are you OK? I thought I heard you talking to someone."

"I'm fine," said Bolt, trying to steady his wiggly, buckling knees.

Annika shrugged. "Well, Blackburn says we should be at Pingvingrad soon. In fact, he's surprised we haven't seen it yet. Although we can't see much of anything."

Bolt looked out into the sea. A thick, impenetrable mist had rolled in so quickly, he hadn't even noticed it approaching.

The fog completely enveloped the ship. It seemed unnatural for fog to come in that fast. It *felt* unnatural, too—there was dread in that mist, as if someone had taken misery and despair and formed it into a cloud. "Do you feel the hate?"

"What are you talking about?"

She might not feel it, but Bolt did. This mist had been

formed by the Stranger—Bolt smelled his breath in the breeze, although it was a very fishy smell and Bolt wished the man brushed his teeth more often. This mist was old—even older than a stale Pez candy—formed by one wispy gust of misery at a time.

It concealed this island from the rest of the world.

But why? What was happening on this island that was so important it had to be hidden?

Loud scraping below the ship startled Bolt, the sound of wood rubbing against rock. The ship floated slowly now, and its hull bumped into something that nudged them to the left. The port side of the ship hit something else, and the ship nudged to the right. They could see nothing through the dense fog.

"We're goin' to be wrecked if this mist doesn't lift!" bellowed Blackburn as the ship scraped against another unseen rock, wood chipping.

6. Mists of Hate

Bolt's feelings of distress were as thick as the fog, which seemed to take the shape of penguins, laughing penguins, beaks wide, taunting him.

He felt cold! So cold!

Meanwhile, more scrapes and crashes jolted the boat.

BANG! went the side of the boat as another invisible rock scraped the hull.

CRZZZTT! A jagged boulder's edge carved a long rut into the starboard side of the ship.

Bolt needed to find a way out of this. But what could he do? He was just a kid unlucky enough to be born with an ugly birthmark the shape of a flightless bird. He was in over his head! Even this whole penguin-verse thing was ridiculous. Bolt wanted nothing more than to run away, close his eyes, and hide somewhere, like in a cave, alongside the great seer Omneseus.

The thought of the seer's chant:

It's love you must trust.

He mouthed those words over and over again, faster and faster: *It's love you must trust. It's love you must trust. It'sloveyoumusttrust.*

Bolt thought of togetherness. Of family and penguins. It made him less afraid. He shook his head, and with each shake, a bead of hate sweat flew off and seemed to evaporate in the air.

"There goes the grog!" Blackburn moaned as a large barrel toppled over the railing and into the sea.

Shake, shake went Bolt's head—shaking with happy thoughts. The air around him felt lighter.

"Me timbers are shiverin'!" wailed Blackburn, a mast cracking.

Bolt kept his eyes closed, continuing to shake his head and thinking more non-hateful thoughts: *Parenthood. Brotherhood. Sisterhood. Anything-hood, really.*

"Look! The fog is lifting!" cried Annika.

The boat wailed with each collision: *THWACK! THUD! THKK!*

Humans and penguins, living in harmony. Happiness. Joy.

"I don't know what you're doin', Bolt, but keep doin' it!" shouted Blackburn.

Love, love, love, love . . .

"Grab that rope, missy!"

As the boat lurched, Bolt opened his eyes. The fog had partly lifted, just enough for them to see the ship's deck and a few yards past it. Blackburn steered to portside, narrowly avoiding a rock in front of them as Annika pulled a rope to straighten the main mast.

The pirate steered to the starboard side, avoiding another boulder.

Had Bolt really cleared the fog? Bolt almost wished he hadn't, as the fog had hid the hazardous mess around them. Cloudy wisps danced among the boulders jutting up from the water, revealing scattered ship remains and wooden planks floating around them. It was like a graveyard of broken boats. If the fog had not dispersed, the *Bobbing Borscht* would have certainly been among them.

Blackburn steered around the destruction. In the distance they could now see a small island through the lingering strands of hate mist.

"That must be Pingvingrad," said Blackburn as the broken mast of a shipwrecked boat nudged against their prow. "Just in time, too."

The *Bobbing Borscht* was near the island now, so close they could see the waves of the Blackest-Deadest Sea splashing upon its snow-spotted beaches and against broken ship parts half buried in the sand.

But the island itself was as thick with hate as the fog was. Dismal worry filled Bolt's brow.

"Your brow is all wrinkly, as if it is filled with dismal worry," Annika said. Bolt could only nod and notice that Annika's brow was just as wrinkled.

Beyond the beach were trees. Somewhere past them, deep inside the bowels of the small island, was the fortress of PEWD. Much of the hate came from there. Bolt was sure of it.

As Bolt scanned the beach, Annika stood next to him. “I don’t see any penguins patrolling the area,” she said.

“They don’t need to,” said Bolt, shivering from the cold he felt inside him. “That mist was the island’s protection. Most ships end up smashed.”

“The mist is mostly gone now,” said Blackburn. “Hopefully, it will never send another boat to Davey Jones’s locker.”

"Hopefully," agreed Bolt, although he wasn't so sure if his fix was anything but temporary.

SCRZZXX! The ship's hull scraped against an unseen boulder in the water underneath them.

"Borscht! I don't dare get much closer to the island. These boulders are everywhere." Blackburn pointed to a rocky crag past the beach, beyond a clump of sea stacks. "We'll go in over there." There was a small cove nestled in front of the cliff wall.

As the ship floated, Bolt stared out into the sea, and the few tendrils of hate mist that remained. How did someone thousands of miles away influence the weather of a remote island? Bolt closed his eyes, reaching out into the cosmos. The penguin-verse *was* everywhere. Could Bolt learn to harness that sort of power, too? He opened his mind and wondered if he could, with enough practice, change the world.

"Are you OK?" Annika asked, and Bolt opened his eyes and was no longer elsewhere. "You have a strange look on your face, like you're here, but not entirely here."

"Yeah, just thinking about the weather," said Bolt. "And the world. Stuff like that."

"Well, stop it. You're creeping me out."

"Sorry," said Bolt. He wanted to tell her more, but she wouldn't understand. How could she? He was a were-penguin, and that was hard enough to explain. How could he describe the vastness of the penguin-verse when he couldn't even describe it to himself?

"Borscht! We'll need to leave the ship in the deeper water and row ashore in our lifeboat," said Blackburn. Bolt and Annika watched as he threw over the anchor and lowered the masts, tied some ropes and untied others, and then began untying more ropes to lower the lifeboat. "While I'm heavin' anchors overboard, tyin' ropes and untyin' ropes, and then lowerin' a boat, ye both can just stand there and gawk. I don't need any help. Really." He threw them a sour look.

Annika and Bolt apologized and helped Blackburn prepare the boat.

A few minutes later the three of them sat in the small craft, Blackburn panting from all his heaving, tying, and lowering while Annika paddled them ashore. Bolt sat, thinking, paddling his mind through the island, trying to feel nearby penguins and sense the werepenguin dentist. But all he felt was the island's hate.

"Paddling this boat is exhausting," wheezed Annika. "Why don't you take a turn, Bolt?"

"I'm doing my own metaphoric paddling," he explained. Bolt felt hate squirm up his sinuses. He forced it away, breathing it out from his nose and, even more impressively, blowing it out from his ears.

Bolt looked at Annika, her face grimacing with her

paddling, but a scowl of determination in her eyes. She was ready for a fight; she always was. Blackburn, while panting, shared her look of fierceness. Bolt tried to scowl, too, but it felt strange to him. What was Bolt doing, floating into a harbor to steal a tooth and maybe fight a terrible werepenguin? He was so much more than he had been, but still wasn't much of a warrior. He doubted he ever would be.

"Something in your eye?" Annika asked.

"No, I'm scowling," said Bolt.

"Well, stop that, too. It's even more disturbing than that look you give when you're here and not here."

Soon they were on the shore, the boat wedged onto the small sliver of sand and its occupants clambered off. Bolt stared up at the cliff's steep face. It rose straight up, hundreds of feet high and every inch covered by a thin layer of ice. The cliff was so tall Bolt couldn't even see the very top. He had never climbed anything before, not even a tree, but penguins are known for climbing ice cliffs.

Unfortunately, penguins are also known for falling off ice cliffs.

Penguins have webbed feet that are good for clinging to rocks, and beaks they can use to puncture small footholds in the sides. Bolt had neither webbed feet nor a beak, of course, but he would try his best. He edged his fingers into a crevice and pulled himself up while jamming a foot

into a small crack. He did the same with another crevice and another crack. And another.

Twenty or thirty crevices and cracks later and he was sweating, his arms and legs aching. Bolt peeked down, although he knew it's never a good idea to look down when climbing something; it can make you dizzy. How high was he?

He had climbed two and a half feet.

"Ah, come on. That's it?" he wailed.

Annika and Blackburn were halfway across the cove. "There's a footpath over here," said Annika. "Why are you climbing that ice wall anyway?"

With a relieved groan, Bolt dropped down to the ground.

The footpath had been carved into the rock face, rising steeply along the edge of the cliff. It was a harrowing walk up the narrow path, where one slip could send you teetering over. The path did not appear to be used often, as patches of snow and ice covered much of it. Bolt wore an old pair of sneakers, and every time they slipped he was convinced he was going to fall to his doom. Fortunately, he didn't.

It was a long hike. Bolt, with his infused penguin blood, could walk for a long time. Annika was in excellent banditry shape. But halfway up, Blackburn looked like he was about to drop.

"Borscht! I need a break," the pirate complained. The path had leveled out, and he sat on the ground, breathing heavily. The pirate removed his boots and massaged his toes. "Me feet hurt terribly. Pirate boots are made for sailin', not climbin'."

As they rested, Bolt looked over the edge, giving himself a mild case of vertigo. The world spun and he gasped for breath, but the feeling was gone in an instant as his penguin senses took over. The cliff jutted out over the harbor, and Bolt could only see half the pirate ship below; once they reached the top of the cliff, it would be completely hidden from their view.

Bolt removed his unicorn-and-rainbow backpack from around his shoulders. He never went anywhere without it now—he was so used to carrying it, he usually forgot he had it on. Fortunately, there were still a few dead fish packed along with his spare clothes. He grabbed one and bit off the tail, fish slime dribbling down his lips. He then put his lips against the fish's body, sucking in some fish guts. Fish intestines clung to his chin.

He looked up, and Annika and Blackburn were staring at him. Annika's face was green. "That's the most disgusting thing I've ever seen."

"I think I'm going to throw up just watchin' ye eat," agreed Blackburn.

"Sorry," said Bolt.

Soon, they were on the march again. The path rose up steadily. Bolt made the mistake of looking down again and had to catch his breath as the world spun—they were so high!—but he cleared his head and kept climbing. Eventually, and after Blackburn had to rest two more times, they reached the top. In front of them was a dark forest, stretching in both directions. They had no choice but to head straight in.

It was silent in the forest. Lifeless. The trees were without leaves, allowing the hazy sun to cast dark and eerie shadows through an endless scattering of gray twisting branches. The plants—and there were only a few—were nearly all brown and withered. It smelled like rot. Bolt and his friends continued forward without uttering a word.

With every step, Bolt was more and more tempted to run back to the ship. But Annika's and Blackburn's determined scowls gave him strength. He considered trying to form his own scowl again, but decided it wasn't worth the effort; Bolt would never be a scowler.

He paused for a moment, sensing penguins, hundreds of them. It was all hazy, and Bolt couldn't lock into any specific thought or mind, but there was no denying there was a lot of evil surrounding them. He could hear malicious penguin squawks and agitated feather rustling. "We're close," he said.

They advanced slower now, and soon they neared the

end of the tree line. They crept to the forest's edge and peeked out from behind a large oak.

It reminded Bolt of sticking your head into a sauna, except instead of hot steam he was hit with a wave of loathing. Fortunately, they saw no penguins—none in the wide dirt road that ran along the row of trees nor in the vast lawn beyond it. That lawn was filled with a smattering of small buildings, sheds, some garages, and, in the middle of them, a domed concrete structure as big as a football stadium.

Bolt thought it might actually be a football stadium until he spotted the giant letters in red on its side:

POOWD

Penguins are poor spellers.

The large building was so gloomy, its gray facade seemed to swallow the sun.

"What do you think is inside that?" Annika asked.

"I don't know," said Bolt. "But whatever it is, it's filled with hate." Thick, terrible hate that crawled up Bolt's skin like tiny ants.

For some reason, staring at the dome also made Bolt feel incredibly hungry.

The entire complex was surrounded by a tall chain-link fence with three feet of barbed wire wrapped around the top. The front gate was about a hundred yards away. It appeared to be unguarded, but seemed like a good place to avoid. If there were any alarms in the fortress, that is where they would be.

Bolt felt penguins lurking inside the nearby buildings, working inside the sheds, and filling the massive concrete dome. He could feel something stronger, too. An evil more powerful than all the other evils around, and he knew it must be Dr. Walzanarz. She was close.

But how close? He couldn't tell for sure, and he also couldn't tell how many penguins were around—not exactly, anyway. It was as if something was blocking Bolt, making everything fuzzy.

He tried to reach through the penguin-verse, to unfuzzy that which was fuzzy.

"You're making that weirdo look again," said Annika.

Bolt gave up. He couldn't break through that strange fuzz.

Annika gestured to a small gate in the fence, not too far from where they stood. It was covered with heavy padlocks and chains. "We can go in there."

"It looks sort of locked," said Bolt.

Annika scoffed and pulled a couple of bobby pins from her hair. "I got it. No problem." Annika was an expert lock-picker.

"But penguins could come out at any moment," warned

Bolt, his birthmark tingling as it often did when danger was nearby. But the fuzziness kept him from knowing more.

"I'll be quick." Before Bolt could protest again, Annika rushed toward the gate. He admired her courage, but was also a little jealous of it. If only he could be that brave!

Bolt let his mind drift through the breeze again. So many penguins were lurking close by! But it was all so, so hazy.

Wait.

Oh no.

He sensed a brute force so close, so vicious, even the fuzz couldn't completely block it. A large group of penguins, two dozen or more, were in a nearby building, and they were about to come outside.

Guards. On patrol.

Meanwhile, Annika had reached the gate. She inserted two bobby pins into one of the padlocks. She twisted her pins, concentrating.

Bolt tensed. As soon as the penguins waddled out of the building they would spot Annika. She needed to get out of there. Now.

Stop! Bolt's mind shouted toward the penguins, but it was like his thoughts were being absorbed by the fuzz before even reaching the birds. Bolt opened his mouth to scream, to get Annika's attention instead, but then shut it.

The penguins would hear his yell—that fuzziness blocked thoughts, not voices. Bolt jumped up and down and waved. He shot out wordless commands toward Annika. *Look at me! Run!* But Annika remained at work, concentrating on the lock. Bolt hopped and leapt, left and right and left.

The door to the nearby building swung open. A webbed foot stepped outside.

Bolt tried to reach into the penguin's head again. *Stop! Go back!*

Nope. Nothing.

The penguin took a second step outside. The open door was blocking its view, but any moment it would see Annika.

Stop! Bolt pushed his thoughts with everything he had inside him toward the penguin. *Stop! Stop! Please, please, please!*

Annika continued playing with the locks, oblivious.

Please! Stop! Bolt begged the penguin.

The penguin stopped, one webbed foot out the door, one still inside. Had Bolt's thoughts wiggled through the fuzz? He wasn't sure of anything; all he knew was that another penguin barked loudly: *Why did you stop? Move out of the way!*

Annika's ears perked up when she heard the bark, and she dropped the lock, her eyes wide. She didn't pause, not for a moment, but sprinted back toward Bolt and Blackburn.

She hurled herself behind the tree line as twenty penguin guards stepped onto the lawn. Remarkably, they had not seen her.

"Why didn't you give a bird whistle to get my attention?" she asked Bolt in a panicked whisper as she huddled next to him behind the tree.

"I jumped up and down," said Bolt.

"Bandits whistle."

"I didn't know that. Next time," Bolt promised.

The penguins marched in a tight formation. They wore head mirrors strapped across their foreheads and carried rifles over their shoulders.

No, wait. Those weren't rifles; they were thick, three-foot-long toothbrushes. Still, they looked powerful. Bolt wouldn't want to be brushed by one of them.

The penguins high-stepped past the spot where Bolt and his friends hid in the shadows of the trees. Annika made a V with her fingers, pointed to her eyes and then to the penguins, and then jabbed her thumb to the left, right, drew a circle with her pinkie, pinched her middle finger, and then made her fingers hop up and down like she was doing the hand movements to "Little Bunny Foo Foo."

"What does any of that mean?" Bolt asked.

Annika sighed. "Sorry. I forgot you don't know secret bandit hand signals. Those locks on the gate are bobby-pin-proof. I was letting you know that I'm going to sneak

up to the last marching penguin, take it prisoner, and force it to unlock the gate. Oh, and then I'm going to sing the 'Little Bunny Foo Foo' song."

"That's a horrible plan," said Bolt.

"Do you have any better ideas?"

"How about we just go in there?" Blackburn pointed to a hole that led under the fence and onto the lawn. "Looks like it was dug by an animal."

The hole was as big as a person and went right under the fence. "But what sort of animal can dig a hole like that?" Bolt wondered.

"Not any sort of animal I'd like to meet," said Blackburn. "Just be thankful it's not here now. Borscht!"

"I'd still like to sing 'Little Bunny Foo Foo' first," said Annika. "I love that song." She quickly hummed the tune, performing the simple hand movements as she did.

A minute later, after the high-stepping penguins had marched out of view and Annika had stopped humming, they scampered from their hiding spot toward the hole. After making sure no penguins were lurking nearby, Blackburn scrambled through. Annika followed, and Bolt prepared to climb under next.

Come in. We've been expecting you, Bolt.

Bolt's spine jumped, and when your spine jumps but the rest of you stays planted, it can be quite unsettling. Bolt looked in all directions. He saw no one.

"Are you coming?" asked Annika, standing next to Blackburn on the other side of the fence. She tapped her foot. "We're sort of waiting here, you know."

The voice in Bolt's head was gone as quickly as it had arrived. The Stranger knew they were there. Was this a trap? Should they run away and make a better plan?

Or maybe Bolt was imagining things. As long as they were careful and avoided alarms, they'd be fine. Pushing aside his worries, Bolt crawled through the hole.

They tiptoed forward, Bolt trying to scan the yard with his penguin-connected mind. *Feel the penguin-verse,* he told himself, but that fuzz was still there, obstructing his connection. He felt a vague presence of penguins, but was unsure where they were. It was all so maddening! "Be careful," Bolt warned as his birthmark tingled. "We're surrounded, I think. Possibly. Just don't trigger any alarms. One wrong move and—"

"Look out!" Blackburn pointed to a small wire that ran along the ground. It was nearly buried in the grass and almost impossible to see.

"Strange," Bolt muttered, reaching out to touch it.

"No, don't!" urged Annika, but it was too late. Bolt tapped the wire, and it snapped. A siren wailed, spotlights shone from every building, and a speaker shouted, "Intruder! Intruder!"

"Sorry, guys," said Bolt. "My bad."

A penguin carrying a massive toothbrush emerged from the side of the building, followed by another penguin, and then another, and another. They were running toward Bolt, Annika, and Blackburn. Bolt stared, frozen in horror.

Even more penguins emerged from the side of the building, all waddling, all growling, and all holding their enormous, deadly-looking toothbrushes.

"Borscht!" shouted Blackburn, reaching for his swordfish. "Well, they won't get me without a fight."

"Me neither," hissed Annika.

"Or we could just run?" Bolt suggested.

"Works for me," said Blackburn, and they dashed toward the hole that led back under the fence.

8. Falling for You

More than one hundred penguins chased Bolt, Annika, and Blackburn as they reached the hole under the fence, dove through it, and popped out the other side, one after another.

"They'll have to go through the hole, too," said Bolt, hoping that would slow the penguins down.

The penguins ran straight into the fence and knocked it over with a *BANG!*

"Or they could just do that," said Blackburn.

Bolt bit his lip and wished his fearful heart weren't racing faster than his legs.

Bolt and his friends fled down the wide dirt road that ran along the tree line, kicking up snow and dirt. The icy ground made running slippery. Penguins aren't fast runners, but their webbed feet make up for it with excellent traction. Bolt and Blackburn kept sliding around on the ice. Annika was as steady as ever.

"Bandits are slippery, but we never slip," she explained as Bolt pinwheeled his arms to keep from flopping onto the ground after an unexpected skid.

Penguins have been known to march fifty miles just to find food, although that's partly because there are so few high-quality penguin restaurants. But that meant Bolt's friends would grow tired long before the penguins did. Blackburn was already wheezing.

In between his running and slipping, Bolt tried to spread his thoughts among the chasing penguin guards, to reach inside their minds and talk to them. They were his family, after all. They were each a part of the mighty penguin-verse.

Peace, my brothers and sisters. You don't want to chase us. Bolt hurled the thoughts at the penguins closest to them. But, like before, his instructions only bounced off, failing to make even a faint impression.

Listen to me! We are family!

The penguins did not listen. Instead, they barked. Bolt understood penguin barks:

"Get them!"

"Stop them!"

"Capture them!"

"Dr. Walzanarz wants the boy! The boy!"

Up ahead, the dirt road forked—one side veering into the forest, the other aiming toward the beach. Blackburn and Annika were ahead of Bolt, and they ran deeper into the forest. "We'll lose them in here!" Annika shouted.

Bolt hesitated.

Bolt always told himself he wasn't brave, not like Annika and Blackburn were, and that he would much prefer to hide under beds than fight monsters. But did that make him a coward, or smart? It was generally safer under a bed than anywhere else.

Still, Bolt didn't need to be brave to do the right thing. Which is why Bolt ran the opposite way. If he took the other path, toward the beach, the penguins would follow him and not his friends. Annika and Blackburn could escape! Or at least he hoped so. Bolt wasn't sure if sacrificing himself to save his friends was terribly brave, or awfully stupid. Maybe it was both.

As Bolt ran, the penguins slowed at the fork. Bolt could hear their barking and their wings flapping. After a few moments of silence, one penguin yapped: *"He went over there! Ignore the humans! The doctor wants the boy! The boy!"*

"Why did I run this way?" Bolt asked himself, finally deciding that had been far more stupid than brave.

The path had ended, and Bolt ran on the beach now.

The sand was filled with dozens of small holes. It's hard to run fast on sand in general, but the holes littering the landscape made for an even slower slog. Bolt's feet kept getting stuck in them and making him stumble.

Bolt's heart continued to race. There were no beds here, or trees, or anywhere to hide out. Just sand, lots and lots of sand. And holes, of course.

Meanwhile, his pursuers were still in the forest. Their pause at the fork had given Bolt a little breathing room, and the trees blocked their view of him for the moment. If only he could run a little faster, maybe . . .

He never got to finish that thought, because he didn't see the hole in front of him: a larger hole than the others on the beach. He stepped right into it.

And heard a *crack*.

"Hey! What? Why?" Bolt sputtered a bunch of other one-word exclamations as the sand gave way beneath his feet, revealing a much larger hole, one as large as the hole under the fence they had crawled through earlier. He plunged downward into darkness, sand raining down on him. For a moment, he was worried that the hole went on forever, a bottomless abyss into nothingness. Although, actually, it only went about ten feet before Bolt smashed onto the hard dirt floor below. *Clomp!* "Ow!"

Dirt floors are not as hard as concrete, but you still

don't want to fall on one. Bolt had the wind knocked out of him, and he curled into a ball, coughing and trying to catch his breath.

His coughing subsided after a few seconds. He wasn't dead. He wasn't injured. Best yet, he wasn't captured by penguins.

Bolt looked up. Branches and leaves had been placed over the hole in the sand, and one of the branches had cracked underneath him when he stepped on it. Sand had poured back over the branches after Bolt fell, leaving only a pinprick of light. The place smelled like earth, but also like horse dung and, faintly, like beets. But it was too dark to see much. He could also hear the faint pattering of penguins up above, in the distance. They were running past the hole. Bolt was no longer in danger.

Or at least he thought he was no longer in danger. Because just then a flicker of lights approached—flames from a torch. No, flames from four torches, hurrying down a long, earth-carved tunnel and toward him. The first torch was held by a short, squat woman with wild dark gray hair standing up on its ends. Her head was round with a big upturned pink nose, and she had two big buckteeth. She wore a loose, long black robe, lined with gold trim near the bottom, a hood flopping behind. She squinted her small gray eyes beneath oversized plastic goggles.

SNIP
SNIP

Three men, wearing similar goggles and robes, also with poofs of gray hair and round pink noses, ran behind her, buckteeth bared.

Maybe Bolt was safe. Maybe these odd but threatening-looking people were friendly.

"Who are you?" demanded the woman. Her voice was squeaky but harsh. "And how dare you invade our home!"

Well, they didn't seem friendly.

One of the men, taller and older than the rest, with deep wrinkles in his long, gaunt face, held a giant pair of scissors. He snipped them back and forth and squawked, "The invader must die."

Bolt yelped. Nope, they weren't friendly, not at all. And Bolt was definitely *not* safe.

Bolt stared up at the odd, torch-carrying woman and her companions, the lump in his throat growing larger with every snip of the scissors held by the tallest man. The man's hands were large, incredibly so, and Bolt soon noticed that all of these people had enormous hands, too. They also had extra-large feet; none of them wore shoes. Their fingernails and toenails were long, pointy, and painted bright red. They all hissed at Bolt.

The tall man continued to open and shut his scissors menacingly. *Snip. Snip. Snip.*

"What are you going to do with those?" gulped Bolt.

"For now, I'll just open and close them in a threatening manner," said the man. His voice was incredibly high.

It reminded Bolt of someone stepping on a rubber duck.

"Wh-what is this place?" asked Bolt, his voice unsteady as he inched backward. His eyes glanced back and forth between the woman standing closest to him and the man with the scissors. Their dancing torch flames added to the general eeriness.

"We will ask the questions," squeaked the tall man. "Who are you? Who sent you? What did you have for breakfast last Wednesday?" The woman glared at him. "Sorry, I got carried away with the questions."

"I'm Bolt. I sent myself. Last Wednesday, I probably ate fish for breakfast."

"Enough," said the woman. Her voice was pitched even higher than the man's. It reminded Bolt of the orphanage where he grew up and where, after meals, the boys had to wash their plates until they were squeaky clean. *Squeak, squeak, squeak.* "No more questions, Topo," the woman squealed.

The man, Topo, bowed his head. "Of course, Zemya. I'll just stand behind you and continue snipping my scissors, if you don't mind." *Snip, snip, snip.* As he stepped back, he glared at Bolt.

Zemya sighed. "Just snip them quietly."

Snip, snip, snip.

The woman, Zemya, looked down at Bolt. "Why are you here?"

“I came to the island on a ship, and then I was running and I fell into a hole. It was an accident,” Bolt explained, his heart beating faster with every snip of the man’s scissors.

“He lies!” roared Topo, who began snipping with even more ferocity as he glared at Bolt and stomped forward. Bolt’s heart was now beating so fast he feared it might bounce out of his chest. “What is your mission?” the tall man demanded. “What are you hiding? How much wood could a woodchuck chuck if a woodchuck could chuck wood?” The man withered under Zemya’s icy stare. “Sorry. I got carried away with the questions again.” He snarled at Bolt. “I’d snip you into strips and then feed you to the alligators, except we don’t have any alligators.”

“Wait a second,” said Bolt. He had been threatened to be fed to alligators before. “Are you related to anyone who lives in Brugaria?”

“I have an older brother named Günter who lives there.”

Bolt thought back to when he had faced Günter, the leader of the Mystical Brotherhood of Whales. “I've met him. You remind me of him.”

The woman peered down at Bolt. Her eyes glared at him from behind her goggles. Bolt stood perfectly still, waiting for her next move. “My name is Zemya. I am the leader of our group.”

“And what is your group?” Bolt asked.

“As if you don’t know!” roared Topo, jabbing his scissors forward. “Let’s cut him into snowflakes! I’ve cut dozens of trespassers into snowflakes!”

“No, you haven’t, Topo!” yelped Zemya. Her voice was so high that her yelp hurt Bolt’s ears, like nails on a chalkboard. “Forgive Topo,” she said to Bolt. “He tends to exaggerate.”

“I exaggerate more than anyone in the world!” declared Topo. *Snip, snip, snip.*

“Look, I came here by accident, I swear it,” yelped Bolt. “And I know I fell into your hole, but really, aren’t you just making a mountain out of a molehill?”

Topo roared. “How dare you!” he snarled. “He mocks us!”

“I didn’t mean any offense.” Bolt felt panic stirring inside him, and confusion—what had he said? He took a deep breath; he needed to control his fear. After all, Bolt had been in worse jams than this and escaped them. Well, on second thought, maybe he hadn’t been in worse jams than this, just equally bad jams. In truth, it was hard to rate his jams in any particular order, but being trapped underground with, well, whatever these people were was high on the list. “What did I do?”

Zemya ordered Topo to stop snipping and looked down at Bolt, shaking her head. “Topo has a point, you know.”

"Actually, I have two points," said Topo, pointing to the ends of his scissors.

Zemya rolled her eyes. "You said you got here on a ship. But if that's true, how did you get past the rocks and the fog?" She peered down at Bolt and gasped. Then she squatted beside him and sniffed around his head. Her buckteeth chattered together, and she poked him on the neck.

"Ow," said Bolt.

She peered so closely, Bolt could smell the woman's robe. It smelled like dirt and worms. She held her torch closer to him and sucked in another breath. Bolt, who was always a little self-conscious about the penguin-shaped birthmark on his neck, instinctually raised his shoulder to hide it.

"He has the mark of the penguin!" she declared. Zemya stepped away from Bolt, wary, but her eyes remained focused on him. "Your white skin. Your long beak-like nose, bushy eyebrows, and your hair, springing up into the shape of horns. You turn into a werepenguin at midnight, don't you?" She scrunched her mouth together and looked away. She appeared to be deep in thought.

"I mean you no harm," said Bolt, his forehead sweaty. He held his hands up in a gesture of surrender and peace. "I'm not a spy. I came here to save the world." Zemya raised an eyebrow. Behind her, the scissor-snipping grew louder. "Honest. We were sneaking into the fortress but set off an alarm and were chased by an army of penguins with toothbrushes."

"We? But you are alone," said Zemya.

"My friends are on the island, too. They'll be looking for me. If they find me, that'll just mean more people falling into your hole. You don't want that, right?" Zemya shook her head. Topo's scissor-snipping slowed. "I just need to sneak into the fortress, steal a tooth, and then travel to the South Pole to stop the evil leader of the were-penguins." Zemya stared at Bolt blankly. "I know it sounds a bit far-fetched, but trust me, I'm on your side."

"He lies. Can I snip him now?" asked Topo, marching forward. *Snip, snip, snip, snip, snip, snip, snip, snip.* The man bent down, and Bolt closed his eyes. The scissors were so close Bolt felt the air next to him being cut in half. "I say I snip him, we lure his friends here, and I snip them, too!"

"Stop!" cried out Zemya. "I don't know if he speaks the truth or not, but it is obvious that he is a were-creature. If we start snipping were-creatures, then we are no better than those who hurt us! No, we must give him the test." The scissors stopped snipping, and after a couple of seconds Bolt, who still had his eyes closed, opened them. Topo was backing away, scowling.

"You're giving me a test?" Bolt asked. That didn't

sound so bad. Maybe Bolt would get out of this mess. He hoped it was a true-or-false test. Bolt was never good at essays.

"We will take him to the antechamber while the test is prepared," said Zemya.

Topo jabbed his scissors in the air. *Snip, snip, snip.* "Follow us. And don't try any funny stuff, got it?"

"I'm not funny," Bolt promised. "I've never been very good at telling jokes."

One of the other men withdrew a hammer from his own pocket and began to wave it in the air, in unison with Topo's snipping. "If he tries any funny stuff, I've got this!"

"And I've got this!" shouted the other man, who then pulled a banana from his pocket. "Sorry," he said, looking embarrassed. "I was about to have a snack when the intruder fell in."

Zemya walked down the tunnel in the direction from which she had come, followed by Bolt, and then Topo with his snipping scissors, and the other two, one waving a hammer and the other holding his banana. But there was nothing funny about any of it.

10. The Underground

Bolt followed Zemya down hand-carved tunnels. The walls were high—even the Omnescian Quad, in his stilts, wouldn't have needed to slouch. The tunnels twisted and turned and branched out to other tunnels. Bolt grew confused as to where they were. Escape was impossible—Bolt would never be able to find his way out of this maze.

They passed two people whispering in the tunnel. The people were dressed the same as Bolt's escorts, with black garments and goggles, and shared the same pink noses and abnormally large hands and feet. They ate something small and wiggly.

Worms. They ate live worms.

Bolt's stomach lurched. Ugh.

But, then again, he ate raw fish, so who was he to judge?

The two worm-eating people moved to the side to let Bolt and his group pass. Bolt slowed, and one of the men behind him shouted, "Keep moving! I have a banana!"

They passed doors, many doors. There was an entire community within these tunnels. They even had electricity, as faint electric lights buzzed from the ceiling, lighting the way, although dimly.

They passed an open room that reminded Bolt of a beauty salon, with barber chairs and sinks and lots of these strange people inside. Some were having their hair cut, while others were getting their nails done.

"Hi, Topo!" squeaked a short woman styling someone's hair with a blow-dryer. "I hope you're enjoying those rubber scissors you borrowed!"

"Wait," said Bolt. "Your scissors are made out of rubber?"

"Yes, but I'm not afraid to use them!" Topo cried. *Snip, snip, snip.* They flopped over to the side. "Thanks for letting me borrow them!" Topo cried back.

They continued walking. After two more twists and three short side tunnels, Zemya stopped in front of a wooden door. She withdrew a small key from her pocket, inserted it into the lock, and pushed it open. Bolt followed her inside.

The room was cold, dirty, and barren of much furniture.

There was a single wooden chair that was missing a leg and didn't look safe to sit on, a standing lamp with a dull, flickering bulb, and a small table with a bucket of dirt on it.

"You should be comfortable here," said Zemya.

"Um, not really," said Bolt, nudging the chair with his foot, and it toppled over.

"Leave us," Zemya instructed the others. "I will speak to our prisoner. You two must awaken Barsuk."

"Who's Barsuk?" asked Bolt.

"I'll ask the questions!" spat Topo. "What's the capital of New Mexico? Why is the sky blue? Do you ever think you're actually a robot?"

"Don't answer," Zemya whispered. "You'll just encourage him." She turned to Topo. "Go."

"I don't like leaving you alone with this boy," said Topo. "It's not safe. Do you want to borrow my floppy, rubber scissors?"

"No, and I'll be fine . . . our tunnels are too confusing for the boy to escape. But send for Grom, please."

"Are you sure, Zemya? The prisoner could try funny stuff!" warned Topo. "I bet he hates whales, too. And you can never trust a whale-hater!"

"You really are a lot like your brother," said Bolt.

"Leave us," said Zemya.

Topo glared at Bolt, but he and the other men left

and closed the door behind them. Zemya bowed her head to Bolt. "I'm sorry that we cannot let you go. But I must uphold our traditions."

Her apology didn't bring Bolt much relief. He pushed aside his urge to hide under a bed, not that there were any beds to hide under, and stood tall. He would take this test. He would pass. And he would save the world. "If I ace this test, whatever it is, then you will let me go?"

"You have my word. And if you pass the test, you will have the same rights and benefits as one of us."

"Which are?"

"Free manicures every Tuesday. All the earthworms you can eat. And tunnels. Lots of tunnels." Bolt failed to feel much enthusiasm for any of those perks. "The test will take place soon. But while you're waiting, can I get you something to eat? You could have a bowl of a hearty soup made out of beets, cabbage, onions, and potatoes. It's quite tasty."

"Borscht?" asked Bolt. Zemya nodded. "No thanks. But I have a friend who would be really excited to be down here right now."

Bolt had so many questions! Who were these strange underground folk? Where were his friends now—had they escaped? If Bolt died, could anyone defeat the Stranger and free the world's penguins without him?

But one specific question had been bugging him ever

since Topo had asked it: What was the capital of New Mexico anyway? Albuquerque or Santa Fe? He wanted answers.

"Who are you people?" he asked, deciding the New Mexico question was not the best one to start with. "Before I take your test, I deserve to at least know that much."

"That seems fair." Zemya leaned in closer and removed her plastic goggles, revealing tiny gray eyes. She blinked rapidly, her pink nose twitched, and her buckteeth chattered. It all made her creepy appearance feel even creepier. "Listen closely to my story. For my story is the story of the Clan of the Moles!"

Bolt thought he heard scary organ music, but quickly realized it was just his imagination.

11. The Story of Zemya

"We come from lands near and far," Zemya began. "Word has spread that our kind is safe here."

"What do you mean by *our kind*?" Bolt asked. "You mentioned earlier something about people hurting you?"

"Yes, but perhaps I should start with my own story. I grew up far away, across the sea, with my mother and younger brother, Grom. We were poor. On birthdays the only cakes we could afford were mud cakes. Although one year I was given a dirt bike."

"That sounds nice," said Bolt. "I've never had a bike."

"No, not a bike. A dirt bike, which is just a small bike made out of dirt. But I didn't mind. I loved the dirt, you see. Whenever I went out to play, I would come home covered in it. Mom would always complain: 'Zemya, you're filthy! You'll catch worms!' I told her she was being silly, and would then quickly release the worms I had stuffed into my pockets earlier in the day. But we never went hungry. For my mother kept a small garden where she grew onions and garlic. That's all we ate."

"I'm guessing you didn't get a lot of visitors," said Bolt.

"No, not many. But I was a normal child, except for two things. First, I was exceptional at Whack-a-Mole. I always had terrible eyesight, so my skill at Whack-a-Mole was surprising. And the second was this." She lifted her robe to reveal a large animal-shaped mark on her ankle. Bolt sat up straighter.

"A birthmark!" exclaimed Bolt. "And it's shaped like a mouse. Are you . . ." He gasped. "Are you a were-mouse?"

"No, and this is a mole, actually. A mole-shaped mole. My mother had one that was similar, although it was the shape of a sloth. Animal-shaped birthmarks are hereditary. Children seldom have the same animal mark as their parents, though."

Bolt had never known his own parents, as they had been killed when he was an infant. Did they have birthmarks? If so, what animals? Maybe his father had a leopard. Leopards were cool. And maybe his mom had a sweet, cuddly rabbit? He would have been disappointed if they had birthmarks of, say, a warthog and a skunk.

"Then, one day," Zemya continued, "we discovered abnormally large animal tunnels under our garden. All our onions were ruined. My mother cried because she was so upset, and she usually only cried when slicing the onions, not losing them. My mother was well aware of my Whack-a-Mole skills, so she gave me a shovel and told me to stand in the garden and bop any moles that peeked out of a hole."

"How long did you stand there?"

"Fourteen hours. Finally, at midnight under the full moon, I sensed something. A mole! I leapt up with my shovel!"

"Did you whack it?"

"Oh no," said Zemya. "This creature was three times the size of an ordinary mole. I knew instantly it was a were-mole. I had seen pictures in storybooks."

"Were-mole pictures are in storybooks?"

"Some."

Bolt gasped, and not just because he had never seen a were-mole in a storybook. No, he gasped because he was surprised to learn about were-moles at all. He had met a were-gull, so he knew there were other were-creatures out there, but had no idea how many different kinds.

"The creature felt endearing, despite its red eyes and long fangs. I gave it a hug," said Zemya.

While some people may think hugging a mysterious

and extraordinarily large mole creature at midnight was strange, Bolt didn't think that. He would enjoy hugging werepenguins if they weren't all so evil.

"The creature spoke, in my head," said Zemya. "It said, *You can be like me. Just let me bite you, and then you will have a new family. A family of moles!* I clapped with joy. It was like a dream come true."

"You have strange dreams," said Bolt.

"I was excited to have a new family—I mean, what sort of mother sends their daughter out to hit moles in a garden for fourteen hours? I agreed to the creature's bargain and became what I am today."

"So, you are a were-mole."

She nodded. "We all are were-moles here. Well, all except for my brother. He does not have the proper birthmark."

It made sense—why these people lived underground, and why they all had odd, mole-like faces and larger-than-normal hands and feet.

"My mother thought I was a monster," Zemya continued. "She couldn't understand why I insisted on sleeping in a hole, or ate five pounds of earthworms a day. She kicked me out of the house."

"I'm so sorry." Bolt didn't know which was worse—to never know your parents, like Bolt, or to have yours turn away when you needed them most.

Zemya bowed her head and wiped a tear from her cheek. "Most of us here have similar stories, I'm afraid."

Bolt understood all too well. He had spent most of his life as an unwanted orphan. And while turning into a penguin had mostly been a curse, at least now he had a family, sort of.

"My brother, Grom, insisted on accompanying me wherever I was heading; we were always close. He and I soon found other were-moles—there is a bustling mole underground, you know. But it's a hard life, always on the lookout for mole traps and extremely large raccoons."

"How did you end up here?"

"A group of us were-moles boarded a ship—Grom is an excellent sailor—and set out to find a new home, far away from civilization. We followed the constellation Talpa the Mole. His tail points to this island."

"The constellation Pepe the Penguin points here, too."

"So do the constellations Skippy the Squirrel and Boris the Badminton Net, although I have never seen a were-squirrel or any were-badminton equipment." She shivered, as if imagining such horrors. "Anyway, we thought we were close to the island when heavy fog rolled in. Our ship was wrecked. Moles are excellent swimmers, so we made it ashore. And our labour built our home."

"Labour?"

"A group of moles is called a labour, just like a group of lions is called a pride, a group of rats is called a mischief, and a group of lion-sized rats is called terribly frightening." She made a sweeping hand gesture. "And this is where we have lived ever since, buried below the earth, unknown to the world. Safe. And that is why we devised a test to ensure only moles, or those with the heart of a mole, would ever leave our burrow."

The door opened and a teenage boy entered the room. He didn't have any of the markings of a mole. His nose was thin and pointy and not short and squat. His hair was dark and straight, although he had quite a bit of it, and it desperately needed brushing. He had normal-sized hands and fingernails, too. His voice was deep, which stood in stark contrast to the high-pitched squeals from the mole creatures. "Zemya, I rushed here as soon as I heard. Topo said you caught a trespasser—some horrible whale-hating spy. I said to him, 'Really?'—you know how much he exaggerates—and . . ." His voice trailed off. He held a bucket filled with dirt and, upon seeing Bolt, dropped it unconsciously. Dirt spilled everywhere. "It's true!"

"I'm not a spy," said Bolt. "And I don't hate whales. I have no idea where he got that idea."

"Bolt, this is my brother, Grom," said Zemya. "Grom, please pick up our dinner." Bolt noticed earthworms wiggling in the freshly fallen dirt. Grumbling, Grom knelt down and scooped them back into the pail. "Grom sneaks onto the fortress lawn to collect worms for us. The soil there is rich with nutrients. He also steals supplies for us when we need them."

"So, you're a bandit!" declared Bolt. "My best friend is a bandit!"

"Just because I steal worms and supplies don't mean I'm a bandit," Grom grumbled.

"Actually, it sort of does," said Bolt.

Grom shot Bolt a dirty look. "Why are you alone with him, Zemya? It's not safe. You coulda been hurt! Maimed! Worse! Do you at least have rubber scissors, or a hammer, or a banana?"

"I have none of those. Yet I am unharmed. The boy says he came here by boat and fell into one of our holes by mistake. I believe him."

"A likely story," said Grom. He narrowed his eyes. "I don't like him. How did he get past the fog? Hmm?"

"Because I'm a werepenguin," said Bolt. What was the point of denying it? If anyone would understand the extraordinary but alienating powers of a were-creature, it would be these people. "But I'm not an evil one." At least he hoped that was true.

"Only an evil werepenguin would claim he wasn't an evil werepenguin," snapped Grom.

"An un-evil one would say the same thing, so I guess

that would be confusing," admitted Bolt. Grom growled. "Look, I mean no harm. I just need to break into PEWD, steal the silver tooth of a prehistoric seal, take the tooth to the South Pole, and use it to end the reign of the world's mightiest werepenguin."

Grom's jaw dropped. He stared at Bolt, and then at his sister, and then back at Bolt. "I gotta admit, if you're a spy, you're not a good one. Not with a tale like that."

"It's the truth," said Bolt.

"I dunno about that, but I know about that tooth," said Grom. "The tooth of the Ilversay Oothtay Ealsay, right?" Bolt nodded. Had everyone heard of this tooth except Bolt? "You'll never get past the PEWD guards. You'd be like, 'Gimmee the tooth,' and then they'd be like, 'How about if we pull all your teeth out instead?'" He stepped closer to Bolt and glared at him. "But we can't let him go, Zemya. He'll tell everyone we're here and . . ."

"Settle down, Grom. Of course not," agreed Zemya. "The boy will be put to the test. That will decide his fate."

Grom buried his fists into his pockets. His nostrils flared as he breathed out, frowning, glaring, and looking just generally displeased. "It's a waste of time. He'll never pass."

"But I could," said Bolt. "Especially if it's a true-or-false test. I'm not good at essays, though."

"It's not that sort of test," said Grom.

Bolt took a deep breath. "Whatever it is, I'm an honorary mole if I pass it, right? And moles help one another, right?

"Yes," said Zemya.

"Grom, you must know the fortress really well if you're a bandit. If I pass, will you help me break into the fortress and find that tooth?"

"I am *not* a bandit," protested Grom. "I'm not gonna help you do nothing, either. You'll be like, 'Help me,' and I'll be all 'Not gonna happen' and—"

"Grom!" shouted Zemya. "He is right. Moles help one another. If he passes the test, you will help him do this thing."

Bolt smiled, just a little. Grom spat on the ground. "Whatever. It doesn't matter. No one has ever passed that test who wasn't a mole. Zemya, you should help the others prepare. I'll watch the prisoner." He crooked a thumb at Bolt and made a fist. "And no funny business."

"I'm not funny," Bolt promised.

Zemya nodded. "Thank you, Grom." As she stepped toward the door, she turned to Bolt. "I owe my brother everything. He gave up his life to help me. It's a debt I can never repay."

"Speaking of which, do you have that five dollars you borrowed from me?" asked Grom.

"No. That's also a debt I can never repay."

Grom waved goodbye to Zemya. When he did, the sleeve of his shirt lifted, just a little. Bolt gasped. Zemya said birthmarks were hereditary, so it made sense that Grom might have one, too. But did Bolt really see what he thought he saw? His glimpse had been quick, so he could have been mistaken.

Zemya closed the door behind her. Grom turned to Bolt, curling his hands into fists. He cracked his knuckles and smiled.

Bolt backed away. "Are you going to hurt me?"

"I don't like you, so I should. But it depends," Grom said. "You want outta here, right? I can help you do that. But you gotta help me first."

12. Refusals and Repercussions

As Grom rubbed his fists together, Bolt fidgeted. "What do you mean?" Bolt asked. He bit his lips despite how chapped they were from his earlier lip-biting.

"I'll help you get outta here and into that fortress. And you don't have to pass no mole test, either."

Bolt's eyes opened wide. Grom didn't seem like the type that would help Bolt. The way he was cracking his knuckles, he seemed more like the type that would hurt Bolt.

"Earthworms are getting scarce," continued Grom. "I found less than two dozen yesterday, and you can't feed an entire burrow of were-moles with twenty-two earthworms. They'd be all 'We want more,' and I'd be all 'Got none, sorry.' But I could find more if I had some help." He raised an eyebrow.

"You want me to help you find earthworms? Sure!" How hard could that be?

"No, I don't want you to help me find worms," said Grom, rolling his eyes.

Bolt's excitement faded to confusion. "I'll do anything."

"I was hoping you'd say that." Grom stared at Bolt, and the more he stared, the more Bolt stared back. Was this a staring contest? Bolt's eyes watered, but he refused to blink, to blink, to blink. OK, he blinked.

Grom didn't seem to care, so perhaps Bolt had been mistaken about the staring contest. Bolt took in the boy's long, thin nose and bushy eyebrows. His hair that sprung up sort of like horns. Grom rested his chin on his hand, and his shirtsleeve lifted again, revealing the birthmark that Bolt had seen before. It was exactly what he thought it was.

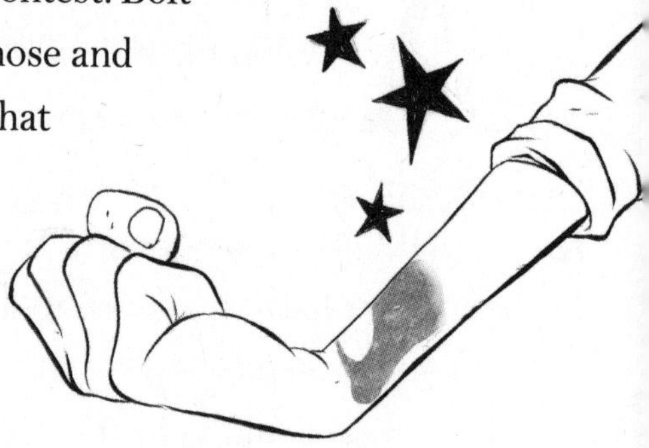

A penguin birthmark.

"No," said Bolt.

"You said you'd do anything."

"Anything but that."

Grom frowned and cracked his knuckles again. "Even if Topo hadn't told me you were a werepenguin, it's pretty obvious with that big birthmark on your neck. I know how it works. You bite me at midnight, and I say, 'Yay, I'm a werepenguin,' and you say, 'Welcome to the club, Grom,' and then I break you outta here."

Biting people was what the Stranger did. And the Baron. They were evil creatures, turning people into werepenguins to conquer the world and join their horrible army. But Bolt was different. He didn't want to conquer anyone. How could Bolt bite someone, cursing them to live forever as a monster?

He couldn't. He wouldn't. Even if it meant flunking a test. "Ask me anything else."

Grom pounded his fist onto his knee. The *slap!* of fist against bone was surprisingly loud, and looked painful, although Grom didn't grimace. He did it again, harder. *Slap!* This time he grimaced a little. "Just think what I could do! I could find worms. I could fight penguin guards instead of hiding from them. I could feel the power of being a penguin!"

"It's mostly just craving fish all the time," said Bolt. "And wanting to rule the world. A lot of ruling."

"One bite," Grom growled. "Even if you fail the test,

they won't execute you right away. I'll get you out in the morning."

"No."

"Oh, come on," said Grom. "Just think how wonderful it would be!"

"It wouldn't be wonderful. It would be terrible."

Grom flexed his fingers and then curled them into fists again, snarling. "I'd hate to have to hurt you."

"It really doesn't look that way to me."

Grom moved toward Bolt. If it had been midnight, and Bolt were a werepenguin, he might have been able to fight Grom. But now? No way. If only a penguin were here to help!

Wait a moment. Grom wasn't a penguin, but he had a penguin birthmark. Didn't that mean he had some penguin blood inside him? Didn't that mean he and Bolt were already linked, and that they shared the same penguin-verse?

Bolt wasn't close to understanding how the penguin-verse worked, but he reached into Grom's head anyway, trying to grab hold of whatever small amount of penguinism might be inside there. *Stop. Don't do this,* he thought. He hoped whatever fuzziness had kept him from reaching into the heads of the PEWD penguin guards was gone. He couldn't feel the haze down in this mole hole.

Grom jumped, slightly. Bolt felt the words burrowing

their way into Grom's head, much like the crawling earthworms Grom had caught earlier.

You don't want to hurt me, thought Bolt.

Grom shook his head and pulled his earlobes. "What are you doing to me?" he yelped.

We are family, in a way. Becoming a werepenguin is not a blessing, but a curse.

"Get outta my head!" cried Grom, hitting his ears and then cocking a fist back. He was close enough to Bolt that one swing . . .

Don't move another muscle!

Grom stopped. Bolt saw that he struggled to move his leg, but it seemed stuck to the ground. He could actually feel the spinal nerves that connected Grom's brain to the rest of his body, suspending the older boy's muscle control.

"Let me go!" Grom howled, but since he couldn't move his mouth it sounded like "Eh ee o!"

A calm cascaded over Bolt, as a deep feeling of penguinism coursed through his body. He sensed a connection to the penguin-verse he hadn't before. The radio waves of fishiness that existed in the molecules of the earth were his to command. This was true power! Why, with those waves of fishiness, Bolt could control the world!

Suddenly, the door swung open and Topo stood in the doorway, snipping his scissors. Bolt came to his senses—control the world? Never!—and released his hold on Grom,

who staggered back, gasping for air. Bolt's connection to the penguin-verse was gone, too, evaporated as quickly as an ice cube in a hot tub.

"What's going on here?" Topo demanded.

Grom glowered but said nothing.

"We are ready," Topo hissed, jabbing his rubber scissors up. "It's time for the Test of the Mole." *Snip, snip, snip!*

13. A Break in the Action

A roar echoed across the ship's deck. The seals had been playing foosball—I had thoughtfully put a foosball table in their cage to help them pass the time during the sea voyage—but the little ball kept bouncing out of their cages. Seals can be temperamental sorts, and they honked loudly until one of the deckhands retrieved the sphere and tossed it back to them.

"Perhaps this is a good time to catch our breath," said the penguin caretaker.

"A breath?" I asked, dismayed. "Don't be absurd. Did Bolt get a chance to take a breath while being imprisoned by those mole creatures? Go on. Please."

"Let's at least take a detour and check on Annika and Blackburn. The last time we left them they were also in a precarious situation. You haven't forgotten about Annika and Blackburn, have you?"

"Who? I mean, of course not," I said, although I had. "They have been a constant source of worry for me," I added, trying to remember who they were. Oh, right. The bandit girl and the pirate. "But must we leave Bolt now, at such a dangerous part of his story?"

"Blackburn and Annika's part of the story was equally dangerous, or soon would be."

"Fine. Go on then," I said. "But tell me—do you enjoy pausing parts of the story and leaving me in continual but annoyed suspense?"

"I . . ." he said, pausing. "I . . ."

"Yes?" I asked, eagerly leaning in.

"It's just that . . ."

"Yes?" I asked, the tension mounting.

"I . . ."

"Just tell me!" I screamed.

"No. I don't enjoy doing that at all."

"I didn't think so," I said, and then he continued his tale after another frustrating pause.

14. The Hero Code

Annika and Blackburn stopped running as soon as they realized they weren't being followed by penguins anymore. How long had that been? A few seconds? A few minutes?

Annika held her knife at the ready, and Blackburn his sword. Annika gritted her teeth, waiting. Maybe this was a trick? Were the penguins sneaking around the side to ambush them? Well, they'd be sorry! As a bandit, Annika was trained to fight. So was Blackburn. Plus, they had Bolt's penguin mind powers. With all that, Annika felt their chances of victory were actually pretty decent, despite being outmanned more than one hundred to three.

"Ready, Blackburn?" she asked.

"Borscht!" he shouted, which Annika interpreted as a yes.

"Ready, Bolt?" she asked. But after this inquiry, there was silence. "You must be thinking penguin thoughts, so just a grunt of acknowledgment is fine," she said, mindful of Bolt's spiritual, slightly peculiar penguin ways. Yet, again, she was met with silence.

"Why, the boy is gone!" exclaimed Blackburn. Annika turned. Blackburn was right. Bolt was nowhere to be found. He'd been trailing them the whole time, running much slower than she and Blackburn, but Annika had made sure to check back every so often to see that he wasn't too far behind. Now he wasn't there at all. It was as if he had sprouted wings and flown away, but of course penguins couldn't fly, and neither could Bolt.

That penguin silence was now even more disturbing. Had the guards captured Bolt and left? Annika tried to retrace the chase in her mind. There had been a fork in the path, and she hadn't thought to look behind her. Had Bolt made a mistake and turned the wrong way?

Or had he chosen the other path on purpose?

The realization that he might have drawn the penguins away to save her and Blackburn hit Annika like a brick. She staggered back.

"Ye look like someone hit ye with a brick," Blackburn observed.

Annika nodded. "We have to help him!" She wanted to run down the path, back to where the road forked, but Blackburn grabbed her arm.

"Whatever has happened has happened," he said. "They either have him, or he's dead, or he's escaped. Hopefully that last one."

"But he's my friend!" Annika protested. "I have to go after him!" She wiggled her arm to break free from the pirate's grip, but couldn't. He wrapped her in a bear hug.

"I can't let ye go. It would be crazy, I'm tellin' ye. The boy's got powers, aye? He can control penguins. Maybe he'll be fine."

Bolt had been getting stronger; that was impossible to argue. But still! Annika wasn't the sort to leave someone behind. "He's my best friend!" Again, she fought against Blackburn's grasp. "Let go of me!"

"Not until ye settle down and agree that running after that penguin horde would be pointless."

"Fine! Just let me go!"

Blackburn did. For a moment, Annika thought about running down the path anyway, but she knew Blackburn was right. Besides, Bolt *was* powerful, in his own way. He was one with the penguins. At least, that's what Bolt said he was trying to do with all that silent meditation on the boat.

"We'll go to the fortress then," said Annika. "If he's

a prisoner, we'll rescue him. I'm not just going to stand here twiddling my thumbs, are you?" She glanced over at Blackburn, who was twiddling his thumbs. When he saw Annika watching him, he stopped.

"And if he's not a prisoner?" Blackburn asked. "Then we've gone there and risked our necks for nothin'."

"If he's not at the fortress, then where could he be?" asked Annika, panic mounting inside her. "He's not dead."

"But if . . ."

"He's not!"

Blackburn raised his hands in surrender. "No. He's not. Of course he's not."

Annika didn't say anything, but the uncertainty spoke volumes. She shook her head. "Well, if something happened to Bolt—and I'm not saying anything did—we can still steal that tooth. I can sail to the South Pole and find the Stranger and free the world's penguins myself."

"Ye'd never find the Stranger. Ye know that. Besides, ye think ye can fight the mightiest werepenguin in the world with a tooth? Maybe Bolt has faith that would work, but not me."

"Well, we have to do *something*."

"Shiver me timbers! I'm not about to risk me life just to do *somethin'*. If Bolt escaped, he'll come lookin' for us. We should head to the boat. That's where I'd go if I had recently escaped a horde of dentist penguins."

Annika slowly nodded. "But what if he doesn't show up?"

"Then we can discuss our next move. In the meantime, we twiddle our thumbs, aye?" Blackburn once again began to twiddle in earnest.

Annika didn't like doing nothing, and she had never enjoyed thumb-twiddling, but she knew the pirate's advice was good advice. At least for now. They walked back down the path, retracing their steps, staying in the shadows to avoid being spotted. Quickly, they found their way to the footpath that led down to their ship in the hidden cove below. It was a long walk, and they said nothing to each other the entire time. Annika was too filled with worry to speak.

When they finally reached the cove, Bolt was not there. Annika plopped down on a rock near the boat. She would wait. For now.

Unfortunately, thinking to yourself *I will wait* is much different than actually waiting. Waiting is very boring. Annika drummed her fingers. She counted to five thousand and then back down to one. She thought about thumb-twiddling but then decided against it.

Blackburn soon abandoned his own twiddling and took out his sword to practice, swishing it this way and that. Annika was tempted to join him, but she was still angry. He was way too concerned about his own safety while their friend could be facing serious harm. Annika couldn't help but think of Blackburn's resistance to travel to Pingvingrad in the first place, unless promised treasure. She was still bitter about it, and maybe a little hurt. She was angry at herself, too—angry for doing nothing but sitting on a rock and not springing into action to find Bolt, despite the pirate's sound advice. Every moment Bolt was away was another moment he could be in trouble.

Annika needed to think about something else. Anything else. So she removed her bandit handbook and some spare pieces of blank paper she had crammed inside it. She gripped her quill and wrote.

THE CODE OF THE BANDIT, CHAPTER 112, SUBSECTION 5

ON BEING A HERO

~~Don't be a hero! A bandit must steal, rob, kidnap, and be extremely nasty. Bandits are also selfish, robbing and stealing for their clan, with total disregard for outsiders. Heroic deeds, which include rescuing people, freeing cities, stopping crime, saving lives (other than your own), putting out fires, cleaning used gum from under benches or school desks, and so on are strictly forbidden. Remember, you are a bandit! (And, BTW, pirates~~

~~aren't heroes either, in case you were wondering about that.) If you want to be a hero, then you are in the wrong profession.~~

~~Let's say, for example, you pass a burning building. You could run inside, save everyone, and be admired around the world for your bravery. But what if the house was set on fire by a giant bullfrog? It's not worth the risk! Get out of there!~~

THE CODE OF THE BANDIT, CHAPTER 112, SUBSECTION 5

ON BEING A HERO—*amended by Annika Lambda*

Bandits aren't naturally heroic, sure. But bandits are clever. And fast. And stealthy. And they have lots of other talents that most people don't have. Why should those talents only be used to rob and kidnap? Can't they also be used to help others who are in trouble?

The answer is yes!

Just because bandits steal and plunder and things like that doesn't mean they can't also make the world a better place. Bandits should help the downtrodden, the poor, and the helpless. It's everyone's job to do that—whether

you're a bandit, or a pirate, or a Viking, or even a were-creature! What sort of world would this be if all anyone ever did was look out for themselves? Not a world I would want to live in, that's for sure.

Besides, what's a hero, anyway?

Yes, it's someone who frees cities from werepenguins, but it is also a friend who keeps a promise, and goes on a voyage to save the world even if she didn't get any treasure from doing it, even when she would rather be home with her father back in Brugaria. A hero can be someone who thinks about her friends before she thinks about herself, and will do anything to protect them.

And why is this bandit book so worried about giant bullfrogs anyway?

Annika Lambda

Annika skimmed over what she wrote. She liked the idea of being a hero, even if bandits weren't traditional sorts of heroes. But heroism wasn't sitting around on a rock and writing in a book. Bolt was depending on them, wherever he was—and he was *not* dead. She had promised him she would help him steal that tooth and defeat the

Stranger. And that's exactly what she would do.

She dropped her handbook back inside her pocket and found Blackburn, who was once again twiddling his thumbs, apparently having grown tired of practicing with his swordfish.

"Bolt should have been back by now. I'm going into that fortress to find him, and if he's not there, then I'll still get the tooth. Even if I can't find the Stranger, maybe I can use it on that werepenguin Dr. What's-Her-Name."

"Dr. Walzanarz."

"Gesundheit."

"Sneakin' into that fortress is a fool's errand."

"You'll get your treasure, don't worry," grunted Annika. "I know that's what you're thinking."

The pirate laughed. "Don't make promises you can't keep, missy."

"I'll keep my end of the bargain." She jabbed her finger at him. "You just keep yours. And I've told you before—stop calling me *missy.*"

Blackburn sighed. "Fine. I'll help ye find that tooth. But I have no intention of fightin' any werepenguins. That was never part of our deal."

"But you will help me find Bolt, right?" Blackburn shrugged, as if disinterested in finding anyone. Annika felt her face turn red, and she clenched her fists. "He's your friend!"

"Pirates don't have friends."

"But—"

"But what?"

"Nothing." Annika crossed her arms and turned away, her eyes watery. How could she convince her entire bandit gang back home to befriend more people if she couldn't even convince Blackburn? Was he really so consumed with treasure that he wouldn't help a friend in need?

Bandits could be friendly! Pirates could be generous!

Couldn't they?

If not, maybe her bandit code rewriting was a big waste of time.

With all those thoughts swirling around her head, Annika marched back up the path and toward the fortress, Blackburn trudging behind.

15. The Test of the Mole

Bolt was barefoot, dressed in a black robe, like his captors. He knelt inside a cavernous chamber where enormous stone pillars with elaborate carvings of moles supported a ceiling so high it disappeared into darkness. Off to the side was a gigantic pile of dirt that also reached up into the darkness above, and was just as wide as it was tall.

The place smelled mostly of earth and mud, but an incredible animal stink, like a stable or a barn gone bad, also permeated the room. Bolt sniffed deeply, and then immediately regretted it. He quickly exhaled, trying to blow out the stink molecules.

Would this be where Bolt's story would finally end?

Was he about to fail some test and also fail the world's penguins all at once? Bolt took a deep breath, hoping the penguin-verse might settle his nerves. All he did was choke on more animal stink.

Zemya stood before him, with Topo, the elders, and a few others from their clan behind her. In addition to their black garments, they each now wore small golden tiaras, which, Bolt had to admit, were quite elegant. "We are set in our traditions," said Zemya in a commanding but steady tone, "like always eating borscht on weekends. But we have a trespasser now among us. And as our laws state, no one is allowed in our burrow unless that person proves themselves to be a mole at heart. But it is not our place to decide such things. That is why we have the Test of the Mole."

A man in a crimson tunic and floppy jester's hat with bells dangling from it stepped forward. He held an old-fashioned lute and began to strum and then sing. His voice, as high-pitched as the others in the mole clan, was also quite lovely.

The Test of the Mole! Right here in our hole!
Will now determine your worth.
Fail and you'll wail, be snipped and then flailed,
Here in our home in the earth.

But if you should ace the test that takes place,

And so your mole heart's confirmed—
Strike up the band! Welcome to our clan!
We'll celebrate and eat worms.

Everyone clapped, including Bolt. The singer bowed and resumed his place among the others. Apparently, his part in the ritual was over.

"Are you ready to take the test, Bolt?" Zemya asked.

Feel the penguin-verse, Bolt thought. But all he felt was panic. "I guess so. But do I need some paper first? Or a pen? How about a number-two pencil?" He was still uncertain of the sort of test he was taking.

Zemya shook her head and pointed to the tall mound of earth to the side. "A single grub has been buried inside that mound. Your task is to find the grub."

That was not what Bolt had been expecting. He stared at the mound. It was big. Very big. Finding a grub in there seemed to be pretty much impossible, and much

harder than even an essay test. Bolt nibbled on his lips. "Is there a time limit?" he asked. His heart slowed a couple of beats when Zemya shook her head. "Are my hands and legs tied?" Bolt's heart slowed even more when Zemya shook her head again. "Is there some sort of trick?"

"There are no tricks, although those are all good ideas," said Zemya, lifting her palms out, as if to show she had no tricks up her sleeves, either. Bolt felt hopeful. "You just need to find the grub before Barsuk does."

Bolt scratched his head. "Who's Barsuk?"

"He is coming now. He is attracted by lute playing."

The room grew silent. The clan members stared at the far wall, which Bolt now noticed had a large crack in it. Rumbling shook the ground underfoot. Bolt's heart regained its frenzied beating.

"Holy Moley!" shouted the lute player, who was then joined by Topo, and soon the entire group was shouting, "Holy Moley! Holy Moley!" as the small crack widened. Soil shifted and crumbled from the wall while it spread farther apart, as if on hinges. Pebbles sprinkled the ground, and then from the dark recesses of whatever was behind that wall, a furry claw emerged, a claw the size of a full-grown bear's, followed by a gigantic furry brown head. The dirt continued to cascade down the tunnel's wall as the animal crawled into the chamber. It shook off its skin, like a dog after a bath.

"Barsuk!" cried Zemya. "The Holy Moley himself!"

It was, quite simply, the largest and most terrible mole Bolt could ever imagine. Bolt's legs felt weak from terror, and his head spun. He almost fainted, but found a small amount of inner strength to keep standing. This beast must have been ten feet long. It let out a loud screech, sort of like a monkey with sinus congestion. Its nose wrinkled, and it rubbed its feet on the ground.

A million things ran through Bolt's mind, and none of them were good. *How can I find a grub faster than this monstrosity? Do moles eat people and, if they don't, will this creature eat me by mistake? Does this place have a bed I can hide under?*

"They say it is hard to find a needle in a haystack," said Zemya. "But finding a grub in a giant pile of dirt is much harder, unless you have the heart of a mole inside you."

Bolt heard a single lute strum and the jester sing out: *"The Test of the Mole! Right here in our hole!"*

"But how am I supposed to find a grub before the . . . the . . . Holy Moley?" Bolt asked, pointing at the beast with a shaking finger.

Zemya shrugged. "I didn't say the test would be easy."

The giant mole growled at Bolt, its mouth opening and closing, revealing a long row of sharp teeth. Bolt clutched his hands into fists at his sides to keep them from twitching.

Bolt gazed at the creature's long snout as it sniffed the ground and snorted. He wasn't sure how moles found food, but that sniffer would seem to be a good place to start.

Penguins don't have a particularly strong sense of smell, unfortunately for Bolt.

"We shall begin on the count of ten," said Zemya. "Ten . . . nine . . ."

The mole shifted on its paws, waiting for the countdown to end, and it made Bolt wonder. If he could control penguins with his mind, did that mean Zemya or one of the others was communicating to Barsuk? It seemed likely, since he doubted the beast could count.

"Eight . . . seven . . ."

Bolt had never even seen a grub before, although he knew they were beetle larvae, which meant they were very small, probably less than an inch long. How was he supposed to—

"One . . . go!"

"Hey, what happened to six through two?" Bolt complained.

Zemya shrugged. "Moles can't count."

Bolt didn't have time to think. The monster charged into the mound of earth, burrowing itself inside with its claws. Bolt took a deep breath and dove in on the opposite side.

It was pitch black, of course. Bolt dug himself inside, deeper.

Fully submerged in the middle of the pile, Bolt heard nothing but his own heart. It was quiet in the dirt. Peaceful, almost. He reached out into the penguin-verse. Maybe, if he cleared his head and focused on the surrounding penguin energy, he could sense the grub. He forced himself to relax. Be the grub. Be the dirt.

All he felt was stupid. He could connect with penguins, not grubs.

He thought back to his days at the Oak Wilt orphanage, where toe-nibbling moles used to crawl out from under the floorboards while the kids slept. Once, Bolt had awoken in the dead of night to discover not one, not two, but three moles nibbling his toes at the same time. Bolt didn't sleep for weeks afterward.

The memory of that moment jarred Bolt now. He had come so far and faced so many monstrous threats. But of all the ways Bolt had imagined dying—and there had been so, so many—being snipped and flailed after losing a mole test hadn't even made his list. He took a breath, which was a mistake since all he did was suck in the powdery dirt. He had to control himself. He could do this. He had to do this. The world was depending on him.

But no. His mind traveled back to the orphanage again; he could practically feel moles sucking on his toes. His mind swelled with panic. He was going to scream!

Wait.

Barsuk!

It *was* sucking on Bolt's toes.

I guess my feet are sort of grubby, thought Bolt, kicking the beast's snout. He felt his mind drifting inside Barsuk. Somehow, he was becoming one with the mole. Was Bolt imagining it, or was he now part of some odd mole-verse? No, it was Barsuk—part of Barsuk was in the penguin-verse. The spirit of a dead penguin, long ago eaten, lingered in Barsuk's bowels.

Maybe Bolt could still ace this test! He could feel the penguin's blubbery remains inside Barsuk and, as a result, could almost smell what the mole smelled, feel what it felt.

And Barsuk felt a desire to lick Bolt's toes, which was not helpful.

The creature stopped licking and darted to Bolt's left. It sensed a grub, and grubs were more delicious than grubby toes. Bolt could feel ravenous hunger filling the colossal mole monster.

Bolt had no idea where the grub was, but he raced forward because Barsuk did. Or rather, he tried to race. Bolt swam with his legs and his feet through the dirt, but it was a very slow crawl.

Bolt was still ahead of Barsuk, but the creature was faster and quickly gaining, its razor-like claws slicing through the soil. Bolt wanted to scream, to cry out: "No! It can't end like this!" And he did open his mouth to scream, and regretted it instantly because his mouth filled with dirt and at the same time Barsuk rammed into Bolt's chin. Bolt flew six inches forward, his mouth filling up with more and more chalky dirt as he went, and he gagged and swallowed a disgusting mouthful of it, and something else. Something slimy and wriggly that slipped down his throat.

The grub.

Bolt feared he was going to have a horrible stomachache later.

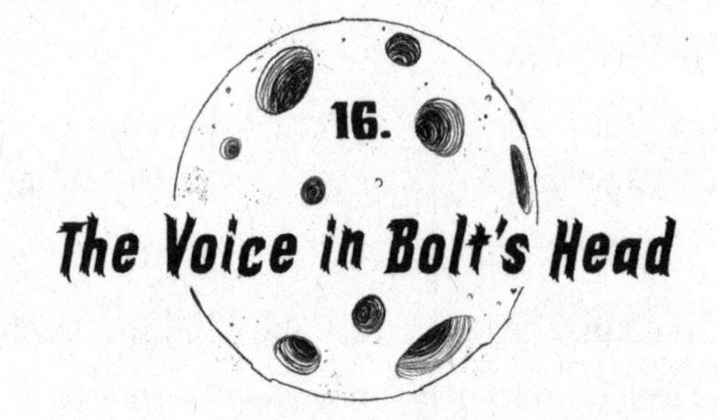

16. The Voice in Bolt's Head

Bolt stood in the large chamber, his stomach unsettled from eating dirt and a grub, but he was relieved he had passed the test, even if he owed his victory to a stroke of luck. Or not. The penguin cosmos was vast, and Bolt was the chosen one. Perhaps he had been destined to pass the test all along.

Zemya smiled at Bolt, her buckteeth appearing more pronounced than usual, although Bolt knew it was just a trick of the light. "Congratulations, Bolt. You have passed the Test of the Mole. You are now one of us. Which means you get all the benefits of being a mole. Care for a snack?" She held out a few worms on her palm.

"No thanks," said Bolt, clutching his stomach.

A few others in the room ran up to Zemya and grabbed the worms from her hand, shouting, "Congratulations, Bolt!" and "Welcome to the labour!" and "Are you sure you don't want any worms?"

But not everyone seemed happy. Topo shook his fist at Barsuk and grumbled, "I can't believe you lost to this spy." The mole hung its head, dejected, and crawled back to its hole. Topo sneered at Bolt and snipped his scissors a few times. "Can't I snip him, Zemya? Just a little bit?"

"We cannot harm him," said Zemya. "We are mole creatures. If we do not keep our word, what are we?"

"Mole creatures who don't keep their word?" Topo guessed. He snipped his shears twice and then slipped them into his pocket. "Very well."

"Grom promised he would take me inside the fortress," Bolt reminded Zemya. His temporary relief faded at the thought of the immense task still in front of him.

Bolt also thought of his friends. They were probably worried about him, wondering where he was or whether he was OK. He was anxious to join them again and just hoped they didn't do something foolish, like go back to the fortress and try to steal that tooth without him.

"Of course. As I promised, moles always help one another," said Zemya. "Grom will happily escort you inside."

"Happily?" asked Bolt, more than a little dubious.

"Well, maybe not happily," she admitted. "But he will. First, we'll celebrate your victory with a party. It's quite an honor to pass the test, and moles are famous for our parties. They are quite fun: we dig holes, we sniff each other, and we dig more holes."

"That sounds like a great time," said Bolt, faking a smile to be polite. "But I really need to get going. And I'm not much of a hole digger, to be honest."

Zemya looked down at Bolt's hands and nodded. "I guess not. Everyone will be disappointed, though. Party's off!" she cried out.

The others in the room mumbled unhappily. The lute player strummed a miserable-sounding note.

"First no snipping, and now no party?" asked Topo, frowning and kicking a rock in frustration. "This entire day has been a waste."

Bolt threw all of them an apologetic shrug, but finding his friends and grabbing that tooth were more important than partying. Zemya instructed Bolt to follow her, and soon they were winding through the dimly lit mole tunnels. They passed an enormous room filled with industrial-sized washing machines. People held large laundry baskets with bundles of black cloth, and every machine seemed to be running.

"It's a lot of work keeping our robes clean while living

in a hole underground," Zemya explained. "But at least we don't have to separate out any whites or brights."

As they continued past the laundromat and down the next tunnel, Bolt felt a sudden buzzing in his skull. It filled his head suddenly, without warning. He stopped and gripped his ears.

What do you want? Bolt thought.

There was a moment of silence and then a burst of static, as if from a walkie-talkie, vibrating in Bolt's head, followed by a voice. *Hello, Bolt, my boy.*

I am not your boy, Bolt thought back.

There was another burst of static, and after a few moments the voice emerged through the noise. *Are you underground or something? We're getting terrible reception.*

Leave me alone.

Oh, I can't do that. After all, we are meant to be together, are we not? Me, here in my ice cave. You in search of a tooth to fight with. As if a tooth could defeat me!

If you're so confident, why don't you come here and get me?

No, no, no. That's not how this works. You will come to me. And then we will work together to conquer the world. If you survive your little trip to Pingvingrad, that is.

Bolt found himself growing angry. Who did the Stranger think he was, assuming Bolt would join his army? *I will fight you. And I will win.*

Bolt, my boy. My poor, deluded boy. You will join me. It is what you were chosen to do. The fates have foretold it. We will rule as one!

"I will never rule! I was chosen to free the world's penguins!"

"Are you all right?" Zemya asked Bolt, looking at him with a concerned expression. "What are you talking about?"

"I said that last part out loud?" The voice inside his head vanished, and Bolt rubbed his temples to remove any lingering intrusions. "I was just daydreaming," he said, forcing a grin. "Can I ask you something, Zemya? Do were-moles ever feel like it would be fun to form a giant army and rule the world?"

She scrunched up her already wrinkled face. "Of course not!"

"Yeah, me neither," said Bolt, hoping the dimly lit tunnel hid the beads of sweat on his forehead and ignoring the part of him that was tempted to welcome the Stranger's evil words.

17. Mission Implausible

The sun was half buried in the horizon by the time Blackburn and Annika trekked up to the fortress. As they had earlier, the two halted just before the tree line and peeked out. There were now hundreds of penguins standing around. PEWD appeared to be on high alert. A large group of birds marched back and forth in front of the main gate. Other penguins were positioned every few hundred feet along the entire fence, as far as the eye could see. Some stared steely-eyed, waiting for trouble. Others ran about barking orders.

The side of the fence that had crashed down had already been repaired, and the hole underneath it had been filled in. There would be no sneaking into PEWD this time, at least not that way.

To make things even worse, every penguin held one of those jumbo-sized toothbrushes over a shoulder. Annika imagined being scrubbed by one. She bristled at the thought of its steel-like bristles.

Then her mind went to Bolt. If one of those toothbrushes had been used to scrub him . . . she pushed the thought away. *He is fine,* she told herself. She wanted to save the world, but she wanted to save Bolt more. Sure, her friend had become more distant over the last week as he explored his powers and the penguin universe thing. But deep inside he was still Bolt, and he still needed Annika.

Annika tapped Blackburn on the shoulder. "Shh," she said, and pointed to her eyes, gestured toward the main entrance, and then wiggled her fingers to mimic walking. She started to mime the "Little Bunny Foo Foo" rhyme, but stopped. Now was not the time for singing.

Blackburn nodded and followed Annika, tiptoeing behind the trees until they came to a stop near the main entrance. Annika had hoped to see an opportunity to sneak in, but those hopes were quickly dashed; there were simply too many toothbrush-toting penguins at the gate. Then she spotted a nearby tree with low branches, perfect for climbing. It was also one of the few trees with leaves, so it provided some coverage. They couldn't risk being seen. Annika scampered up limb by limb to get a better view of the grounds as Blackburn lumbered up behind her,

scraping his hands and nearly falling twice. "Borscht," he exclaimed. "I'm glad there are no trees to climb on pirate ships." He shook a thumb at the guards. "If these birds brush their teeth with those things, I'd hate to see their dental floss."

Annika nodded, and an image of Bolt being angrily flossed filled her head. *No.* She had to stop thinking these kinds of things. If she was going to get into PEWD, she needed to concentrate on the job ahead.

She and Blackburn kept completely still as a group of penguin guards approached them, marching in formation down the dirt road. The guards passed just underneath Annika and Blackburn. One of the penguins paused for a moment, and Annika was convinced she and Blackburn had been noticed. She reached for her knife and grabbed its handle; she wouldn't go down without a fight. But then the penguin continued marching past.

"Who knew penguins could march so well?" marveled Blackburn.

"Penguins do all sorts of things I never thought they could do," admitted Annika.

"Aye," said Blackburn. "But we can't stay up in this tree all day. I'm going to take a closer look."

"Let me do it," said Annika. Blackburn didn't have her clandestine banditry skills.

"Nah, I need to get down. This hard branch is hurting

me bum." Before Annika could object, Blackburn dropped to the ground beside the tree with a loud *thud!*

"Shh!" hissed Annika. Fortunately, the patrolling penguins were now quite a bit past them and hadn't heard the pirate. None of the penguin guards positioned along the fence looked in their direction either. Hopefully, Blackburn could sneak closer without making his presence obvious. He took a quick step forward around the tree and . . .

Snap!

His foot broke a twig in half.

"Quiet!" whispered Annika in alarm, looking left and right. Still, no one paid attention to them. But that didn't mean they were in the clear.

Blackburn took another step forward and toward the road. "Ow!" He hopped up and grimaced. "My bad. Didn't see that rock." Annika threw him a dirty look. He took another step.

Pip! Pip! Pip! He stepped on some Bubble Wrap.

Pwwffft! He stepped on a whoopee cushion.

La de da! He stepped on an accordion.

Annika glared at Blackburn as he scrambled back up the tree, but not before stepping on a bike horn. *Hoot!* Annika shook her head in dismay. Miraculously no penguins seemed to have noticed.

"At least I avoided those alarm clocks," said Blackburn,

pointing to a group of clocks lying in a small hole next to the road.

Annika jabbed her thumb down the tree line. "Look!"

Blackburn had climbed back up the tree just in time. Another band of penguins was coming up the dirt road, pulling a large wagon. Annika could smell seafood—the entire back of the wagon was filled with silver glistening fish, several feet deep. Some even still wiggled. She covered her nose with her arm to keep the horrible stink away.

Annika nudged Blackburn, pointing two fingers at the wagon, then three fingers up, then making a circle with her thumb, and then wiggling her fingers.

"Yer not suggesting we jump into that wagon, hide under all that fish in the back of that cart, are ye?" Annika nodded, grateful that Blackburn could interpret her bandit gestures better than Bolt could. Blackburn didn't look happy with the plan, but nodded anyway.

The wagon would come directly underneath them when the penguins passed. They could drop right into the cart. Yes, it would be smelly and slimy. Yes, they would both need long showers afterward. But sometimes smelly and slimy and shampoo were the best options.

They needed the cart to stop or slow down for a moment, so they could land in the fish without mistiming

their drop. In the Brugarian forest, a bandit could topple a tree onto the road to slow down a carriage, allowing bandits to climb inside and rob it. That's how Annika had first met Bolt. But she didn't think she could cut down a tree quickly enough for that plan to work now. She hadn't thought to bring an ax or a saw anyway.

The cart drew closer, and Blackburn sneezed. Annika cringed, but the cart was loudly creaking as it rolled, and no one else heard him. Still, Annika glowered at him.

"Sorry." Blackburn shrugged. "Allergies."

The cart was nearly underneath them now, and Annika needed to figure out a way to stall it. Carefully, she plucked an acorn off the branch next to her. It wasn't much, but she didn't have many options. She flicked the acorn at one of the penguins marching in front of the wagon and held her breath.

Doink. The acorn bounced off the penguin's beak.

Unfortunately, penguins have hard beaks. The penguin didn't even flinch as the acorn bounced off. Annika silently cursed herself. She watched as the acorn popped up into the air. It landed on one of the bird's flippers and then spun, flipped up, bounced twice, and then rolled to a stop in a hole along the road, smacking against one of the alarm clocks Blackburn had noticed earlier.

Brriiiinnnnngg!

The sound jolted Annika as much as it did the pen-

guins. As the birds halted, surprised by the jarring noise, Annika moved fast. She pushed Blackburn off the branch and then released her own grip and dropped down.

Splunge! Fwssst!

They both landed in the cart, amid the soft, squishy bodies of dead fish.

Annika held her breath, partly because she wasn't sure if someone had spotted them and partly because she was lying inside a giant bed of smelly fish. She didn't relax until the carriage began to move again.

Being buried in a giant pile of fish is not a particularly fun way to travel, but at least it cushioned the hard wooden floor of the wagon, which bumped and creaked on the uneven path. Annika didn't dare move in case a penguin saw her, which was frustrating since she had a fish in her earhole that she desperately wanted to dislodge. Somehow, despite the rocking of the carriage and the countless bumps, the fish remained stubbornly in place.

The cart stopped for a moment, but soon began moving again. They must be through the main gate and on the other side of the fence by now! Fortunately, the stop and start of the carriage jiggled the cart, and the fish in her ear fell out. Unfortunately, another fish somehow wedged itself into one of her nostrils, and that was even worse. She really wanted to sneeze it out, but that would only blow their cover.

The cart stopped once again, and Annika heard rusty creaking, like old chains lowering a garage door, followed by a thump. Soon, there was the sound of their penguin entourage waddling away, and a door banging shut in the distance. Then, silence.

"Borscht," mumbled Blackburn. "Can I move now? I've had a fish stuck in both my nose and my ear since we fell in here."

"Sure. I think we're alone." Annika and Blackburn sat up, removing various wedged-in fish.

They were inside a large storage warehouse with a slanted wooden ceiling and sheet metal sides. There were no lights, but there was plenty of sunlight streaming in from cracks and seams in the walls. Four or five carts, just like the one they now sat inside, were fixed along a wall, each one filled to the brim with fish. The stink in this room was so thick Annika's eyes watered. "Let's get out of here. I've never smelled anything so horrible in my life."

"Ye've obviously never been on a ship with two hundred unwashed pirates before."

Annika jumped down from the cart, wet and disgusted by the coating of raw fish slime covering every inch of her. Blackburn was in a similar state. Next to the warehouse's delivery door from which they must have entered was a smaller door. As they walked toward it, Annika—normally sure-footed—slipped on some rogue fish. She regained her balance and grabbed Blackburn's elbow when he almost teetered over himself. But they soon reached the door, and she grabbed the doorknob and twisted.

"It's stuck." Annika jiggled the knob and pushed, but it wouldn't budge.

"Let me try," said Blackburn. Annika moved out of the way, and the pirate grabbed the knob, straining to twist it, grunting from the exertion. "Ugh! Omm! Errr!"

"Shh," urged Annika.

Still struggling, Blackburn moved his feet back to gain

more leverage, and stepped on a toy fire truck. It let out a loud siren squeak. *Weeeeeooow!*

"Quiet," Annika whispered urgently.

Blackburn continued to push. He stepped back and into a cardboard box filled with glass plates. *Crack! Crsnk! Glzzzz!*

As Blackburn continued to struggle, the door groaned, rusty metal practically screaming in agony. Annika buried her face in her hands.

Finally, the door opened wide, and Blackburn fell forward, landing on a pile of cowbells.

Ring-a-ling-a-ling!

Annika and Blackburn were on the lawn of the PEWD complex, across from the main domed concrete building. They spotted no one. Maybe luck was on their side. Skipping forward, they crouched behind some bushes. Annika pointed to a snare drum and a tuba nearby. Blackburn stepped gingerly out of the way to avoid them, and backed up onto a cotton ball.

Thft.

Spotlights beamed onto the lawn, shining from giant lights positioned at the top of every building in the compound. Three dozen toothbrush-wielding penguins rushed toward them, seemingly from out of nowhere.

"Really? They heard *that*?" moaned Annika.

The penguins surrounded them, snarling, clomping

their beaks together and waving their toothbrushes in the air. But Annika was not the sort to go quietly into the night, which is quite different from sneaking quietly into the night, which was something she could do well, unlike Blackburn. She unsheathed her knife. Blackburn withdrew his swordfish.

Annika waited for the penguins to attack, but they didn't. Annika continued to wait. And wait. She was growing a little impatient. And then a few penguins parted, and a tall, statuesque woman strode into their circle. She wore a white dentist's coat, plain except for a fluffy cheetah-fur collar. The woman was pale, almost as white as her coat, which contrasted sharply with her charcoal-black hair. She was attractive despite her long beak-like nose and bushy eyebrows. "Vat is this? Voo are you? Vy am I saying vords with a *V* instead of a *W*?"

"Because you have a Germanic accent?" Annika guessed.

The woman shook her head. "Nope. It's just fun to speak that way. I mean *vay*. Any*vay*, I am Dr. Valzanarz."

"Gesundheit," said Annika. "But do you mean *Walzanarz*?"

"Of course. Now I'll ask again, voo are you?"

Annika blinked. "What?"

"Voo? Voo?" the dentist demanded.

"Do you mean *who*? With a *W*?" Dr. Walzanarz nodded.

Annika held out her knife. "All you need to know is that we're here to steal a silver tooth. Give it to us and we won't hurt you."

Next to her, Blackburn made a *Z* with his swordfish.

Dr. Walzanarz looked unimpressed. She glanced behind her, where the penguins continued to snarl and wave their toothbrushes. Dr. Walzanarz stared back at Annika and Blackburn. "You won't hurt *me*? I have fifty penguins carrying dangerous toothbrushes. There are only two of you. Am I missing something?"

Annika scowled. "Toothbrush-carrying penguins are no match for the greatest bandit who ever lived—or at least I will be someday—and a fearsome pirate! We'll never surrender! Right, Blackburn?"

Blackburn dropped his swordfish and raised his arms up. "Actually, I'd rather surrender, if that's all right with you, missy."

The woman smiled, displaying perfect—and perfectly golden—teeth. Annika had to shield her eyes from the glare. "I've noticed you don't have bushy eyebrows nor long, thin noses, so neither of you are the guest I vas expecting." She turned to the penguins: "Throw them in the vaiting room. I'll deal vith them later."

No one moved. The penguins remained snarling in a circle. Dr. Walzanarz turned to them, her face blooming red. "Don't just stand there! I said I vant them in the vaiting room!"

The penguins still didn't move. Finally, one of the penguins barked. The dentist groaned. "Fine. I want you to throw them in the waiting room. With a *W. Want* and *waiting*, not *vant* and *vaiting*. Are you satisfied now?" She frowned. "And it's so fun to speak in pretend accents, too."

18. Dinnertime. Or Is It Breakfast?

Bolt changed back into his clothes and then followed Grom, Zemya, and Topo through the dark mole tunnels. Grom kept shooting Bolt furtive, hostile glances. He had agreed to keep his promise and help steal the tooth, but didn't appear to be all that happy about it. In fact, his exact words were: "I'll help you, but I'm very unhappy about it."

After a while, they climbed out of the hole and emerged onto a quiet stretch of beach along the lapping sea, the moon and stars overhead. Bolt was glad for the fresh air against his face, to smell the salt water, and to feel the fish in his pores. He stretched his arms. Penguins were meant to be outside, near water, near seafood.

A few scattered ship parts littered the sand. The full

moon above was so bright and large that it bathed the island in light. At midnight, Bolt would turn into a penguin and his new friends would turn into moles. Only Grom would remain human.

The boy sidled up to Bolt. "You can still bite me tonight."

"Not happening."

"Have I told you I don't like you?"

"Not in the last few minutes," Bolt mumbled to himself.

The thick Pingvingrad air swirled around them, the dense hate hammering Bolt's ears and blowing into his mouth. He burped.

Bolt closed his eyes and concentrated on clearing the wispy fog, like he had on the pirate ship. He couldn't repel all the hate mist—it seemed to go on forever—but he thinned it enough so that it no longer made him want to belch.

"We have many tunnels into the fortress," said Zemya. "But most lead into the gardens. We will need to dig a fresh hole into the main building so you will not trip their alarm system. The beach is a good place to start digging."

"Thank you. But sorry for all the extra work."

"We love to dig," Zemya said with a shrug. "A regular mole can dig up to eighteen feet in an hour, and we're very large moles. Still, it will be a long tunnel. It will take all night."

Topo snipped his rubber scissors a couple of times and then handed them to Bolt. "Sorry for threatening you earlier, my new mole brother. While I dig, can you hold on to these for me?" Bolt held the scissors up, and they flopped over. "They can't actually cut anything," admitted Topo. Bolt slipped them into his pocket.

As Topo and Zemya huddled to discuss their digging strategy, Bolt thought about Annika and Blackburn. If the tunnel took all night, could he run back to the cove and look for them?

No. His blood was churning. It was almost midnight. There was no time.

Besides, he and Grom would run through the tunnel in the morning, grab that tooth, and rush back. It would be fast, easy. Bolt would see his friends after. He would proudly show them the stolen tooth. Wouldn't they be surprised! Even Annika—Bolt knew she had her doubts about his ability to fight and succeed in his quests—would be impressed. Then they would go off to find the Stranger.

As Topo and Zemya spoke together, Grom stood off to the side, his hands buried inside his pockets. Bolt hadn't thought about it before, but it must be lonely for Grom being the only one who didn't dig tunnels, or eat worms, or turn into a were-creature at midnight.

Bolt knew what it was like to be lonely and to feel different. He felt that way himself, first as an orphan and

now as a werepenguin. But maybe things *would* be better if Bolt decided to bite Grom. They could become were-penguin friends. They could fish together. Fight together. Rule! Conquer! All hail Bolt's penguin army!

Bolt shivered. What was he thinking? He didn't want his own penguin army. And he certainly couldn't curse another person into becoming a were-creature. There must be some hate mist lingering in his nostrils, making Bolt think evil thoughts. Yes, that was it. Just evil hate mist.

Bolt's blood began to splash inside him now; blood splashing was never a good sort of feeling. There were no clock chimes here, no ringing bells, but Bolt knew it was midnight. How could he not: the spine tingling, the foot prickling, the elbow buzzing—always the elbow buzzing before his arms vanished and sprouted into wings.

Meanwhile, Zemya and Topo were undergoing their own transmutations. Their abnormally large fingers and fingernails became claws, as did their toenails. Their cheeks grew as their faces became rounder. They had removed their goggles, and their eyes now glowed blue. Fur crept up their bodies. Their clothes fell away, untorn. Apparently, that was why they all wore loose-fitting robes. *I will need to get one of those*, thought Bolt as his pants ripped down the seams.

With a loud snort, Zemya, now a giant mole, dove

into the sand to dig. Topo joined her. Their paws plunged into the soil, moving as fast as a penguin's wings in water. Sand flew into the air, and Bolt stepped back to avoid it being flung into his penguin face.

Grom eyed Bolt, but his expression was unreadable. Envy? Anger?

It didn't matter to Bolt. Only one thing did.

Dinner.

While the were-moles dug, and Grom stood off to the side sulking, Bolt waddled away, toward the sea.

Come to me, come to me, the sea seemed to say, and Bolt swatted at his ears. He was sick of hearing voices in his head, although this one was sweet and harmonic.

Soon, Bolt swam under the waves. As he went deeper into the sea, farther away from the coast, he was joined by a group of penguins. These penguins did not wear head mirrors or hold giant toothbrushes, and Bolt smiled at one. He didn't feel completely like he belonged—Bolt never did—but it felt good swimming with his own, away from problems, away from hate.

How could any penguin feel hate when they were swimming in the sea, feeding on the ocean's riches?

"I hate humans," yelped a penguin swimming by.

"Oh, me too," responded another.

OK, so Bolt was wrong about the feeling hate thing.

A small family of carp swam by. Bolt dove under the

water to grab one for a snack, but two penguins were closer. It is the way of penguins to never fight over food; there is always more than enough fish in the sea for everyone.

Bolt stopped and gasped, which forced him to cough up seawater. Up ahead, a penguin grabbed a carp's head in its beak, and another penguin grabbed its tail. Courtesy would indicate one should let go, or both penguins should. Instead, one of the penguins snarled at the other; it's difficult to snarl with a fish in your mouth, but snarl it did. It tried to yank the fish for its own, but the other penguin didn't let go either. Their wings met, jabbing each other, as their mouths held their grips on the carp's head and tail.

There are plenty of fish here, Bolt thought to them.

Mine! Mine! their thoughts hammered back.

Eventually, the fish ripped in half, and the penguins growled, chomping down their own half portions while glaring at the other.

Feed, my penguins! Feed and fight! You are too mighty to share!

Those words did not come from the penguins, nor from Bolt, but they slammed into his head and—evidently—the heads of all the penguins in the water. More carp swam by and more penguins fought, slapping each other, reaching out for a fish only to have another penguin snatch it away.

The sound echoed: *feed . . . fight . . .* in Bolt's head,

like bees buzzing in a hive. The Stranger, it seemed, was everywhere.

Fight, my children. Fight! After we conquer the world, nothing will stop us.

Bolt wanted to flee from those thoughts, and he kicked his feet forward, propelling himself away from the commotion, farther away from Pingvingrad, away from the voice.

I'm coming for you soon, Bolt thought, but he did not aim his thoughts at the Stranger, for the voice was gone now, faded away as quickly as it had come. But his thinking gave him strength. *And when I do, I will be ready.*

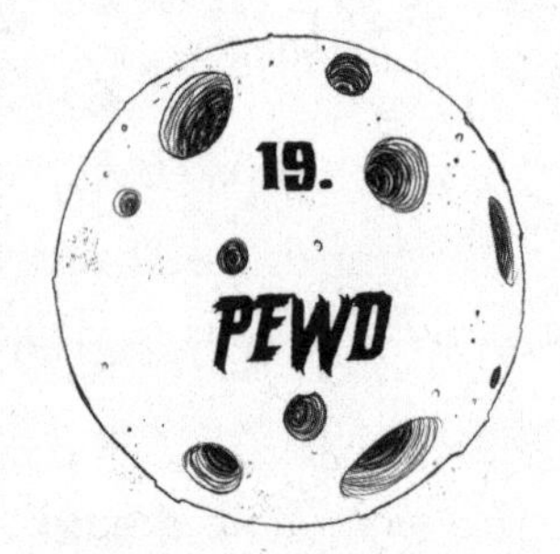

The next morning, when all the were-creatures were human once again, Bolt stood near the entrance to the freshly dug mole tunnel. Zemya and Topo were covered with dirt. Bolt handed the rubber scissors back to Topo, who eagerly accepted them, although not before carefully inspecting them for scratches.

"Good luck," said Zemya, wiping a crust of dirt from her upturned nose. "And be safe. You too, Grom."

"I will," Grom said. "We'll be back soon." He glared at Bolt. "Follow me and keep quiet. If we're lucky, most of the penguins will still be sleeping. Just don't forget: I'm helping you because I promised and not because I like you."

"I won't forget," Bolt assured him. He took a deep

breath to steady his always jumbled nerves, and followed Grom into the tunnel.

The tunnel was crudely made, but for being dug in one night, it was impressive. It was so tall that Bolt barely had to duck. The ground was uneven in spots, but Bolt's penguin eyes noticed the divots. Grom kept whispering, "I should let you trip on that divot because I don't like you" and "I should let you stumble on that rock, person I don't like," which also helped Bolt avoid the small holes, although unpleasantly.

They walked longer than Bolt would have guessed they needed to, and the tunnel curved and twisted several times. "I think we've gone in a circle," said Bolt finally.

"Two circles," said Grom. "That's the problem with digging underground. You never know where to end it and pop back up. You're like, 'How about now?' And then, 'Or maybe now,' and then, 'Nope, wrong again.' Anyway, we're here, so stop complaining."

"I wasn't complaining, I was just remarking."

Grom hissed at him. "Did I mention I don't like you?"

Above them, a thin shard of light peeked through a crack. Grom reached up and pushed aside a small rug that had covered the hole, before pulling himself up and out. Bolt followed.

They stood behind a reception desk in a cavernous room at the front of the building. As Grom had guessed,

it was too early for anyone to be working; the room was empty of people or penguins. Bolt had never been to a hospital—the orphanage treated every injury with Band-Aids no matter how severe, including broken bones—but this is what he imagined the waiting area of a hospital might look like. There were long rows of white plastic chairs, potted plants, and some television sets hanging from the ceilings. There were also two vending machines selling sugar-free fish snacks, but Bolt didn't have any coins to buy any. His stomach rumbled.

Grom sneered at Bolt. "Stop thinking about food. We have to go in there." He pointed across the room to a large door made of solid steel. "It's probably locked, and looks way too strong to break down."

"Then how do we get past it?" asked Bolt.

"We wait."

"What do we do while we're waiting?"

"You could twiddle your thumbs," Grom suggested. "I hear some people enjoy that."

Bolt scanned the area, trying to sense nearby penguins. But all he could pick up was fuzziness. Last night, as he swam in the sea, Bolt read penguin thoughts, even though those thoughts were horrible and disturbing. Why then were the PEWD penguins' heads so difficult to read? As if they were blocked somehow?

But there was . . . something. A penguin guard.

Bolt couldn't scan its head, but he sensed it coming. He motioned for Grom to be quiet. They ducked down to avoid being seen, and peeked over the desk. A moment later the sound of webbed feet flopping against the ground confirmed Bolt's suspicion. The penguin wore a lab coat, and a head mirror was strapped across its forehead. Bolt gently tried to dip inside the penguin's head, to control it, to speak to it.

Nope. No success.

The penguin stopped in front of the steel door. There was a small electronic device on the wall, and the bird stared into it. A red laser flared from the gizmo, fanning up and down across the penguin's head. A retina scanner! The door clicked open, and the penguin stepped inside.

"Quick," said Grom, jumping out from the desk and toward the door. "Before the door closes."

Bolt stretched his mind toward the penguin. *Hold the door. Don't let it close.*

But the penguin didn't stop, and the door clicked shut before Grom reached it. Grom pulled the handle, but it didn't budge. "Too late," Grom muttered in frustration. He glared back at Bolt. "You coulda tried to help."

"I did try," said Bolt, still confused why his thoughts couldn't penetrate the heads of the PEWD penguins.

He joined Grom by the door. Bolt didn't know much about scanners, but he did know it would be difficult to

program a scanner to read every set of penguin eyes in the complex; there were hundreds of penguins here, and penguins don't like to stand still for long periods of time. That's why there are so few penguin portraits in art galleries.

It would be easier to program a scanner to read penguin eyes in general, as they were quite distinctive from the eyes of people. Bolt's eyes were human, or mostly so, but they were also part penguin. Would that be enough for them to work with the scanner? He put one of his eyes in front of the small machine. If he was wrong about this, an alarm might sound and they would probably be immediately captured. His heart beat faster. He blinked, blinked again, and then forced his eyes open. Retina scanners don't work well with blinking eyes.

A laser crisscrossed Bolt's retina. Nothing happened, but no alarm sounded either. That was promising. Bolt's heart still pounding, he blinked again and then refocused.

A laser flicked across Bolt's eye once more. Again nothing happened.

And so it continued.

Blink. Scan. Pounding heart. Blink. Scan. Pounding heart.

"I'm waiting," said Grom, tapping his foot.

Blink. Scan. Blink. Scan.

The machine's lights twinkled; it seemed confused.

Blink. Scan. Blink. Scan. Faster and faster.

Buzz.

Click.

The door opened.

And Bolt's heart slowed to a steadier pace.

Grom danced through the open door, and Bolt danced after him. Grom shimmied along the side of the hall. Bolt shimmied, too. Grom sidestepped. Bolt sidestepped. Grom galloped. Bolt galloped.

"Can't we just walk?" Bolt asked.

"I thought it would be more interesting to dance, shimmy, sidestep, and gallop," said Grom. "But whatever."

They continued down the empty hallway, listening for sounds. Bolt tried to send his mind ahead of them, through the penguin-verse and down the hall, but sensed nothing. He wasn't sure if that meant that there was nothing, or if that mysterious fuzziness blocked him.

Up ahead, the hallway forked. One way was dark and dingy, with yellow paint peeling off the walls. A sign read:

THIS WAY TO THE TOOTHBRUSHING ROOM,
THE TEETH-POLISHING ROOM, THE GOOD ORAL
HYGIENE ROOM, AND THE EXTRA-FANCY
TOOTHBRUSHING AND TEETH-POLISHING
AND GOOD ORAL HYGIENE COMBO ROOM.

"It doesn't look like this hallway is used much," said Bolt, feeling uneasy. "But if they aren't brushing, polishing, and practicing good oral hygiene, what are they doing here? I thought this was a dentist's office."

"A dentist's *fortress*," corrected Grom. "I've never been in this building, but I don't think they do much dentistry. It's just a front for their real purposes."

"Which are?"

Grom gestured toward the very next sign, which pointed down the opposite hallway, a hallway that was bathed in light and looked like it had recently been painted. According to the sign, this hallway led to:

THE WORLD'S BIGGEST FISH FRYER, THE UNIVERSE'S GREATEST TOOTH COLLECTION (FEATURING THE TOOTH OF THE ILVERSAY OOTHTAY EALSAY), AND OUR SECRET-PLAN-TO-RULE-THE-COSMOS ROOM.

"Wow," said Bolt. "The World's Biggest Fish Fryer! How big do you think it is? How many fish do you think they can fry at once? Let's go there!" His fear dulled, quickly replaced by hunger pains. Bolt was suddenly famished.

"We need to go to the Universe's Greatest Tooth Collection and then get outta here," said Grom firmly.

"Right. Of course," said Bolt, but he couldn't mask the disappointment in his voice. How big *was* the World's Biggest Fish Fryer? Maybe they could come back for a tour later?

Ignoring his grumbling stomach, Bolt followed Grom past more doors and down the corridor. As they walked, the air grew hotter and more humid. Bolt felt sticky. Up ahead, the tight hallway widened into a vast open atrium with a large floor-to-ceiling window aquarium crammed with fish. The fish made up a kaleidoscope of colors: emerald greens, cobalt blues, and bright golds.

As Bolt stared into the glass, he wondered if he could jump into the aquarium and grab a snack? It would only take a few minutes. His growling stomach was interrupted when the fish scattered away, frightened by something approaching.

From the dark depths of the water came a giant white whale.

That aquarium must be massive, thought Bolt.

As the whale swam closer, passing only a few inches from the edge of the glass, Bolt noticed a white sling wrapped around its mouth. A low disgruntled murmur rumbled from the mammal.

Bolt put his hands up to the glass, trying to feel through it and into the penguin-verse, wondering if his powers extended to other sea creatures. After all, penguins and whales and fish had lived together for eons. Surely they were connected somehow?

And they were, faintly. Bolt didn't feel any fuzziness either. He couldn't understand much—Bolt's connection with the whale was not as deep as it would be with a penguin. But he sensed the whale's sadness—sadness for being kept in an aquarium, sadness for being away from other whales, and, mostly, sadness for having very sore gums.

"All its teeth are missing!" exclaimed Grom, gasping. Sure enough, the whale was entirely toothless, and obviously quite unhappy about it.

I'm so sorry, Bolt thought.

Tell me about it, complained the whale.

The whale softly moaned and slowly swam away from the glass, back into the murky depths of the aquarium. Its space in the tank was quickly replaced by colorful fish.

Bolt's neck birthmark burned, something that only happened when he was in danger or something was threatening nearby. There was more to these missing teeth than a few whale cavities. "I don't like this."

"Well, I don't like you," said Grom. "But let's keep going."

Just beyond the aquarium was an open staircase that disappeared into a billow of smoke. As they stepped

forward, they were engulfed in a wave of wet heat; it felt as if they had walked into a sauna. Bolt's skin was not only wet but oily to the touch. There was a sign on the wall. In order to read it, Bolt had to wipe off the condensation that coated it.

WELCOME TO THE WORLD'S BIGGEST FISH FRYER.
CAUTION: FLOORS SLIPPERY WHEN WET
AND OILY, WHICH IS ALWAYS.
EXTRA CAUTION: WEARING CLOTHES MADE OF
VEGETABLE OIL IS NOT RECOMMENDED.

Bolt's mouth watered. The fryer was so close! He closed his eyes and inhaled the glorious aroma. Rather than the hot stickiness bothering him, Bolt embraced it, sucking in the intoxicating scent of fried bread crumbs, although they were a bit over-peppered, and he almost sneezed. Maybe they could run up the stairs and grab breakfast? He took a step up the staircase.

"Where are you going?" Grom asked.

"Getting breakfast?" Bolt paused. *I have to keep my eyes on the prize*, he reminded himself. He gritted his teeth and took a step back down. "Um, never mind." They needed to get the tooth! Still, as they walked away, Bolt had regrets.

They hadn't gone far down the hallway before spotting

a cluster of glowing bright lights shining from the end of the hallway.

"That must be it," said Bolt.

"Really? Do you think so?" asked Grom, rolling his eyes. "What gave it away? The giant neon sign?"

Above the door, an enormous sign blinked and crackled:

YOU'VE ARRIVED AT THE UNIVERSE'S GREATEST
TOOTH COLLECTION (FEATURING THE TOOTH
OF THE ILVERSAY OOTHTAY EALSAY).
COME ON IN!

As they approached, Bolt's knees buckled. He and Grom hugged the wall. They inched forward. Slowly,

slowly. There were no penguins around. Nothing stopping them. Could this really be as easy as Bolt had hoped?

They peered inside the doorway. Bolt steadied his knocking knees.

The room was filled with standing glass display cases, like in a museum. But rather than holding Aztec vases and ancient artifacts, the glass shelves were lined with sets of teeth. Bolt was amazed at their many shapes and sizes: he spied large elephant teeth, medium-size turtle teeth, small anteater teeth, and even teeny-tiny bee teeth.

"I didn't even know some of these animals *had* teeth," admitted Bolt.

But the most prized tooth in the collection was straight ahead. A red carpet led right up to a pedestal topped with a glass dome in the middle of the room. A spotlight shone down upon it. The silver tooth inside the glass glistened. It looked as long and sharp as a knife.

Bolt rushed down the red carpet. This was it. He would simply grab the tooth, run back down the hall, past the whale aquarium, maybe take a peek at the fish fryer—no, scratch that—and head back through the tunnel behind the desk. He had expected guards! Alarms! What a relief he had been wrong. He reached his arms out to lift the glass dome covering the tooth, when—

"Wait a second," Grom whispered loudly. "It could be a trap."

"Good thinking." As Bolt rested his fingers on the glass, his birthmark felt like it was on fire. Bolt's birthmark burned when there was trouble nearby, but it also burned if he had a really huge mosquito bite on his neck.

Slap!

Bolt turned around to see Grom rubbing his palm against his shirt. "Sorry. I think I killed a mosquito. Lots of bugs here."

Bolt stared at the glass. Of course it could still be a trap, but Bolt didn't see anything that looked trap-like, such as a large net overhead or giant lasers pointing at him. He just needed to be quick! So, ignoring his increasingly aching birthmark—just a mosquito bite, he told himself—Bolt lifted the glass lid. Nothing happened. He rested the glass gently on the floor. Still nothing happened. He then reached out and touched the edge of the silver tip of the tooth. It was so sharp, it punctured Bolt's finger on contact, and a drop of red bloomed from the spot.

Bolt froze, his neck now so hot that he had to bite his tongue to keep from howling. He inched backward. His birthmark screamed at him: *Stop! Go! Run!*

Slap!

"Another mosquito," said Grom from behind Bolt, wiping his hand on his shirt again.

Ignoring his neck as best he could, Bolt stepped forward and lifted the tooth.

"Never mind," said Grom. "Those weren't mosquitos. They were fruit flies."

A thousand lights—maybe a million—lit the room, moving and twirling and blinking like an insane disco. An alarm sounded, a foghorn so loud it hurt Bolt's ears.

Bolt held the tooth in his hand but looked up to see twenty penguins dashing into the room, each wearing a head mirror and armed with one of those humongous steel toothbrushes. Standing among them was a tall woman with jet-black hair wearing a white doctor's jacket lined with a fur collar. With her long nose and bushy eyebrows, there was no mistaking who she was.

"Velcome, you must be Bolt," said the woman. She sounded vaguely European, perhaps Russian, or German, or the accent could have been entirely made-up. She smiled, golden teeth glinting off the lights in the room. "My name is Dr. Valzanarz."

"Gesundheit. But is it Valzanarz or Walzanarz?"

The woman sighed. "Walzanarz. With a *W.* Ah, never mind." When she continued, she no longer had an accent. "I've been looking forward to meeting you. You came alone?"

"No, I . . ." Bolt turned around. Grom had disappeared. Bolt scanned the room but saw no sign of him. "Yeah, just me."

Had Grom run away? The boy had seemed brave, but at the first sign of trouble had he abandoned Bolt? So much for "moles help one another." Well, as he had made quite clear, Grom didn't like Bolt anyway.

Bolt was alone now. Fine. This was *his* mission. He'd find a way out of it. Maybe.

"You're much scrawnier than I thought you'd be," said the woman, eyeing Bolt up and down, frowning.

"I may be scrawny, but I'm . . ." Bolt hesitated. What was he? Fierce? Mighty? No, he was neither of those things. As he stared at the dentist and her penguin guards, he felt a familiar helpless panic crawling up his spine.

"I think you have something of mine." Dr. Walzanarz

held out her hand and sneered. “I want my tooth back. Now.”

Bolt spied the silver tooth in his palm. For a brief moment, he considered leaping at Dr. Walzanarz, stabbing her with it. He could defeat her, just like that!

Or not. Bolt was no killer. Instead, he was going to be brushed to death by one of those steel-bristle toothbrushes, or something equally unpleasant. The mission was over. Why did he think he ever stood a chance? His legs felt like jelly. He just wanted to hide, hide, hide forever.

But. There was one thing he *could* do. Control penguins. He might not be a natural-born fighter, but he was tightly bound to the penguin-verse. He needed to get past whatever was standing in the way of his connection to these penguin guards. He had to find a way to reach into their minds. *We are family. Stand down!*

The penguins inched forward and growled. *Stand down!* Bolt repeated. But still, nothing.

“The tooth!” Dr. Walzanarz held her hand out expectantly.

“I don’t understand why I can’t talk to the penguins,” groaned Bolt. His shoulders slumped and he handed Dr. Walzanarz the tooth, his head bowed.

“Thank you, dahling.” She slid the silver tooth into her front coat pocket. “By the way, every member of my penguin patrol wears a silver-plated head mirror.”

Bolt stared at Dr. Walzanarz blankly. "So?"

"You don't know?" She looked at Bolt, eyes wide open, surprised. "I was wondering why you kept scrunching up your face and staring at my guards like you were trying to reach into their heads. All werepenguins hate silver."

"Because they clash with our beaks. I've heard. But I don't hate silver. I'm not very fashionable."

Dr. Walzanarz chuckled. "Fashion isn't the only reason we hate silver. It's because our minds can't penetrate the metal. Silver makes everything fuzzy. Our thoughts just bounce off it."

"Always?"

"Yes, dahling. Yours, mine, even the Stranger's. A penguin with silver surrounding its head is a penguin that can't be controlled."

Bolt had feared something was wrong with *him*, that he didn't possess the penguin powers he thought he did. But that wasn't the case at all. Still, one thing didn't quite make sense. "If you can't talk to them, then why are they growling at me?" Bolt asked, his voice unsteady, uneasy, as the penguin guards stood at command. "How are you controlling them?"

Dr. Walzanarz held up a small transistor radio and spoke into it. "Attention, my penguins. I command you to growl louder." The penguins' hissing and snarling rose ten decibels. "Raise your toothbrushes in a fearsome, intimidating way." They all raised their toothbrushes and waved them fearsomely. She put the radio back into her jacket pocket. "I've attached earphones under their silver head mirrors. As long as I speak into my radio, I come in loud and clear."

Bolt was impressed by her ingenuity. Horrified, but impressed. This whole place was a marvel. And it contained the World's Biggest Fish Fryer!

"I won't help you," said Bolt, ignoring his excitement over the fish fryer, and tapping into whatever small drip of resolve he had left, although it was a very, very small drip. "I told the Baron that. I told the Earl that. I told the Stranger that. Why won't anyone listen to me?"

"Maybe because your stomach is making loud hunger gurgles? Perhaps you'll change your mind after lunch."

"Why would I change my mind then?"

"Humor me."

Bolt had no desire to humor the doctor, but he didn't really want to argue against eating lunch. He was famished.

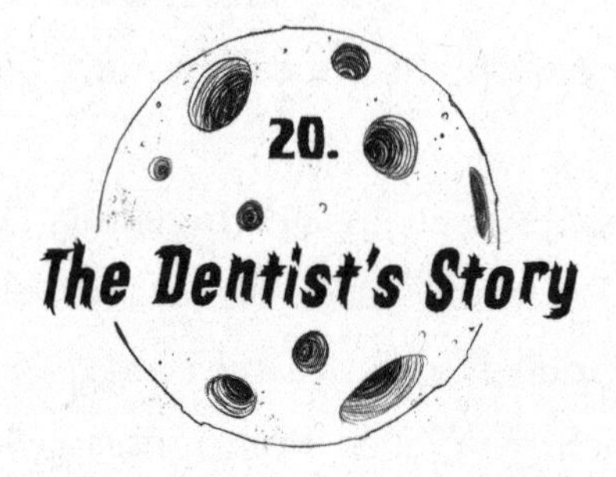

20. The Dentist's Story

"While we eat, we can get to know each other a little better, dahling," said Dr. Walzanarz. She smiled at Bolt, but it wasn't a reassuring smile, not when they were surrounded by growling toothbrush-carrying penguin guards.

Bolt and the doctor sat at a large oak table filled with several large platters of fish sticks, as well as fish rings, fish squares, and a bunch of other shapes, all fried to a golden brown. Bolt's tongue watered at the sight.

He still hadn't seen any signs of Grom. The boy must be long gone, back in the mole hole with his sister. If Bolt was going to survive, he was on his own. Which meant he probably wouldn't. Survive, that is.

If only Bolt could hide under the dining room table!

He could bolt under it right now and close his eyes and hope everyone would leave him alone.

Or he could sit in his seat and fill his empty stomach. That sounded like an even better idea.

"It's been so long since I had someone to talk to, Bolt," said the doctor. "The Stranger speaks to me, in my head, but it's not really the same thing. And while it's enjoyable to order penguins around all day, they aren't great conversationalists. But now you're here! Please eat. I've prepared this feast for you, after all. You'll find our fish shapes are vonderful."

"They're what?" Bolt asked.

"I mean *wonderful*," said the dentist with a sigh.

Bolt didn't need to be asked twice. He tried a fish triangle first. Exquisite! Then he ate a fish circle; it was even better. "These *are* wonderful" Bolt agreed, his fear giving way to delight as his taste buds hummed with happiness.

"Much of our work at the institute is about making fried fish, you know."

"What does whale dentistry have to do with fish frying?"

"We'll get to that later. For now, I'd much rather talk about you. The Stranger has asked me to convince you to join our army."

"There's nothing you can do to convince me," said Bolt, sticking his chin out in defiance. If he acted powerful and courageous, maybe he would feel that way, deep inside. It was what he had been doing for most of his quest. Sometimes it worked, briefly.

"Think of it, Bolt. A lifetime of ruling!"

"I don't care about ruling."

"A lifetime as a king!"

"I don't care about kingdoms."

"A lifetime filled with eating trapezoid-shaped fish fillets!"

"Really? You have trapezoid-shaped fish fillets?" Bolt asked, his stomach growling. "I mean, I don't care about trapezoid shapes!" Although he did. Very much.

He took a bite of a parallelogram fish stick. The thought of ruling horrified him, but he found himself nodding anyway, his brain forcing his head up and down as a hungry smile spread across his lips.

Yes, Bolt. Join us. Fish octagons can be yours!

Really, fish octagons, too? thought Bolt. *I mean, that sounds horrible!*

The Stranger's voice echoed in Bolt's head, again jumping in without warning. Bolt knew he should fight against the voice, drive it out, but instead, he picked up a fish shape with more sides than he could count. So crunchy! He could eat like this forever. Maybe Annika and Blackburn would join him for dinner. He smiled at the thought.

Wait. Annika! Blackburn! Thinking of his friends jolted Bolt, breaking whatever spell he was falling under. They were out there somewhere, counting on him. He needed to concentrate. He needed to free himself and his mind of hate. And he needed to free the world as well. He put down the fish shape without taking a bite.

Then, he picked it back up and ate it. Fighting evil would be easier on a full stomach.

Yes, now he was ready.

Bolt narrowed his eyes. The Stranger's voice drained out from his ears.

"Oh, Bolt, dahling," said Dr. Walzanarz. "How disappointing. You started to smile, but now you're glaring at me again." She leaned back in her chair, licking her long fingers. "I was like you once, you know."

"Really?" asked Bolt. "You were a twelve-year-old former orphan boy whose best friends were a pirate and a forest bandit?"

"Well, no. I meant I didn't always think about ruling the world. Many years ago, the only thing special about me was an odd penguin birthmark I had on my back tooth. It was very hard to see. All I wanted was to grow up and be a dentist. As a young girl I caught toads and pulled out their teeth to study."

"Toads don't have teeth," said Bolt.

"I know that *now*, dahling. But that's only because I'm

a professional whale dentist. Still, I spent my days dreaming of pulling teeth, the bigger the better. What child doesn't dream of that?"

Every other child in the world, thought Bolt, but he kept his thoughts to himself.

"Then, one night, there was a knock at my door. It was far too late to see patients, and besides, whales seldom knock. Still, I answered the door. Cautiously.

"'I'm sorry, we're closed,' I said to the tall, thin man in the doorway. His eyes glowed red. His face was covered in scars. He let out a loud, evil laugh. 'Come on in!' I said. And we talked."

"Why did you let him in if he had glowing red eyes and was laughing evilly?"

She shrugged. "Something about the man spoke to me."

"What about him spoke to you?" Bolt asked.

"His mouth. He was talking to me. Aren't you listening? Anyway, he explained that my birthmark meant I was special. He told me that if I let him bite me at midnight he would help me build a whale dentist fortress on a remote island, as long as we also built the biggest fish fryer in the world. I jumped at the opportunity, of course. As will you."

"Never!" Bolt crashed his fist on the table and almost knocked over his plate.

Dr. Walzanarz shook her head, her lips pressed tight.

"Oh, Bolt, Bolt, Bolt," she mumbled, and then abruptly stood up. "Come! Let me show you something. I think once you see our fish fryer in person you'll feel differently."

"I won't," said Bolt, although he drooled a little bit. Those fish nuggets *were* delicious, and he very much wanted to see the fish fryer.

"Come, dahling." Dr. Walzanarz held up her transistor radio. "And don't try any funny stuff."

"Why do people keep saying that?" said Bolt. "I'm not funny."

21. A Fine Kettle of Fish

As they entered the fish frying room, billowy steam slammed into Bolt with such power he almost flopped backward. The vapor dissipated as he stepped farther inside. They now stood atop a raised metal platform that hung over what would have been the biggest swimming pool in the world if it had been filled with water. Instead, it was filled with thick, yellow, bubbling oil.

Bolt's mouth dropped open. Sure, he had pictured a large fish fryer—but not something as big as this!

Also on the metal platform were a dozen penguins, each wearing head mirrors, lab coats, and goggles, operating a computer console that nearly reached to the top of the domed concrete ceiling. The console was filled with hundreds of red and green blinking lights and emitted random beeping blips.

"What do all those buttons and lights do?" asked Bolt.

"They blink and blip randomly," said Dr. Walzanarz.

A layer of oil—the vapor from the pool—left a thin sheen of grease on just about everything in the room, including Bolt's skin. Two penguins mopped the floor, although as soon as they were finished cleaning an area, it almost immediately grew oily again.

Dr. Walzanarz rubbed her hands together. "The haddock, my penguin dahlings. Who has the haddock?"

A penguin holding a single dead haddock ran to the edge of the platform, where a long metal walkway slowly extended over the oil. Hydraulics hummed and gears clanged as sections of the walkway unlatched from other sections, creating a retractable pier that reached to the middle of the bubbling pool. As soon as the pier had ceased retracting, the penguin waddled down it. About halfway across, the penguin lost its footing—the metal grating was covered with oil, and there was no railing—and spun twice in place before regaining its balance.

"Oh, do be careful," called Dr. Walzanarz. "Fried penguin sticks just aren't my thing."

The penguin, no longer spinning, reached the end of

the walkway and tossed the haddock into the oil before scampering back.

The penguins standing at the control panel slapped buttons haphazardly. Some beeped, some didn't. A couple of buttons whistled. One tooted.

"Most of the buttons just make fun noises," admitted Dr. Walzanarz.

Electronic whirring rose up from the bottom of the pool. Bolt now noticed an enormous machine sitting on the pool bottom, with rotating cogs, a moving canvas belt, and large slicing knives that chopped up and down.

The oil in the pool began to splash and form tall, bubbling spouts of steaming liquid that sprayed over the retractable metal walkway.

"Our fish fryer is completely automatic," said Dr. Walzanarz. "It debones, breads, fries, and even slices."

The oil churned and spun, fizzed and frothed. The haddock was sucked down under the bubbling surface.

"Now comes the fun part," said Dr. Walzanarz, clapping.

The entire room vibrated. Loud whirring sounds spat out from the machinery inside the pool, followed by loud hacking sounds, a few clacks, a clink, and then a loud hiss.

Something shot straight up from the oil and into the air. It hurtled toward Bolt. Bolt put his hands up but Dr. Walzanarz stepped in front of him and caught the projectile on a dinner plate. "A fish pentagon!" she announced, adding a sprig of parsley to the plate. "Want one?"

Bolt stared down at one perfectly cut and fried five-sided fish shape, still sizzling with oil. He looked at it, amazed, and then picked it up carefully and popped it into his mouth. It was hot, but fresh. "Delicious," he admitted. Oh, so delicious!

It also tickled his nose. He scrunched his lips. He held his breath. He rolled his fingers into fists. He gritted his teeth. Then, he sneezed.

Honk!

It was a very loud sneeze.

"The latest batch of bread crumbs was over-peppered." Dr. Walzanarz rubbed her nose. "We're still working out the kinks, I'm afraid. That fried haddock was merely a demonstration for you. We didn't build a fryer this big just to fry a single haddock." She held up her radio and commanded, "Bring it in."

A large metal panel along a far wall lowered, rusty chains clanking. Bolt squinted—a dull oil mist filled the room—as a loud motor roared, grinding and popping.

A giant metal claw—it reminded Bolt of a claw that pulled prizes from an arcade game, although a thousand times larger—slid along a track in the ceiling. It rattled and creaked as it moved closer.

Hanging from its metal claws was a brown leather harness. And inside that harness was a whale.

It was the same whale Bolt had seen earlier, still wearing the bandage around its toothless mouth, still looking as unhappy as it did before. No, even less happy now.

But as much as the whale seemed to hate being dangled from a crane, the metal claw seemed to enjoy it less. Its tips were bending and the metal warping from the mammal's immense tonnage. Behind Bolt, at the control console, four penguins in lab coats slapped blinking buttons.

The claw stopped sliding, and the whale hung directly above the middle of the oil pool. The harness swayed in place, the claw holding it continuing to bend. Bolt wondered if the claw would snap in half.

"You're not going to . . ." Bolt began. "You can't . . ."

"Of course I can. Dahling, what did you expect? Once we rule the world we'll have to feed millions of penguins. One haddock can't feed all of us."

"You'd fry a whale?" Bolt asked, horrified.

"Of course. Fried whale is delicious."

Bolt fidgeted. Sure, whales ate penguins. They were natural penguin enemies. But whales were also honorable creatures. Honest. If they borrowed something from you, they always returned it, promptly. Frying them into seafood sticks just didn't seem right.

"Imagine eating fried whale every day!" shouted the dentist, raising a fist, her mouth curved into a crazed grin.

"Or fried walrus. Or fried anything! Last week I fried a helicopter, just because I could. Isn't it marvelous? What would you like to fry?"

This was anything *but* marvelous. It was terrible! Bolt was so upset that he couldn't even speak. He merely shook his head and muttered a grumbling "Harrumph."

"Fried harrumph? I can't say I've tried that, but why not?"

Oil continued to boil in the pool. The whale thrashed. The claw creaked. Penguins squawked.

Bolt reached into the mind of the whale, sensing confusion, anger, panic. Meanwhile, the crane began to lower closer to the oil, metal screeching.

It'll be OK, thought Bolt, trying to soothe the creature.

Really?

Well, probably not.

The whale's panic became Bolt's. His throat tightened, and his heart raced in his chest. "You know, I'm not really all that hungry."

"A werepenguin not hungry? Don't be absurd, dahling. You think haddock pentagons are tasty, wait until you try a whale equilateral triangle!"

The crane jiggled from the weight of the mammal. The gears cracked. The whale swayed.

"You can't!" shouted Bolt.

"But I can. And I will."

The penguins at the control deck all wore head mirrors, and there was no way to get through to them. But Bolt had to do something!

Penguins have excellent eyesight, and so did Bolt. As he stared at the nearest penguin he noticed a small crack in its head mirror, a jagged line running all the way through it. Bolt concentrated on that crack, carefully wiggling his thoughts through it. He could feel his mind curling inside, like small vines twisting around a trellis.

Stop!

The penguin continued to press buttons. The whale was only ten feet from the oil, the crane slowly lowering it ever closer. Eight feet. Five feet.

Bolt jammed his thoughts harder inside the crack. *Stop! Stop! Stop!*

The penguin smashed its wing against a button, and the crane screeched to a halt. The crane began to reverse, raising the whale higher and higher, away from the oil. The metal claw screeched, warped, and cried out in agony.

"What's happening?" asked Dr. Walzanarz. She jumped up and down and yelled into her radio, "Fry it! Fry it!"

The crane lowered again.

Dr. Walzanarz didn't know what Bolt was thinking—he was careful to keep his vine-like tendrils of thought inside the penguin and away from her. *Stop. You don't want to hurt that whale. Go up.*

The penguin slapped another button, and the metal claw changed direction again with rusty screeching.

"I want that whale fried!" Dr. Walzanarz shouted. She glared at the mammal, and so didn't notice the penguin at the console, shaking its head and twitching.

The crane lowered.

Up! urged Bolt, keeping his thoughts firmly wedged into the head mirror's crack.

The crane went up.

"Fry it!" demanded the dentist.

The crane went down.

Up!

"Fry it!"

Up!

"Fry it!"

The crane jerked up, down, up, and then with a loud *BANG!* shook, and stopped. The whale hung in its harness, five feet over the pool, swaying. The penguin at the control console stopped twitching and barked, "Gears are jammed."

Bolt stood, sweating, eyes watering, and not just from the oil.

Dr. Walzanarz grunted with displeasure. "Not sure what happened there, Bolt. But I see your eyes are watering

you're so upset. Don't worry. We'll have plenty of time to fry whales later. Besides, frying the whale isn't even the best part of our plan. Well, maybe it is the best part. There are two parts, and I can't quite decide which one is better. Let me know what you think. Come with me, my dahling Bolt. You'll love the next room." She cackled.

Bolt threw her a dirty look. He didn't like it when seers cackled, and he liked evil werepenguin dentists cackling even less, although he would have welcomed a lifetime of cackling if it meant no more whales being fried.

Still, he had saved the whale! At least for the time being. Sure, he had just gotten lucky. But he needed his luck to continue if he was going to not only save the whale but himself. And the world.

You'll be OK, thought Bolt, taking one last look at the whale.

Really, dude? You're not the one hanging over a steaming pool of oil.

As Bolt followed Dr. Walzanarz out of the room he said, "The whale was toothless. Which means you pulled all its teeth, right?" Dr. Walzanarz nodded. "But why bother, if you were just going to fry it anyway? Is it just because you're an evil dentist and enjoy hurting helpless whales?"

"Well, that's partly the reason, sure. But not the main reason. You'll see for yourself in a minute!" They walked

down a back stairway, through a narrow hallway, and stopped in front of a steel door. Bolt glanced at the sign over it:

OUR SECRET-PLAN-TO-RULE-THE-COSMOS ROOM.

Dr. Walzanarz grinned and pushed open the door. "Victims first." She cleared her throat. "Sorry. I mean *guests.* Guests first."

Bolt entered the dark room, wondering what horrors he might see next.

22.
The Whale Teeth

Fluorescent lights flickered from the ceiling, revealing a spacious laboratory filled with microscopes, test tubes, and, most of all, dozens of large teeth, maybe hundreds of them.

Dr. Walzanarz picked up one of the teeth. It must have been six inches long. She rubbed it gently against her cheek. "Whale fangs," said the dentist, closing her eyes. She seemed to be lost in the moment. Then, as if remembering she wasn't alone, she opened her eyes and chuckled. "Did you know that some whales have nearly two hundred and fifty teeth? Of course, some whales have no teeth at all. But a whale without a tooth is like a werepenguin who doesn't want to rule the world. Pointless." She gently rolled her finger over the edge of the tooth, sighed, and then placed it back down. "Whale teeth can be all sorts of sizes, dahling. The narwhale only has one tooth, but it's nine feet long. That's a bit *too* long for my needs, but still interesting, or at least interesting if you're a whale dentist." She beamed. "In whale dentistry school I got an A on the Guess the Size of the Whale Tooth test. It was the only test I passed in school."

"If you flunked all your other tests, how did you become a dentist at all?"

"I didn't say I was a *good* dentist, did I? Besides, whales seldom ask to see diplomas."

A group of dental chairs, each as big as a whale, sat on the opposite side of the room. Next to each of the large chairs was a much smaller, mini dental chair. "Are those for baby whales?" Bolt guessed, shivering. Pulling the teeth of adult whales was horrifying enough. But little whale calves?

"Do I look like someone who would pull the teeth of baby whales?"

"Sort of. Yeah."

"I guess you're right," agreed the dentist. "But those little dentist chairs aren't for babies. No, they are the key to our entire operation." She giggled. "Get it? I said *our operation*, and this is where I perform mysterious whale operations? Oh, I'm so clever. But those chairs are the size of something else. Can you guess what?"

"Inflatable clowns? Smallish mannequins? Very large cantaloupes?"

"Not even close, dahling. Take a look over there." She pointed just beyond the chairs.

There wasn't a wall on the far side of the room but a small metal railing overlooking a vast expanse of darkness. Dr. Walzanarz clapped her hands, and a light turned on.

Bolt approached the railing and looked down onto a room with gray walls and a bare gray floor except for a small rainbow-colored plastic kiddie pool in the middle of it, and a large mound of fish skeletons.

Next to them was a penguin. It looked up at Bolt. Bolt looked down and gasped.

This penguin was an ordinary, run-of-the-mill penguin except for one horrible feature. Or rather, two horrible features. Twin six-inch fangs hung down from its beak. The penguin hissed.

"But penguins don't have teeth!" Bolt cried out.

"They do now!" said Dr. Walzanarz, clapping, and the lights turned off. "Sorry." She clapped again, and the lights turned on. "As I was saying, yes! Whale fangs! It took a while to get them to stay in place—they fell out every time we implanted them. Finally, I tried dental glue instead of masking tape. And ta-da! If I hadn't flunked the How to Put in Tooth Implants test back at dental school,

I might have figured that out sooner. But better late than never, dahling."

Bolt thought *never* would have been far better than late. This was a monstrosity!

"Imagine how marvelous our penguin army will be when all the penguins in the world have giant whale fangs!" exclaimed Dr. Walzanarz. "Sure, our penguins can probably take over the world without them, but penguins with fangs are so much better than ordinary ones—just like fish hexagons are better than your basic fish sticks—don't you agree?"

The penguin wasn't wearing a silver head mirror, so Bolt confidently reached out with his thoughts into its head—*Are you OK? Does your mouth hurt? I'm so sorry they did this to you!*—but his thoughts bounced back at him. Again, he shot out his questions. Again, they went nowhere. The penguin's twin teeth shone brightly. Too brightly.

"Its teeth are silver!" Bolt exclaimed.

The dentist smiled. "Yes. Inspired by the silver tooth of the Ilversay Oothtay Ealsay." She tapped her jacket pocket, where the Ealsay tooth Bolt had handed to her earlier remained. "It makes penguins harder to control, of course. And the teeth implants make them so cranky, they just want to destroy everything. But that's OK with me!"

Bolt tried to force his mind into the penguin's head again, but to no avail.

"What do you think, dahling? Option one: join our army, help lead our penguins to victory, rule the world, and eat whale sticks forever! Option two: be bitten to death by a whale-toothed penguin. It's a pretty easy decision, I think."

Bolt set his jaw. "You're right. It is an easy decision. I will never help you!"

Dr. Walzanarz took a deep breath. She shook her head and sighed. "I didn't expect *that* answer. The Stranger will be disappointed. Are you sure you won't change your mind?"

With whatever bravery he could muster, Bolt glared at her. "Yes, I'm sure. That's not a penguin down there—it's an abomination!"

"A shame for us. A bigger shame for you. Kiki hasn't had dinner, you know. She's a bit hungry."

Dr. Walzanarz shoved Bolt in the back and—not expecting to be pushed—he stumbled forward, his stomach banging hard into the railing. Bolt flipped headfirst, his momentum carrying him over the side. Reaching back, he attempted to grab the rail, but failed. His fingers touched nothing but air.

For a moment Bolt felt weightless while he toppled

down. His stomach lurched. But then the feeling subsided and he landed hard, directly inside the kiddie pool.

Splash!

Bolt stood up, dazed. Cold water cascaded off his clothes, his drenched shirt clinging uncomfortably to his body. The penguin snarled at him, saliva dripping from its fangs.

From above, Dr. Walzanarz cried out, "Bolt, meet Kiki. I'd love to stay and watch her eat you, but I hate the sight of blood. Another reason why I flunked dental school. I'll leave you two to get acquainted. Goodbye, Bolt dahling. It's a shame that things didn't work out for you here. But, frankly, I would have been surprised if they had."

"N-nice to m-meet you, K-K-Kiki. You've got really nice fangs," said Bolt, stepping out of the pool as water rained off him. His voice shook, and he raised his hands in a sign of peace. Bolt spread his thoughts toward the fanged beast. *We are family.*

But as he expected, the words did nothing but bounce off the penguin's teeth.

Kiki looked angry. Bolt couldn't blame her: he would be angry, too, if whale teeth had been implanted in his mouth. Kiki jabbed forward with a wing. She was quick, but Bolt hopped backward and out of the way. As he did, one of the penguin's fangs nicked Bolt's arm, leaving a small gash. It wasn't deep, but it hurt.

The penguin rushed at Bolt, fangs first. This time Bolt

twisted to his side and the fangs missed him completely. Bolt shot thoughts of love and kindness, but they merely deflected off the creature's teeth. Bolt's foot slipped on some water from the kiddie pool, and he fell.

He landed on the hard ground, bruising his butt.

Kiki stood above Bolt and roared a ferocious roar. "Please don't hurt me," Bolt whimpered.

The penguin roared again.

Bolt cringed, waiting to be eaten or at least hurt badly, as Kiki howled over him. He couldn't blame Kiki for her madness. If anything, he felt sorry for her—warped and deformed for some evil werepenguin purpose. He only regretted he couldn't help her. But then again, he couldn't help any of the penguins if he was eaten by Kiki. "I'm sorry I couldn't save you. I couldn't save anyone," mumbled Bolt as the penguin lurched forward, beak first, and Bolt closed his eyes.

And then Kiki collapsed on top of Bolt.

Bolt squirmed out from under the unconscious penguin. He opened his eyes to see a figure standing in the shadows, shuffling toward him. Bolt tensed, ready to fight again.

"Just because I saved your life doesn't mean I like you," said Grom.

"What? Why? Where? How?" Bolt had so many questions and they all wanted to come out at once, so it sounded

more like *WhWhWhyHuh?* "I thought you abandoned me. I mean, I wouldn't have blamed you if you had."

Grom put down a metal wastebasket that he had used to knock Kiki out. "As I ran down the hall and back toward the mole hole, I thought about what you were doing. Moles help one another, even if I'm not a mole myself, just the brother of one." Grom looked down at Kiki, who lay unmoving. "What's with the fangs?"

"Implanted. If they put more silver whale teeth inside the mouths of penguins, nothing will be able to stop the Stranger's army."

"Then I guess we not only need to steal that seal tooth you want, but also destroy this lab."

"And the fish fryer, too. This whole place is evil." Bolt could barely believe the words coming out of his mouth. Destroy the fish fryer? That could mean he would never again eat a fish dodecahedron!

No. He had to destroy it. And steal that tooth. Bolt took a deep breath. This was more important than eating.

Bolt could do this, too. He and Grom. Together! *I'm not the boy who bolts every time there's danger,* he told himself. *Not anymore. I'm ready to fight.*

"Let's go," said Bolt. "We have work to do."

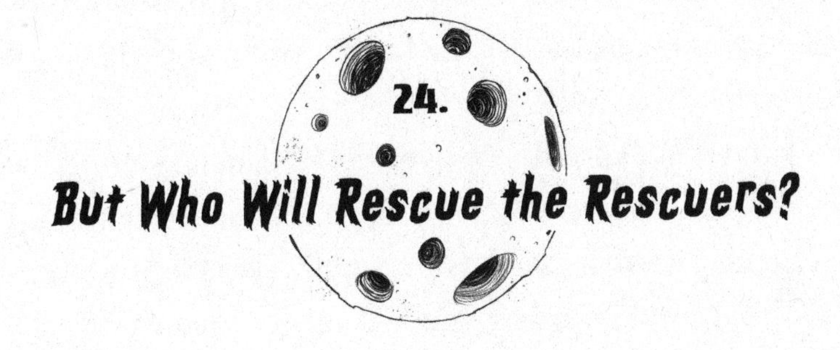

24. But Who Will Rescue the Rescuers?

Annika sat on the floor, her back resting against a cinder block wall in the PEWD waiting room. They had been stuck here for a day and a night. "We need to get out of here."

"What's the point?" said Blackburn, twiddling his thumbs. Annika had to admit he was quite good at it. "Bah, I knew this was a mistake. I should never have agreed to come with ye. I wanted to quit adventurin', and I should have."

"You're a pirate. Adventuring is what you do."

"In me youth, maybe. I'm too old for this sort of thing."

Annika looked away. She was still mad at Blackburn for surrendering so easily. Once locked away, the pirate said it was better to live and fight another day, especially the part about living. To Annika, that sounded like a poor excuse. Bandits never surrendered! It was written in the Code of the Bandit, and she had no plans to change that section.

And what of Bolt? While they sat here, waiting, he could be anywhere. Captured. Hurt. All alone. He needed her; they were a team! He couldn't defeat someone as powerful as this werepenguin dentist without her help. "Arrgh!" she screamed in frustration. It was the eighteenth time she had screamed in frustration that morning. "Arrgh!" she screamed again. Nineteen.

The waiting room was big but sparse. It had ten long plastic sofas, each the length of a whale. There was also a television in the corner that didn't work, a telephone with no dial tone, and a radio that played only shrieks of terror. After turning it on, Annika had switched the dial off. There were layers of dust everywhere, and spiderwebs, and it smelled like mold.

There was one door into the room, but it had been locked after Annika and Blackburn had been pushed inside. They could hear a penguin guard on the other side of the door, wheezing. The guard had snored for a while, and Annika thought that was her chance to pick the lock and escape. But as soon as she had inserted her bobby pin into the keyhole, the penguin began wheezing again.

She heard commotion outside—a horde of penguins barking and running—and tensed. Maybe the birds would rush inside the room. If so, she would fight them. Although she didn't have her knife—that had been taken away, as had Blackburn's swordfish—she still had her bandit training.

But the outside sounds trailed away. Was something going on? Maybe something to do with Bolt?

She stood up, rigid, and went to the door, pressing her ear against it. She couldn't hear any sounds now, not even heavy snoring. Had their guard run off, too? If she and Blackburn were ever going to escape and help Bolt, this was their chance!

She glanced at Blackburn, still twiddling his thumbs but in the other direction now. "I'm going to make a break for it." She slipped a bobby pin from her hair.

"And then what?" asked the pirate. "Stealin' that tooth is crazy. I say we go back to our boat and get out of here."

"And leave my best friend?" She inserted her pins into the lock. "Never."

"Can I tell ye a story?"

"We're kind of in a rush," said Annika, maneuvering the clips, listening for a click.

"I knew a pirate once," said Blackburn as Annika continued to play with the lock. "Fancy John, they called him, because he always wore jackets with frills and silk shirts.

But he had no time for the ladies—for he was obsessed with findin' the Buried Treasure of Barney the Terrible. Ye've heard of it, yes?"

"Nope." She almost had the lock, she thought. She felt it giving way.

"Fancy John had a treasure map, and he traveled across the world to find that treasure. And ye know what happened then?" Annika shook her head. "He found the treasure and retired."

"And what does that story have to do with you running back to the boat?" demanded Annika.

Blackburn scratched his chin. "Never mind. That was the wrong story. I meant to talk about Redbeard the Pirate. He died searchin' for treasure, so the moral was supposed to be somethin' about wasting yer time searchin' for things instead of livin' yer life and escapin'." Blackburn scowled. "Let me start over again. I knew a pirate once . . ."

"Got it," said Annika, removing her bobby pins from the doorknob as the door swung open. "Come on."

"Fine. But yer missin' a great story." Blackburn trailed Annika into the corridor. "I'll follow ye for now, mind ye. But I'm not doin' any fightin'."

"Then I'll fight without you, and thanks for nothing," said Annika, letting her frustration boil over. Why was he acting like this? Bolt was counting on them. The world was counting on them! She knew Blackburn could be heroic, so why was he choosing to be a coward now of all times?

They rushed down the hallway. Thankfully, it was empty. Annika ran soundlessly in her well-padded bandit boots. Blackburn was loud, but at least there weren't any accordions or alarm clocks on the ground for him to step on.

Flppt! Pop! Snap! Blupp!

"Sorry," said Blackburn, after colliding with a bunch of balloons and bursting most of them. "Didn't see those there."

Penguins approached from a different corridor—Annika could hear their floppy webbed feet—and she and Blackburn hugged the wall to avoid being seen. Annika stood still, as quiet as she could. Blackburn belched.

Fortunately, the penguins hurried past them without stopping.

Annika turned left, following in the same direction as the penguins.

"Shouldn't we run the opposite way?" Blackburn asked.

"If Bolt's here, the penguins could be running to capture him."

"Exactly. So we should go the opposite way."

Annika didn't answer and kept her pace down the

hallway. She was both surprised and glad that Blackburn followed her. "I'm still makin' no promises about fightin' and savin' people," he reminded her.

She hoped, when the time came, the hero she knew was in him would come out.

As they made their way down the hallway, the air felt muggier. Steamy. They saw vapor clouds, and Annika sneezed.

The hallway opened into a large concourse with a glass tank that might have held a million gallons of water and was filled with thousands of colorful fish. Just beyond that was a staircase that led up into a thick, misty cloud. A sign read:

UPSTAIRS. FISH FRYER.

"I'm heading up," Annika whispered to Blackburn. "Whatever is going on here, that fish fryer seems to be the key."

"There could be hundreds of penguins in there."

"And maybe Bolt, too."

"Then runnin' headlong into the room would seem like a poor way to free him, aye? What about over there?" He pointed to a set of doors underneath the staircase. There was nothing particularly interesting about those doors, they didn't have any sort of sign indicating where they led to, but Annika noticed why Blackburn had pointed to them. A puff of steam wiggled through a small crack between the door and the floor. "That must be another entrance into the fryer, aye?"

Annika rushed across the hallway. Blackburn hesitated for a moment, sighed, and joined her. She jiggled the door handle, but it was locked, and there was no keyhole to pick. "Drat! We will need to find a different way in."

"All this sneaky bandit stuff is fine and dandy, but us pirates have a few tricks, too." Blackburn nudged Annika aside and rammed his black pirate boot against the door. The door squeaked. He kicked again. The door thudded. He raced toward the door and smashed into it with his shoulder, breaking it off its hinges with a deafening *bang!*

"Could you *be* any louder?" Annika complained.

"At least I didn't step on any of those." He pointed to a mound of cotton balls on the floor.

They entered a large walk-in kitchen pantry, which was crammed with dozens of plastic buckets. Curious, Annika dug her fingernails into one of the bucket lids and peeled it open. She dipped a finger inside. "These are filled with bread crumbs." She sneezed twice. "Way too peppery, though. Why would they need this many bread crumbs? Are they planning on frying a whale?"

"Don't be ridiculous," said Blackburn, also sneezing, although his sneeze was much louder than Annika's had been.

They continued through the pantry, navigating around the tubs, trying not to sneeze, until they reached a set of swinging doors at the end. They could hear bubbling liquid from the other side, and penguin barks.

Annika pushed the door open gently and was hit by a wave of moist air. She blinked a few times as a cloud of wet, hot mist sprayed onto her face. She wiped her eyes and, when her vision cleared, stared at an enormous swimming pool, bubbling, steam rising from it.

Blackburn peeked through the crack of the door, just over Annika's head. "Why would someone need a swimming pool filled with hot oil?" he wondered aloud.

They looked up, and their question was answered. A whale, an actual whale, hovered over the pool in a harness attached to the arm of a large claw. The whale had a white sling over its mouth and did not look happy to be there. "That's not a pool, it's a fish fryer! And I think they plan to fry that whale," said Annika. "The poor thing!"

"Aye," agreed Blackburn. "Whales are no friends of pirates, mind ye. A whale attacked me pirate ship once, but that's another story. Still, the creature doesn't deserve to be boiled alive."

Annika scanned the rest of the room. A large control console, so tall it reached the ceiling, stood on a raised platform. Dr. Walzanarz was there, along with a group of toothbrush-carrying penguin guards, and penguins in lab coats pressing buttons amid the blinking lights of the computer. Every penguin wore a head mirror.

On the platform, but also on the sides of the pool, other penguins mopped the oil-splattered ground. One of those mopping penguins was only a few feet away from Annika.

She shrank back to avoid being seen.

"I want to fry that whale! And I want to fry it now!" screamed Dr. Walzanarz into a walkie-talkie. A few penguins yelped back. Annika didn't speak penguin, but from Dr. Walzanarz's frustrated squawk, she wasn't happy with their responses.

The crane moved, an inch and only an inch, and then that was followed by a rusty squeal and a loud *POP!* One of the buckles in the harness snapped open. The whale dangled on its side, still hovering over the pool, but the rest of its binding looked dangerously unsteady. Another buckle could burst any second, and the whale would be a goner.

Annika needed to do something. She couldn't stay here, hidden. Bolt needed her! The world needed her! And right now, this whale needed her! Could Annika reach Dr.

Walzanarz without being spotted? She needed to run up a metal staircase to get to her, so the odds were low. But she had to try.

There was a flash of movement on the opposite end of the platform. A penguin guard had been standing there, Annika was certain of it. As a bandit she could scan a room and immediately remember everything about it. But now the penguin was gone. After a pause, part of a head popped up from behind a stack of boxes.

A pair of eyes peeked up. Annika squinted.

She didn't recognize those eyes, but they were definitely human. And maybe a hint of something else . . .

Then a second set of eyes popped up, and Annika's heart leapt.

Bolt! Annika would recognize his twin horn-shaped hair bulges anywhere. Yes, those were definitely his bushy eyebrows. He was alive! And not even a prisoner! Annika gave a yip of happiness. What was Bolt doing here?

Fortunately, no one heard Annika's yip because at that exact moment, Bolt sneezed, and the sound of his sneeze echoed across the entire room. "Why is it so peppery in here?" he asked.

Dr. Walzanarz stared at Bolt, as did every penguin in the room. Bolt stood up, and so did the boy, a teenager a couple of years older than Bolt, with hair as unruly as his and a nose just as big. Had Bolt found someone to help them? It seemed so, as Bolt and the boy strode across the platform, toward Dr. Walzanarz's perch.

"You!" the dentist shouted, her voice echoing across the wide-open room. She held up a small radio. "Kiki? My silver-fanged beauty? Kiki? Come in!" She stomped her foot. "Come in, my dahling penguin!"

"She's indisposed at the moment," Bolt growled. "And now it's time *you* cooperate with *me.* I want that silver Ealsay tooth!" He pointed at Dr. Walzanarz. A glimmer of light bounced off something shiny and reflective in her chest pocket.

The dentist screamed into her radio: "Stop him, my dahlings! I command you all!"

A group of burly penguins with toothbrushes that had been standing guard near the doorway behind Dr. Walzanarz rushed toward Bolt.

"Out of me way, missy." Blackburn pushed open the swinging door and rushed into the room. In one motion, he grabbed a mop from the penguin janitor near them and swept it at the bird's feet, toppling it over.

"I thought you promised you wouldn't fight," said Annika.

"Well, maybe just this once. Besides, pirates never keep our promises. Ye know that."

Blackburn looked out of shape, what with his big gut and clumsy, noisy gait, but when he fought, he was a different person. The hero in him had finally come out.

Holding his mop with one hand, he rushed up the stairs two at a time, his boots clomping loudly.

"En garde!" Blackburn cried as he reached the top of the stairs and faced a toothbrush-carrying penguin. The pirate twirled the mop handily. It whistled and whipped through the air like a sword. The penguin swung its toothbrush at Blackburn—which could have easily sent Blackburn over the railing and into the hot oil below, had it connected—but Blackburn ducked out of the way and jabbed the penguin in the stomach with his mop. The penguin keeled over. Another penguin rushed toward the pirate, but the heavy toothbrush slowed it down. Blackburn was faster. He swung his mop like a baseball bat, hitting one of the penguin's wings. The penguin dropped its toothbrush, and then Blackburn sprung up, feetfirst. His feet collided against the penguin's belly, and he bounced off the bird as if it were a trampoline.

Penguin bellies can be quite springy.

"Son of a biscuit-eater!" Blackburn roared, continuing to swing the mop handle, striking three more penguins.

Annika hadn't joined the fight yet. She had been too surprised to do anything but watch: that helpless whale

hanging above the pool, Bolt and his new friend emerging from their hiding spot, Blackburn rushing into the fray. She didn't know who was at greater risk.

But Annika was done being a spectator. She pushed open the door of the pantry to join her friends, but after only one step, she felt a heavy bang on the back of her head.

The world spun. She blinked, trying to regain focus, her head aching as she fell to her knees.

When she turned her head, she saw the nastiest penguin she had ever seen. The penguin bellowed at her, snarling, angry. Vicious. But the worst part of this creature was its whalelike fangs, whalelike fangs sticking out of its beak. And they both seemed to be made of silver.

"You must be Kiki," said Annika with a loud gulp.

25. Crumbling Plans

B*lackburn!* thought Bolt. *He's here!* Bolt hadn't spotted Annika, but she must be nearby, too. If not . . . he wouldn't think about it. She *was* fine. She had to be. But Bolt wouldn't be fine if they couldn't dispatch the dozen toothbrush-wielding penguins standing between them and Dr. Walzanarz. He became more optimistic, though, with every shout of "Borscht!" and the panicked penguin squawk that inevitably followed.

But even Blackburn's impressive fighting skills wouldn't be enough to take down the whole platoon of penguins on their own.

"Can't you control them?" Grom asked, fists up. "I thought you were like, 'Do this, I'm a penguin,' and they'd be like, 'Whatever you say'?"

"Yeah, I'm working on it," said Bolt, but his thoughts still went nowhere. He had to push his mind past those silver mirrors somehow.

The penguins hissed and stomped forward. As one of them swept a toothbrush forward, both Bolt and Grom leapt backward.

No! We are family! Love! And other things like that! Bolt thought. But it was no use. Bolt's commands bounced off their heads. He could send his thoughts to the whale instead—that poor whale—but that wouldn't do much good.

What else was part of the penguin-verse?

Werepenguins! Werepenguins were part of the penguin-verse, of course. Dr. Walzanarz didn't wear a head mirror. Bolt sent his thoughts hurtling toward her. *You can be a force of good. Of love. You don't have to rule!*

"I am a werepenguin!" bellowed the dentist. "Ruling is what I do."

It doesn't have to be. Life can be wonderful. Or vonderful. You can even speak with a strange fake accent.

"Really?" said the dentist, and Bolt felt her anger subside, just a smidge. There was still, like, 95 percent anger in there, but Bolt felt a small indentation cutting through her resolve.

You can't persuade her, Bolt. The dentist is mine. They are all mine!

That voice was not Bolt's, nor Dr. Walzanarz's, but it rattled inside both of their heads. The Stranger, wherever he was, had joined the fight.

Bolt fought back, sending his thoughts soaring at the whale dentist. *No. You don't need to do this. Forget about this giant fish fryer.*

"But I like fried fish," said Dr. Walzanarz, pouting.

Well, we'll figure something out then.

No! The Stranger shouted into their heads once more. *We are better than humans. We are meant to fight and hate! Our silver-toothed penguin army shall rule!*

Don't listen to him! You can be a source of goodness! insisted Bolt.

"I can?" Dr. Walzanarz asked, confused. "Are you sure?"

Yes, definitely! Bolt maintained his bombardment of voiceless arguing. *Listen to me. Do what I say! Stand your army down and give me that silver tooth in your pocket.*

"You might be onto something," the dentist admitted, moving her hand toward her breast pocket.

See, Bolt? The Stranger's voice echoed inside Bolt's head and his head alone now. *Doesn't it feel good to take control? Doesn't it feel good to control all penguins?*

Bolt had to admit it did feel sort of nice. Maybe he could get used to controlling other werepenguins, and penguins, and whatever else he could think of. Everyone would do what Bolt wanted. He would be in charge!

What was Bolt thinking? That wasn't what he wanted! *Snap!* His connection with the dentist severed, and the Stranger seemed to have drifted away, too. Bolt blinked, breathing heavy—controlling minds was draining.

Meanwhile, Blackburn had joined them, fighting his way through the throngs of penguins. But there were so many more!

"Borscht!" said Blackburn. "If we survive this, I'm definitely retirin'."

"The good news is we probably won't survive this," said Bolt. "So you won't have to worry about it."

Penguins stomped forward, head mirrors firmly in place, angry scowls on their faces. Bolt backed up, reaching the long, retractable metal pier that stretched into the middle of the pool. Grom and Blackburn backed up next to him.

"I'm Grom," he said to the pirate. "You got very nice sideburns."

"Thank ye for noticing," said Blackburn. "That's what I'd like on me tombstone, by the way: *Here lies Blackburn the pirate. He had very nice sideburns.* It looks like I'll be needing that tombstone sooner than I'd like, though. Borscht!"

They walked backward down the pier, hot oil bubbling along either side of them. A drip landed on Bolt's shoulder and immediately burned through his shirt.

They reached the end of the gangway, where, above them, hung the whale. Bolt could hear its leather harness tearing, the claw's rusty metal screeching, and the nuts and bolts straining.

Blackburn stood in front of Bolt and Grom, poised to fight, as a penguin soldier rushed forward and barreled right into his stomach. Blackburn stumbled back and swung his mop wildly, arms flailing, accidentally knocking the penguin's head mirror off.

The penguin raised its toothbrush as if it were some sort of battle-ax. Blackburn was still off-balance, and raised his mop weakly to try to parry the blow, but the effort looked like it would be futile.

Bolt blinked and glanced at the penguin's head mirror, now sitting on the ground.

Don't! Don't hit him! Bolt thought, his orders clear, with nothing to block them.

The penguin swung its toothbrush to the side, missing the pirate by a good two feet.

Blackburn regained his composure while the penguin blinked in confusion. Bolt could read the penguin's thoughts as clearly as you are reading this chapter. They were hurtful thoughts, ones wanting to obey the dentist and harm others. Bolt twisted them around inside its brain. *This is not you.*

Other penguins stepped forward, at least twenty of

them. Bolt hadn't thought he and his friends had a sliver of a chance to survive. But that's exactly what they had. Slivers. And cracks.

"The head mirrors!" Bolt shouted. "Go for the head mirrors!"

"Then how will they see our back molars during a dental appointment?" Blackburn asked.

"Just do it!" Bolt shouted.

Blackburn swung his mop at the nearest penguin. Glass shattered from a broken mirror.

"You don't want to hurt us!" Bolt shouted, both out loud and through his telekinetic powers. The penguin lowered its toothbrush, looking around, dazed, as if waking up from a midday nap.

Grom jumped next to Blackburn, swinging fists toward other penguins who waddled forward, dodging toothbrushes and slapping head mirrors askew.

In the middle of the brawl, Bolt noticed some commotion off to the side of the pool. Annika! Bolt would have been overjoyed to see her had he not also seen who she was fighting: the silver-toothed penguin monstrosity, Kiki. Annika had fled up the metal staircase but was down on the ground now, the penguin crouching, ready to leap on top and crush her. Bolt couldn't lose Annika. Not his best friend!

"No!" he cried, spreading desperate thoughts into the

fanged beast's head. *Leave her be! Stop! Back away!* His thoughts bounced weakly off Kiki's silver teeth.

Or did they? Did the beast hesitate, just for a moment? Had Bolt somehow broken through silver? No, that was impossible. Werepenguins couldn't do that.

Before Bolt could tell for sure, a sudden bark turned Bolt's attention back to his own situation. Grom lay on the ground, moaning, his leg bleeding—a penguin guard must have overpowered him and now was headed for Bolt. But its head mirror dangled atop its head, shattered. Without thinking, Bolt screamed words into its head.

Freeze!

The penguin halted, frozen like a block of ice, just like Bolt had frozen Grom the day before, when they were in the mole hole.

Bolt stared at the penguin. It was breathing but otherwise completely still. Bolt flicked his fingers, and the air seemed to curdle around them.

Bolt felt the room inside him. It was as if the heat had sucked up penguin perspiration, and Bolt could feel every molecule in the air. The penguin-verse was here. It was everywhere.

He held his hand up into a fist as a few more penguins rushed forward. *Freeze!* They stopped dead in their tracks. But there were still many more guards working their way around their unmoving comrades.

"What are you doing?" shrieked Dr. Walzanarz, who had walked up the pier behind her penguins. She held her walkie-talkie and screamed into it. "I vant them vounded! Vrecked! Viped off the face of this earth!"

The penguins didn't move but instead looked back at her, blinking.

"Want, wounded, wrecked, wiped," said Dr. Walzanarz with an unhappy sigh.

Many penguins remained still as statues, but others surged forward, toothbrushes high. Grom stood, grimacing, trying not to put any weight on his leg. Together, he and Blackburn inched back, and Grom bumped into Bolt.

"Watch it," said Bolt, nearly falling backward. The heels of his feet hung off the metal grate and over the bubbling pool.

Freeze! Bolt commanded, and one of the penguins froze. But more kept coming, more than Bolt could count, and these penguins had head mirrors firmly in place. Bolt knew shooting out commands was futile. He started to take a step back before reminding himself he was already at the edge of the retractable pier.

"It was nice knowing you guys," grunted Grom. "Well, not so much you, Bolt. I still don't really like you."

Blackburn reached into his pirate frock and removed a large squeeze bottle, grinning. "Not so fast, fellas. I got me some floor wax from one of those mopping penguins.

And lucky for me, I know plenty about floor waxin'."

He squirted the bottle, and wax gushed from its spout and onto the metal grating in front of them.

Penguins charged forward and onto the waxy floor. Their feet slipped. Two banged into each other, bellies first, and they bounced off and flopped to the ground. Two more penguins did the same. Heads collided into heads, smashing head mirrors.

Dr. Walzanarz screamed and ran forward, jumping over fallen penguins. She then sprung off a penguin's stomach, flying up into the air and toward Bolt. "You are no longer my dahling! You are going to ruin everything!"

She landed next to Bolt, her fingers curled, long nails scratching at him. He kicked her—he was crouching and holding his hands out to deflect her sharp-looking manicure, so a kick was the only thing he could do. It wasn't much of a kick, really. But Dr. Walzanarz wobbled, just a little, forcing her to lurch backward, and she stepped right on a puddle of wax.

She did a complete pirouette, her hands waving up and down to keep herself upright. She reached out to steady herself and clutched Bolt's arm. For a moment he thought she might fall into the oil and take him with her. He looked up, staring into the eye of the whale dangling above them.

Then Dr. Walzanarz's bony fingers slipped from Bolt's arm. Grom, who had been wrestling a penguin, broke

away and shoved the doctor. Her feet slipped on more oil, and she spun once, twice, three times—an impressive triple axel, really—before colliding with a penguin next to her. The penguin's bouncy belly sent her hurtling up, into the air.

For a moment she seemed suspended over the hot oil, extending her arms as if they were wings and she wanted to fly, flapping them incessantly.

She couldn't fly, but one of her fingers caught the edge of the white sling covering the whale's aching mouth. Somehow, she held on. "Help!" she cried.

All action below stopped, as everyone stared up at the dentist. Blackburn lowered his mop, and Grom his fists. Penguins who still had head mirrors in place—there were only a few of them now—stopped swinging their toothbrushes. Even those penguins with shattered mirrors, many of which had seemed confused, stopped their aimless blinking to gaze at the swinging legs of the dentist.

The only sounds were bubbling oil from the pool around them, a random penguin sneeze, and Dr. Walzanarz's panicked screeches.

A loud bang shook the walkway. A series of explosions came from the fryer's controls, flames shooting out. Penguins scurried out of the room.

And at that exact moment, the metal pier began to retract, taking Bolt and his friends, and the penguins near

them, back toward the safety of the raised metal platform.

"Wait! What about me!" howled the doctor, still dangling over sizzling hot oil. "Don't forget about me!"

At that moment Bolt realized, *What about Annika?* He had been so wrapped up in fighting he had momentarily forgotten about her! Through the rapidly rising smoke, he couldn't see much of anything at all.

26. One Last Fish to Fry

So, what *was* happening with Annika? Well, three minutes earlier, she had backed up through the pantry doorway, the silver-fanged penguin following, chomping her beak and gnashing her dangerous fangs.

Annika's foot collided against one of the many barrels of bread crumbs that filled the room. Kiki charged, and Annika leapt out of her way. The penguin missed Annika and crashed into the wooden bread crumb barrel, which splintered into pieces, spilling crumbs across the floor.

Annika sneezed. "Why is this so peppery?" she complained.

The creature turned and dove at Annika again. Again, Annika jumped out of the way, and Kiki rammed into another barrel of bread crumbs. And again, Annika sneezed.

She grabbed a broken wooden slat. It was about the same size and weight as her practice sword. Perfect.

Annika swished her new weapon to the left and then the right. She jabbed. She poked. "En garde!" she cried. She had no idea what that meant, but she had heard Blackburn say it a few times, and it sounded cool. "Borscht!" she cried, but cringed. *En garde* was a far more appropriate battle cry.

Kiki snarled. Annika's pokes and jabs did nothing but make the penguin angrier. And Kiki looked plenty angry already.

Annika swung her slat, and it made a satisfying *thwack* against one of the penguins' wings, but the creature barely seemed to notice. Annika lunged, but the slat bounced off the penguin's belly. Finally, she thrust forward and smacked one of the penguin's fangs with a loud *crack!*

The wooden plank broke in half, and Annika dropped it to the ground. Had she effectively loosened the tooth? Annika didn't have time to find out, because at that moment Kiki leapt. As Annika stepped out of the way she grabbed a fistful of bread crumbs from a broken barrel and tossed them into the air. Kiki began sneezing, slashing out with her wings to get at Annika, but momentarily blinded.

Annika sprinted back through the swinging doors and out of the pantry. Kiki sneezed twice more and gave chase while Annika raced up the metal staircase, hoping it would slow down the monstrous penguin pursuing her.

It didn't. Kiki ran right up after her, snarling, fangs chomping.

Annika reached the top of the stairs and surveyed the room. There were other penguins on the platform near Annika, but they were too busy pressing random buttons on the enormous control panel to pay attention to her. Some of the buttons they pressed made lights blink and horns buzz. Other buttons seemed to do nothing.

Below her, Bolt, Blackburn, and every other penguin stood on some sort of metal pier that extended into the middle of that bubbling fish frying pool. Dr. Walzanarz was there, too. Above them dangled the whale—that unfortunate whale—moaning unhappily. Annika wished she could help them, but they were too far away, and she had her own problems to deal with anyway.

Kiki hopped up the final staircase, snorted—and few things are more disturbing than a penguin snort—and rammed into Annika with surprising speed. Annika fell to the ground.

Lying there, Annika caught another glimpse of Bolt, down below. He was looking at her, his mouth twisted in a pained expression. *It was nice knowing you,* Annika thought

as Kiki crouched, preparing to belly flop on top of her like a professional wrestler, before plunging her fangs into Annika.

"No!" cried Bolt. His voice reverberated through the room.

Kiki sidestepped. Strangely, she seemed to freeze for a split second, but that was all the time Annika needed to scamper back to her feet.

Whatever had slowed this fanged monstrosity wasn't slowing her down any longer, though. The penguin rubbed her webbed feet on the ground, preparing to charge like a raging bull.

Annika kept her eyes trained on the penguin. She tucked her head down to pick up speed, but that also meant she couldn't see where she was going. She snaked left and right, getting closer and closer. At the last second, Annika deftly moved to the side. But not before one of the penguin's fangs sliced painfully through her thumb.

Tears threatened to fall down Annika's cheeks. But bandits are tough. They seldom cry, and never during fights. That was in the bandit code and everything, although Annika wondered if she should rewrite that part, too.

No. That part would stay. She would not cry.

What happened next happened so quickly, Annika would have to sort it out in her head later.

Kiki dashed toward Annika, head down once more.

Annika leapt in the air, legs out, spinning. Her foot collided against the penguin's beak, cleanly knocking one of Kiki's fangs out of her mouth—perhaps the one she had loosened earlier—and it flew up and embedded itself into the control panel behind Annika.

Annika saw sparks. She heard a bang. Flames erupted from where the tooth was impaled into the fish fryer control panel. The flames spread, growing larger, and metal began to curl from the heat.

Behind Annika, Kiki lay on the ground, groaning.

Meanwhile, the fire burned out of control. Part of the console collapsed within itself. The smell of burning rubber and charred steel spread through the room. Loud snaps and booms erupted from inside the computer bank as the fire raged within its wires. Steam and smoke gushed out. Metal smoldered. The blinking lights began to shatter—*Pop! Pop!*—like popcorn. Random toots bellowed, garbled and slow, like a melting radio.

The platform shook. The oil in the pool next to her bubbled and frothed, with small mini oil explosions erupting at random. Penguins scampered for the exits.

Bolt! Blackburn! That teenager who looked somewhat penguin-ish! They were still on that metal pier! Annika hadn't seen what had happened there, but surprisingly, Dr. Walzanarz hung in the air, her hands clutching the white sling wrapped around the whale's mouth. Annika dashed to the end of the pier and smashed her hand against a big red button. The pier retracted toward her.

"Hurry!" she shouted to her friends. "This place is gonna blow!"

Fissures spread on a steel girder above Annika, which collapsed to the ground only a few feet away from her, amid a bed of glowing ash. A series of hanging lights shattered, one after another. *Crack! Crack! Crack!*

Penguins with and without smashed head mirrors ran

off the pier and toward the exits. Bolt and Blackburn came next. The boy who looked penguin-ish limped between them—his leg was cut.

"Hurry!" Annika shouted as they rushed toward the exit. Annika could barely see anything but smoke. It was billowing everywhere, and she blindly staggered forward in the general direction of *out*.

She heard someone, maybe the older boy she didn't know, cry out, "Get down!" and then—

BOOM!

Annika felt a blast of hot air ram into her, sending her flying off her feet. And then . . . nothing.

Bolt saw stars, but his ears didn't seem to work. He was covered in white. Angels were white. So were clouds. He must be dead, that's it. Death was sort of peaceful, actually. Still, he would have much rather been alive.

But the silence became a hum, and Bolt's numb joints ached, and he realized that soot was also white, and when he stood up the white flakes fell off him and he coughed. He also sneezed from all the pepper in the air. The explosion had dulled his hearing and senses for a moment, but things were now growing in volume, and his vision was clearing. It was nighttime, and ashes burned in the sky, flames jutting up from the parts of the fortress that still stood, although most of the building was completely gone.

Bolt had been thrown clear onto the lawn, as had most of the fortress. Giant concrete slabs and broken machinery were feet deep, everywhere.

Annika leaned over him. She was bleeding from a dozen small cuts on her face and arms, and her clothing was also covered in ash. "Are you OK?"

"I guess it sort of depends on what you mean by OK," said Bolt. "Achy all over and filled with soot? Is that OK enough?"

Annika wrapped her arms around him. "It's good enough for me. I thought we might have lost you."

"I feared I had lost you, too," Bolt croaked back.

Annika and Bolt had hugged before, but only with large groups of people. Bolt became aware that they were hugging only each other now, and Annika must have become aware of it at the same moment, because she quickly released her hold and stared awkwardly at the ground. "All right then. Good," she mumbled.

"Borscht! That was close!" said Blackburn, standing near them. Part of his waistcoat was burned, and he was missing one shoe. His cheeks were black and blue, and an eye was swollen shut. Still, it was a miracle they had survived. It appeared all the penguins had, too; they stood in groups of two or three on the lawn, agitated but unharmed. There was no sign of Dr. Walzanarz or of the whale—Bolt had no idea where either had gone.

Bolt looked back at Blackburn and Annika, still barely believing their good fortune. He was alive! His friends were alive! And the horrible fish fryer was destroyed.

But, despite this, Bolt didn't feel happy. He had failed.

They had risked their lives for nothing. The Stranger was still out there, and the Ealsay tooth was gone—destroyed or buried under feet of rubble, lost forever.

The Stranger would live. The world would fall to his penguin army.

Bolt wiped soot from himself, his nose filling up with congestion. "It's gone. It's *gone*," he mumbled. His shoulders slumped. "The tooth is gone."

"We won't give up," Annika said with a look of bandit-like determination. "We'll find another way to defeat the Stranger. As long as we stay together, we'll fight. Right, Blackburn?"

Blackburn looked away. "Well, about that. Remember when I was talking about retiring . . ."

Bolt didn't hear the rest of what the pirate said, as a small explosion from part of the fryer shook the ground.

Bolt straightened, his heart rocking.

"Grom! Where's Grom?" asked Bolt. In the confusion of the blast, he had momentarily forgotten about his new non-friend. But now, Bolt felt panic. Grom rescued Bolt from Kiki. Grom shoved Dr. Walzanarz, keeping her from dragging Bolt off the metal pier. Grom even shouted, "Get down!" right before throwing himself on top of Bolt to shield him from the blast.

Grom had complained he didn't like Bolt, but in the end, he had risked his own life to save Bolt's.

"Grom! Grom!" Bolt yelled. No one yelled back. "You have to help me!" Bolt yelped to his friends, lifting random rocks and sheets of metal from the ground. Nothing. Over there? More nothing. And more nothing.

Wait—what was that moving under that pile of large concrete stones? Bolt darted over to them. "Give me a hand!" he cried out. In a heartbeat Blackburn and Annika were there, lifting. "Hurry!" Bolt urged. The stones were heavy, and every part of Bolt's muscles ached from the blast and the exertion, but he finally lifted one. And another.

But all that they saw underneath was more rubble.

Bolt moved from rock to rock, asphalt chunk to asphalt chunk, and so did Annika and Blackburn. Every time they didn't find a human arm, Bolt was relieved—and more frightened at the same time.

It would take weeks—months, maybe—to lift up every boulder. And then what? Bolt reached out his mind, hoping to connect to Grom's, to sense his penguin blood, feel his breath, hear his beating heart.

He heard nothing but silence. Deadly silence.

Bolt sat down on a chunk of concrete and cradled his head in his hands. Grom was dead. There was no other

explanation. And he had given his life to save Bolt's.

Bolt wiped wet debris from his eyes, ashes mixed with tears.

"Wait. What's that?" Annika asked.

A low moan rumbled from across a pile of crushed metal, long tangled wires, and ragged hunks of cement. Bolt leapt to his feet and followed the noise, not sure where it came from and less sure what was making it, not daring to hope.

Bolt moved aside some rocks only to reveal more rocks. He slid over a metal sheet. Under it was another metal sheet.

"Look at all this silver!" cried Blackburn from a few feet away. "You could fill a treasure chest with this stuff."

Bolt was beside Blackburn in a microsecond, hands digging, moving a large silver brick to the side. Under it was a space, a hole, as big as a person.

And there was Grom, his face bloody, one eye half open. "About time," he mumbled.

Blackburn and Annika helped Bolt heave a concrete slab out of the way so they could get Grom out of the hole. Bolt's relief was tempered by the painful squeals trembling from Grom's lips as they gently moved him.

"Grom, these are my friends. This is Annika, the band—"

"Ahem . . ." Annika cut in.

"Sorry," Bolt said. "This is Annika, the *greatest* bandit who ever lived."

Annika grunted her approval.

"The boy and I met already," said Blackburn. "He admired me sideburns, he did."

"Well, guys, this is Grom," said Bolt.

"Nice to meet you," Grom said through painful groans. "Did we win?"

"Sort of," said Bolt. "We destroyed the fortress, but the tooth . . ." He couldn't say any more. Grom was alive, and that was more important than a silly silver tooth.

"You mean this thing?" Grom asked, unfolding his hand to reveal the famed tooth of the Ilversay Oothtay Ealsay. He handed it to Bolt.

Bolt stared at the tooth, his eyes wide with shock. "What? How?"

"I grabbed it when I shoved the dentist lady," said Grom.

"You picked her pocket?" asked Annika, obviously impressed. "Are you a bandit, too?"

"Just because I can pick pockets don't mean I'm a bandit," Grom mumbled.

"It sort of does," said Annika.

Bolt felt like hugging Grom, except it would have been even more awkward than hugging Annika earlier. Besides, Grom still looked to be in bad shape.

But Bolt couldn't dwell on his relief. Grom coughed, and blood splattered onto Bolt's shirt. "You know, I really don't dislike you. I was just saying that," said Grom, and then he collapsed into Bolt's arms. He was still breathing and reopened his eyes. "Sorry. I feel so weak."

A short series of explosions rumbled the ground, and a few metal shards flew into the air and landed near them.

"We best get out of here," said Blackburn.

Grom's eyes barely fluttered open. He wrapped his arms around Blackburn's and Bolt's shoulders, and they weaved their way across the rubble. Bolt bit his lips with worry every time Grom moaned, which was pretty much continually.

"Over there," said Grom, motioning toward a boulder. When they approached it, Bolt saw a small hole peeking out from behind it. Annika slid the rock to its side, revealing a larger entrance and a tunnel heading down into the earth below.

"What's down there?" Annika asked.

"Home," Grom mumbled.

28. Another Break in the Action

The foghorn from the ship disturbed my already disturbed thoughts. The animals were being led to their temporary homes aboard the ship—the journey would take a week, but the monkeys had video games to keep themselves busy, the rabbits had Ping-Pong tables (everyone knows rabbits are the animal kingdom's finest Ping-Pong players, just like hippos are quite skilled at macramé, although I had accidently left the macramé sets behind, so I worried the hippos might get bored), and other animals had equally well-prepared amusements.

The sun was still high; nighttime was far away. My previous discussions with the penguin caretaker had been in the evening and had ended at midnight. Both times, at the stroke of twelve, the man had turned into a penguin, or so I believed. I had never fully witnessed a transformation, just hints of one.

"Why did you stop talking?" I asked as the penguin caretaker paused in his narration. "Grom is gravely injured. Our heroes are far from finding the Stranger. I am at the edge of my seat!"

I had pulled up a chair, but the boat slightly rocked and I fell off the seat, landing on my rear on the ship's deck. "Well, I had been on the edge of my seat."

"Next time, you should sit in the middle of the chair," said the caretaker. "But why did I stop my story? I thought this would be a good time to leave our heroes and check in on the Stranger. See what he's up to."

I stared at the man, my lips sputtering. It took me a second to still their sputter. "The Stranger? Who cares about him? I want to know about Bolt. Grom. The others. Are they safe? I agreed to take your penguins and all the animals to my zoo," I reminded him, "but only if you told me the whole of your story, not a story left with mole holes."

"We will return to our heroes shortly, my friend. But the story is about the Stranger as well, and we have spent so little time with him. Of course, the less time spent in the company of such an evil being, the better."

"Just keep the next chapter brief then," I said.

"I'll do my best."

29. The Stranger, Part 1

"The Stranger sat on an ice throne in an ice cave in his home in the icy South Pole. Meanwhile, back in Pingvingrad . . ."

"Wait," I said, interrupting the penguin caretaker. "That's it? That's the entire detour to visit the Stranger?" The man nodded. "The chapter doesn't have to be quite that short. If we're going to stop in and see the Stranger, we might as well linger a little longer."

"Good," said the man. "I hate to skip interesting back-story. We shall continue with the Stranger in Chapter Thirty."

30. The Stranger, Part 2

The Stranger sat on an ice throne in an ice cave in his home in the icy South Pole. It had all been built by penguins and carved from glaciers. An ice throne wasn't very comfortable; the Stranger would have liked a seat cushion, but the penguins' attempts at carving a seat cushion had been unsuccessful. When the Stranger ruled the world, he would get a seat cushion. It was near the top of his to-do list, right after putting all humans in dungeons, and making lots of fish sticks.

The Stranger hadn't always been called the Stranger, but he couldn't recall his real name. He was pretty sure it had rhymed with Tim. Or maybe Dave. Or Doug. He hadn't used a proper name for a long time.

Tim, or Dave, or Doug, or whatever his name was stood up from his throne, ice crystals stuck to his rear, although he barely noticed them, and walked out a back exit. He had built the exit in case of a fire, but really, how likely was a fire in an ice cave? It led to a ridge overlooking a chasm, where thousands of penguins had gathered, waiting for him.

He looked down at them. His children. His family. Oh, how he hated them all! They looked up, ready to obey, eager to please him. They would do anything: sing, dance, juggle. Often, he just made them poke other penguins in the eye. Today he wanted them to tickle one another.

He didn't need to say anything. Instead, he merely thought the word: *Tickle!*

And they did. Penguins rubbed their wings under wing pits, pecked the bottoms of webbed feet, and softly caressed under beaks.

The Stranger clapped. He should probably train them to fight instead, but tickling was far more entertaining. Who needed video games, or a television, or a computer when you could order an army of penguins to tickle one another for no reason?

But the war would start soon, and that would be just as fun. Yes, very soon.

Or would it?

He had felt a disturbance in Pingvingrad but had not been able to reach Dr. Walzanarz. Ashes and dust sometimes hurt his reception, but so did rain. And, of course, silver.

And what of Bolt? Alive? Dead? He couldn't reach the boy, either. Bolt had been getting better at keeping the Stranger out of his head, but this was different. Something had happened.

The Stranger assumed the boy was alive and that he would eventually find his way to the South Pole. Sure, the Stranger had ordered Dr. Walzanarz to convince Bolt to join the penguin army, and if not, she was instructed to kill him, but the Stranger had never given the dentist much of a chance of succeeding at either task. It was more of a test than anything—if Bolt survived, he was the chosen one. If not, then the Stranger had been wrong.

The Stranger thought back to when he had first learned of the chosen one. Back then, the Stranger was just your run-of-the-mill werepenguin. He had been content feeding with penguins at night and doing the occasional card tricks for them. Since he could read their minds, he could always guess what card they were holding; oh, how he amazed them! But he was also immortal, and after guessing penguin cards correctly about ten thousand times, it grew tiresome. Surely he was meant to do more than this! He had heard rumors of a fortune teller, a woman who knew all. Maybe she could give him a hint about what he was meant to be.

He traveled a long way to see her, but see her he did.

"Come in," the Fortune Teller said as he peeked into her tent within her nomad caravan. She curled a finger, beckoning him to enter. "You want to know your purpose in this world, yes? Sit. And see."

He sat, and she laid out her tarot cards on a small table covered with a red lacy tablecloth. She flipped the first card over to reveal a picture of the moon. The card read: *Night.*

She flipped a second card. It had a picture of a tornado. *Power.*

She flipped a third card. The card was blood-red. The caption on the card read: *You are a werepenguin and will take over the world.*

"Wow, that card is eerily specific," said the Stranger.

The Fortune Teller flipped over three more cards—one had a picture of a yardstick. *Ruler.* One showed a boy with a penguin sitting on his head. It read: *Boy with a penguin on his head.* The last card showed a seesaw and said, appropriately: *Seesaw.*

"What do they mean?" the Stranger asked.

"They can mean many things. One, that you enjoy

measuring things, walking around with a penguin on your head, and seesaws." The Stranger nodded. He did enjoy all those things. "Or, they could mean you are meant to rule penguins—you will wear a crown as their king—except . . ." She squinted. "No. Accept."

"*Except* or *accept*?" asked the Stranger. "Those are quite different words, although they sound alike."

"Yes, I'm aware of what a homophone is," she said. "When placed next to the ruler and the boy-with-a-penguin card, the seesaw card means your future is unbalanced. You will rule forever! Except! Or accept."

"Except or accept what?" the Stranger asked, confused.

"The boy-with-the-penguin-on-his-head card is the key. You will rule the world *except* there is a werepenguin boy who will defeat you. Or the boy will *accept* his place by your side and help you rule the world. These tarot cards are disappointingly vague and also filled with mistakes, so it's hard to say." She showed him a card with a disgruntled penguin on it. "See? Read this card! It is supposed to say: *Beware the penguins*, but instead it says: *Behind the pengoes.* What does that even mean?"

When the Stranger had left the tent, he was excited but also bewildered. He would rule! He would have an ally who would *accept* the Stranger, or maybe *except*? Eventually, he settled on *accept* as the far more likely prediction. After all, who could ever defeat the Stranger? He

RULER.
BOY WITH PENGUIN
ON HIS HEAD.
a.
b.
SEESAW.

was way too powerful. And when the boy joined him, the world would be theirs.

The Stranger spent many years searching for the boy, looking for anyone born with a penguin birthmark. He had also spent that time turning others into were-penguins, like the Baron, the Earl, and Dr. Walzanarz. Any good army needed lieutenants, after all. None would be generals, however. No, that rank was the Stranger's rank. And reserved for the boy.

Despite traveling the world twice over, the Stranger never found the one he was searching for. But the Baron did. The Baron had always been the most powerful of the Stranger's spawn.

The Stranger looked down at the penguins now, tickling one another, and thought, *The Stranger says* stop. All the penguins stopped what they were doing. *The Stranger says* tickle. They tickled again. *The Stranger says* stop . . . *The Stranger says* tickle . . . *Stop. Ha, ha, I didn't say,* The Stranger says.

Such playing around had amused him once, but now it bored him. *Eat dinner,* he thought, and they all ran off to find fish.

He closed his eyes and felt the penguin-verse. It had taken a long time, but he had managed to implant a nugget of hate into every penguin in the world. Most weren't

even aware of it. All he needed to do was awaken that hate nugget and they would revolt. They would take over zoos and water parks. They would invade fishing villages. They would conquer bowling alleys.

As soon as the boy came, the war would start. The cards had foretold it.

Or, rather, the war would start as soon as the boy came—and the other one. The three of them would rule. Two generals and one lieutenant.

His eyes still closed, the Stranger gently reached out halfway across the world.

Hello, Bolt.

He waited for a response.

Nothing.

I said hello, Bolt.

Again, nothing.

Well, the boy would join the Stranger soon. And he would *accept* who he was, with no *except*ions allowed.

PART TWO
The Tundra

31. If You Can't Beet 'Em . . .

Annika sat, thinking. Bolt was a werepenguin, of course. But he was also becoming . . . something else. And that *something else* made her uneasy. He was prone to staring off into space, his eyes rolling into his head. It was disturbing. Bolt said he was trying to feel the penguin cosmos, whatever that was. He could sense penguins from miles away, but it was hard to do and required tremendous concentration. He admitted he still didn't quite understand how it all worked.

She suspected Bolt was more powerful than he realized. If he did discover all his powers, would he remain her friend or would he become just like the Stranger and want to rule them all?

No. He was Bolt. He would always be Bolt. It was silly of her to think otherwise.

It had been three days since they had first come to this underground burrow by wandering through its confusing tunnel system. Grom had been half-conscious, but just awake enough to direct them. Bandits created tunnels in Brugaria—tunnels were helpful for sneaking about and escaping from trouble—but these tunnels were far more intricate than any Annika had seen. When she got back home maybe she would improve the bandit tunnel system.

If she got home.

No, *when* she got home. *I have to remain positive,* Annika thought.

But for now, she sat on a sofa in a surprisingly comfortable underground apartment. The apartment wasn't all that different from a regular apartment, except for some distinctive differences. There were no windows. The lights were dim; moles don't like bright lights. There was a large tree trunk in the middle of the apartment—"to sharpen our claws," Zemya had explained. And the entire apartment smelled like nail polish—these mole creatures were serious about their nails. Oh, and there was hair everywhere, too. Moles shed a lot.

But the people were odder than the room. They were friendly enough—well, all but the man Topo, who

kept threatening everyone with a pair of floppy rubber scissors—but their large pink noses and constantly chattering buckteeth were hard to look past. They had offered Annika one of their black robes to wear, but she preferred to keep her regular bandit clothes on, even if they smelled like fish and needed washing.

Because Annika and Blackburn had helped save Grom and destroy the fortress, they both were named honorary moles. Apparently, it was a big honor. Some of the perks, such as free earthworms, didn't seem particularly helpful. But others, like "we won't kill you," were appreciated.

Annika felt a small cut just over her lip. It would be gone in a few days, just like most of her remaining cuts and bruises, which had been carefully cared for and bandaged by Zemya. Blackburn's wounds were healing as well. But Grom had been injured much worse.

Annika didn't know Grom at all, but he had saved Bolt's life. He had probably saved all of their lives. She hoped he would survive; they said it was a miracle he was still alive.

Blackburn emerged from the kitchen with Zemya. He had been spending nearly all his time with her, much of it in the kitchen. They made an odd couple—a pirate and a were-mole—but somehow it seemed to work.

Blackburn approached Annika holding a bowl, a spoon,

and a big smile. "Borscht?" he asked. "I brought ye breakfast, missy."

"Thanks," said Annika. She was so hungry she didn't even argue about Blackburn calling her *missy*. She slurped up some broth. "It's delicious."

"Aye, Zemya is a marvelous chef, as long as you like beets. And worms. On the seven seas we ate plenty of grub, but we never actually ate grubs. Who knew they could be so tasty?" He flashed Zemya a thankful grin, and the woman blushed, her pink nose turning a deep maroon.

Were they holding hands? Annika squirmed uncomfortably.

"A pirate like me could spend the rest of his days eatin' your borscht and worms," Blackburn cooed to Zemya. Annika continued to squirm.

"We have some leftover beets," said Zemya, smiling shyly. "Would you care to help me make some roasted beet juice and snail tarts?"

"Sounds delicious!" said Blackburn. "And I can show you how to make grog." He held out his arm. Zemya hooked it with hers, and they strolled back to the kitchen. Annika, who couldn't squirm any more than she was already, turned away so she wouldn't have to watch them.

At once, the front door to the apartment banged open and Bolt entered, panting. Annika popped open her eyes.

He had been gone since the night before, feeding in the sea. He said that penguins weren't meant to be underground. Then again, neither were bandits.

"How's Grom?" Bolt asked.

"Zemya says his fate is in the hands of the great moles in the sky," said Annika. "I'm not really sure what that means, but it doesn't sound good."

Bolt stayed by the door. He couldn't stop bouncing his legs. He glanced behind him, as if he was expecting someone to enter the room. "We have the tooth," he said, breathing hard. "We should leave and finish our quest. Find the Stranger."

"Maybe in a few more days?" Living in an underground mole hole wasn't a great life, but at least they were safe from harm here. Most importantly, Bolt was safe. She cared more about his safety than her own—as the world's greatest bandit she could take care of herself. But Bolt was, well, he was Bolt. Even with his growing penguin powers, she worried for him.

Staying here in the hole, he would be fine. *Just another week*, she thought. *Or two weeks. Two weeks where we don't have to face any threats for a while.*

Annika had to admit that although she was daring and fearless, the Stranger scared her. Not that she would ever tell anyone that.

"No. We should go," said Bolt, glancing back at the door, legs bouncing more violently. "Now."

"What's the rush?" *You're safe here.* "And why is your leg bouncing so much?"

Was that sweat dripping from his forehead? "Just anxious, maybe?" he said.

"Do you even know *where* we're supposed to go?" Annika asked. Laughter trickled out from the kitchen, and the pirate cried out "Borscht!" at least twice. "And I'm not sure if Blackburn will be so eager to leave."

"Look. We really need to go. Now or . . ."

Bolt's words were interrupted from shouts outside the room. Yells and commotion. The sound of glass breaking. Penguin barks. Bolt stared at the closed door. His legs quivered. "Too late," he groaned.

"What's going on out there?" Zemya asked, hurrying into the room with Blackburn, a red apron around her black robe. Blackburn wore a matching apron around his waistcoat.

The door burst open, and Topo tumbled inside. He slammed the door behind him, his face twisted in wild panic. "The penguin dentists! They've found us!" He tossed a pair of rubber scissors onto the floor. "I tried to stop them, but these are no help at all."

32. Three's Company

"There are three million penguins in our hallway!" Topo cried out. Zemya arched an eyebrow. "Well, maybe twenty."

"They must have found one of our holes," said Zemya. "It's a miracle they didn't find us years ago."

No, it was me, thought Bolt. Guilt poured into his head like an April shower.

The last few nights, while swimming in the sea, he had spoken with many penguins. He had learned a lot, both good and bad. Mostly bad.

The good news? The whale had survived—which was a big relief—and was seen swimming in the sea with other whales. It didn't have teeth, but whales can swallow quite a bit without needing to bite anything.

But in the bad news category, Dr. Walzanarz had also survived the explosion. She was living with a waddle of penguins that remained loyal to her despite their head mirrors being smashed. She was angry, demanding Bolt's head on a platter or, since all her platters had been broken in the explosion, in a seashell. Really, the container that kept Bolt's head wasn't as important as the head itself, which she hoped would be breaded and fried even though she no longer had a fish fryer.

"Be careful," one of the penguins in the sea had warned Bolt as they sat on the beach, bellies full after a festive feeding.

"I'll be fine," Bolt assured the penguin. "I'm staying underground with some moles, but I'll be gone in a few days." The dentist would never find him.

But then Bolt saw a glint in the distance. Squinting into the sun, he saw it reflected off a massively large toothbrush. The penguin carrying the brush took off in the opposite direction now, too far for Bolt to catch up.

Had the penguin seen Bolt? Had it overheard his conversation? Was it running back to Dr. Walzanarz, to tell her he was living underground with moles?

Bolt's heart raced. He had been foolish to talk so openly. He and his friends needed to leave. Even if the conversation had not been overheard, the longer he stayed, the more danger he brought to the labour of moles. Bolt had

been careful to keep his thoughts guarded, especially from the Stranger, but werepenguins can sense one another. Eventually, Bolt would let his guard down and they would be discovered.

It took Bolt a while to find his way back to the mole hole. There were many holes, but most didn't lead anywhere. By the time he scampered down the right hole and found Zemya's apartment, half the morning was gone. His birthmark had tingled the entire time, and it tingled more now.

They needed to go.

But he had been too slow. The penguins had found them.

More barks rang from the hallway. A terrified scream. Running footsteps. Someone yelled, "Grab a handful of worms and flee!"

Bolt headed toward the door, but Annika grabbed his hand. "You're not going out there, are you?"

Bolt shrugged off her hand. "If I surrender, maybe they'll leave everyone else alone."

Annika held a knife, a gift from Zemya. "Then we'll both go. What you did earlier—when you ditched Blackburn and me when we were running from the penguins? That wasn't OK. We're a team, Bolt. Promise you'll never do that again."

Bolt didn't answer. They had promised to never lie to each other. So instead he merely smiled.

But as Bolt reached for the doorknob, Zemya shouted: "Stop! You're a mole now, and moles stand together."

"But it's me they want," explained Bolt, "not you."

"Zemya is right," said Topo. "I may seem scary with my menacing floppy rubber scissors—"

"Not really," said Annika.

"—but I'm a mole, and proud. Moles are solitary creatures, usually. But we support one another. That's one of the things that makes our clan special. If we have to fight to save you, then we'll fight."

"No," declared Zemya. "What we need to do is leave."

"What about your home?" asked Bolt.

"And what about our beet tarts?" asked Blackburn. "They're still in the oven."

"We'll have to leave the tarts," said Zemya, and Blackburn groaned. "And we can always build another home. No, we must go."

"They'll track me," Bolt warned. "I can hold off the penguins for a time, but eventually I'll be discovered."

"That's why you're taking your ship, leaving this island, and going far away," said Zemya. "If you're gone, they'll leave us alone. But it's Grom I worry about. He won't make it through the tunnels with us. He can barely move. You need to take him with you. He's a good sailor. If he survives, he could be helpful."

"Of course." Bolt already felt terrible for luring the

penguins down into this hole. He certainly couldn't refuse Zemya's request to take Grom with him.

They followed Zemya to her back bedroom. Bolt hadn't seen Grom since the day they'd arrived in the burrow. He was thinner now, his face greenish, his long, thin nose droopy. Bags were under his eyes, so big they were more like shopping bags. Bolt and Blackburn helped Grom to his feet, but he could barely put any weight on them. It was like holding up a sack of potatoes.

They could still hear loud noises from the main tunnel. Bolt felt a group of penguins hesitating outside Zemya's door, about to burst it open. Bolt closed his eyes. *Go away. We are not here. We are not the droids you're looking for.*

He wasn't quite sure why he thought that last part.

The commotion muted as penguins continued racing down the tunnel. It would take the penguins a while to search the entire burrow. The moles would make their escape. Most probably already had.

Zemya instructed Blackburn to slide the nightstand in the corner out of the way, which revealed a large dark hole dug into the earth. "All of us have emergency escape holes," Zemya explained. They scurried down it, with Blackburn and Bolt carrying Grom.

They turned left and right in a seemingly random way, but Topo and Zemya appeared to know where they were

heading. The tunnel was smooth, without divots, and so wide it fit three people side by side.

"We are almost there," said Zemya.

Sure enough, they soon pushed aside some branches that had been laid across the hole's entrance as camouflage, and emerged into the daylight. They were now in the cove where Bolt and his friends had first landed. The pirate ship was still anchored in the harbor, and the smaller rowboat they had used to get ashore was resting on the sand.

Blackburn carried Grom to the rowboat and carefully placed him inside it.

"Good luck to you all," said Zemya, bowing. "Take care of my brother."

"Yes, good luck!" cried out Topo, holding out his scissors. *Snip, snip, snip.* "Would you like to take my scissors with you?"

"No thanks," said Bolt.

"Borscht!" said Blackburn, walking over to Zemya and Topo and waving to Bolt and Annika.

"Hurry up, Blackburn," Annika said as she and Bolt pushed the small craft back into the water.

Blackburn stood where he was. He glanced at Zemya and Topo and then to Annika and Bolt. He glanced back and forth again. He smiled at Zemya, and she returned it.

Finally, he turned to Annika and Bolt. "Find the Stranger," he said. "Save the world and all of that, aye? I'll miss ye both."

Annika rolled her eyes. "Stop joking around and give us a hand with this boat."

Blackburn still didn't move. "I'm goin' to stay here and live underground with Zemya and the other moles. I might not be the fighter I once was, but I can help protect them. I think this is what I was born to do."

"Really?" asked Bolt. "You were born to live underground and protect a bunch of mole creatures? That seems like a rather odd reason to be born."

"Perhaps," agreed Blackburn. "But then again, ye were born to free the world's penguins, and that's odd, too." Zemya was now walking back to the mole hole with Topo. She turned and exchanged a knowing glance with Blackburn. A loving glance? "A lifetime eating borscht and worms. What more could an old pirate want?"

"Adventure?" guessed Annika. "Sunlight? Just about anything else? No offense to Zemya, who seems very nice, but she turns into a mole every night."

"Well, we all have our quirks," said the pirate. "For example, I sometimes get bunions on me toes."

"You can't abandon us!" Annika rushed to Blackburn and clasped her hands in his. "You're a pirate. The sea and adventure are in your bones!"

"Having sea in yer bones is actually quite uncomfortable," admitted Blackburn. "It's better to have bones in yer bones." Annika still held his hand and tried pulling Blackburn toward the boat, but he didn't budge.

"How will we defeat the Stranger without you?" Annika asked, her voice tiny and desperate.

"Ye are a mighty swords-girl and an even cleverer bandit. Bolt is a powerful werepenguin with a silver fang. And perhaps Grom will recover. I told ye I wanted to quit the adventurin' life."

Annika had tears in her eyes. She let out a loud, creaky wail that sounded, sort of, like a heart breaking. "But I thought you were just complaining because sometimes it's fun to complain. I didn't think you were serious about quitting. Not really. You've still got plenty of pirate in you."

Bolt didn't quite share Annika's surprise. He had doubted the pirate would join them in their voyage to find the Stranger all along. Still, Bolt wished he had been wrong.

"Ye don't need me," said Blackburn.

"But we do need you!" Annika insisted, her watery sniffling turning into choked-up sobs. "*I* need you. You're like a fourth father to me. My adopted father is my second father, and his assistant bandit chief, Felipe, is like a third father to me. You're right up there, though."

"And yer like a daughter to me, although I never really

wanted a daughter. Still, if I had one, ye would be it."

"But what about the treasure I promised you?" Annika asked, although it sounded more like a pleading than an asking. "I still owe you treasure chests."

"It was a treasure having ye as my friend. That's enough. Besides, there is so much silver from cracked head mirrors around here, I could buy a dozen treasure chests. So I'll give ye a treasure: me pirate ship. I'll miss her, and I'll miss ye, too. And I'll miss calling ye *missy*, missy."

"You can call me *missy* anytime you want, if only you'll come with us!"

Barking interrupted the conversation. Penguins marched down the cliff's edge, along the path. Bolt and his friends had been discovered. The penguins would be upon them in a few minutes.

"Go!" Blackburn ordered.

"But . . ." Annika began.

"Go!" Blackburn said

again, swiping his hand from Annika's clutches and turning to join Zemya. Topo had already disappeared down the hole.

Grom moaned from the bow of the small boat as the sounds of approaching penguins grew louder. The tops of their heads could be seen bobbing along the footpath.

Bolt and Annika didn't have time to linger. They finished pushing the small rowboat into the water. Grom groaned, only half awake.

As the boat splashed into the waves, and as Annika picked up the oar to paddle them to the pirate ship, Bolt looked back at Pingvingrad one last time. Part of him wished he were escaping down a mole hole too, and not heading across the sea to fight the most powerful were-penguin in the world.

Neither Annika nor Bolt were experienced sea travelers, but both took turns at the wheel.

"Two degrees starboard," said Bolt.

"What does that mean?" Annika asked.

Bolt had no idea; the directions just seemed to come to him. He was linked, somehow, to the wind and air. Or maybe it was the Stranger—it was as if the Stranger were a magnet, pulling Bolt toward him.

They had been on the sea for two days but were still far from the Stranger's polar home. They both thought of Blackburn often—everything in the boat reminded them of him. After all, the entire deck smelled like grog, there was a treasure chest filled with eye patches and old borscht recipes in the hold below, and a sign over the main cabin read:

THIS IS BLACKBURN'S BOAT. DON'T FORGET ABOUT ME!

Annika seemed to miss the pirate more than Bolt did. Blackburn and Annika had grown close; while Bolt was thinking of penguins, they would be practicing sword fighting or arguing about whether bandit codes or pirate codes were more admirable. And Bolt now had the entire penguin-verse to keep him company. Annika spent much of her day looking over the railing, staring out into the water. Bolt did the exact same thing, but he was reaching out to the penguin cosmos at the same time.

Grom lay in a cabin down below. He had turned a seaweed-green color that was fitting for the sea but not for a person. There was not much Bolt and Annika could do for him, as they knew even less about medicine than they did about navigating a ship.

His groans wiggled up through the wood and onto the deck. "He won't live much longer," said Annika. "It's a miracle he has survived this long—the guy's a fighter, that's for sure—but he's not getting any better. Seaweed-green people seldom do."

Bolt nodded slowly, scratching his chin. "I could save

him, you know." He had thought about it ever since Grom had first been injured.

Annika stared at him. "What are you talking about?"

"I could bite him. Turn him into a werepenguin. He'd live. All of his wounds would heal." Another moan floated up from down below. "But then I'd just be creating another monster. All werepenguins are monsters."

"But you're not a monster."

"I sort of am. I'm just good at ignoring the eagerness to be evil that's inside me. If I bit Grom, I could be creating another Baron, or Earl, or Dr. Walzanarz."

"Gesundheit."

"And I'd be just like them then, spreading more rottenness in the world." Bolt shuddered at the thought of creating evil.

Annika laughed. "Bolt, don't you see? You're not the same as them, I mean, other than turning into a penguin at night."

"That's a lot to have in common."

"I guess so," agreed Annika. "But think about it. The Stranger bit the Baron out of hate. The same thing with the Earl. That's why they are evil. But you would be biting Grom out of love, out of a desire to save him. How could a werepenguin born out of love be the same as those monsters? How could a werepenguin born from love be controlled by the Stranger? He couldn't, because he would

be different. Because he would be a part of you." She tapped his chest. "He'd have your penguin-ism, sure. But he'd also have your heart."

"Do you really think that? That my heart isn't crusted with evil?"

"Of course I do. You're not filled with evil; you're filled with love, Bolt. Don't you think so?"

"Maybe. Kind of. I don't know."

The seer had sung, way back in the first chapter:

> *But you won't win unless you take this advice—*
> *Born from love may entice, but a bite's twice as nice.*

And now, here was Annika using the same words: *born from love.* Coincidence? Perhaps. But the next part—*a bite's twice as nice*—still didn't make much sense.

So Bolt remained unconvinced as the ship bobbed along the waves.

Annika went down to check on Grom as Bolt set the wheel on its course. The sky had turned dark. Bolt stood near the railing and closed his eyes, feeling penguins across the sea. He sensed small nuggets of hate in every one. Bolt tried to pry some of those hate chunks out, but they were too deep, too tightly wedged.

Bolt had always felt a barrier between the penguins and him, a cavernous gulf he could never cross. That barrier came from the Stranger's dark, misguided evil-nugget planting. Was there any way to dislodge it? Bolt didn't know.

Bolt kept his eyes closed, feeling the air around him, sensing penguins near and far, dipping into their minds to say hello before jumping out. As the sky continued to darken, the moon rose and filled the nighttime sky. It was a full moon. This was not an unnatural, always full moon like the ones in Pingvingrad, but an ordinary one, smaller but also purer. This moon was not evil; it just was.

"Grom isn't doing well," said Annika, emerging from the cabins below. "His seaweed green is now more of an emerald green. It's actually a very nice shade on him, although I suspect it means he won't last through the night."

Bolt pointed to the sky. "It's almost midnight. And it's a full moon."

Once, Bolt would have worried about turning into a werepenguin while on a boat in the middle of the sea. What if he hurt Annika? What if he attacked her? But he did not worry about that anymore. He could control the evil, mostly. At midnight he would go into the sea, feed, and return in the morning.

But his turning meant more than feeding, didn't it? It meant he could spend time with his penguin family. Sure,

it was a flawed family with hate nuggets, but it was still a family he could love.

Love. There was that sappy word again. Love, *born from love,* and all of that. Was Annika right? Would a good werepenguin be created if it came from such a wonderful emotion?

Bolt closed his eyes and let the feeling of love spread over him, warming him. The love of Annika, his best friend. The love of the mother and father he never knew but who had loved him regardless. The love of all penguins, everywhere, even despite the hate in their heads. Love was part of the penguin-verse, wasn't it?

A werepenguin *could* feel love. Bolt was proof of that. Maybe *born from love* did mean something.

"I'm going below," said Bolt.

He brushed by Annika, walked down to Grom's cabin, and knocked. A groan answered Bolt, and he entered the cabin.

Moonlight lit the room, shining directly from the porthole and onto the bed.

Grom was now somewhere between an emerald green and shamrock hue. He stirred, his eyes fluttering open. "What do you want?"

Bolt reached into Grom's head, feeling whatever small amount of penguin spirit was inside. There was a trickle,

like the drip of a faucet. It started in Grom's wrist birthmark and flowed everywhere. Was there love in there? Goodness? And if so, would it remain? Or would Bolt's bite transform that love into hate?

Bolt took a deep breath and knelt over the boy. "I need you to agree." Bolt wasn't sure why that was important, but he knew it was. Victims needed to be bitten freely. Grom nodded. "No. I need you to say the words. I need you to say *yes.*"

"Yes." *Cough, cough.* "Yes. Yes. Yes."

Bolt bit his lips as a clock chime rang silently in his head—one, two, and up to twelve—and he felt the familiar tingling in his body as he transformed, first his legs, then his arms and body, and last his head.

He barked a loud, deafening bark before lowering his werepenguin fangs.

34. The Journey

Grom did not leave his cabin the next day. Bolt was asleep for nearly twenty-four hours when he was first bitten, so he was not surprised when Grom did the same. The only time Grom stirred was when Bolt brought a plate of dead fish into the room, and even that didn't wake him.

Instead, Grom groaned, pretty much continuously, but the groans were softer and less raspy than his earlier ones. He was no longer green but had turned a deathly white. That was a good sign. All werepenguins were deathly white. His cuts and bruises were healing, too. A big gash on Grom's head had closed itself.

"How's he doing?" Annika asked Bolt when he returned to the deck after checking on Grom.

"His eyebrows are bushier, his nose is a little longer, and his hair is standing up, like horns. So, he's doing good." Those were all signs of a werepenguin. "But we should know for sure tonight. Tonight, he will change." Full moons lasted three days, so there would be a second one tonight.

But when Grom changed, what would happen? Would Grom be a ruthless killer or an ally? Bolt couldn't help but worry.

There wasn't much to do for Grom but let him sleep, so Annika spent much of her day writing in her bandit code notebook while Bolt sat on the prow, practicing his mind control. He was getting better at it, his mind dashing further and further across the waves. He could jump inside a penguin's head and see the world from its eyes. But penguins have rather dull lives—they mostly just stand around—so looking through their eyes wasn't very interesting.

Once, Bolt dove into a penguin's head and tried to chisel out the evil nugget embedded inside it. It was slow, tedious work, and after a couple hours and only a few crumbs chiseled, he gave up. Stopping the Stranger was the only way to completely free the birds.

As the waves lapped against the boat, Bolt sat with his eyes closed, scanning the cosmos. He felt the presence of penguins everywhere, from the emperor penguins who ruled their portion of the sea to the mountain penguins near the clouds. He felt penguins swimming free in the frigid deep and those performing in water shows.

I am here, Bolt sang to them, his voice soothing and calm. *Can you feel me?* He reached his voice out in a wide circle, like a penguin radar, trying to reach as many penguins as he could. But he wasn't sure if any heard him.

I hear you! Yoo-hoo! Me! came a voice that was neither soothing nor calm. The Stranger. *I'm so glad you are well! I lost track of you for a bit. But we shall be together soon.*

Bolt cursed himself for his clumsiness. If he controlled his thoughts, kept them narrow, he could avoid the Stranger's touch. But reaching out to the cosmos? What had he been thinking? *Leave me alone!*

But we are meant to be together, arm in arm and wing in wing.

No! Bolt pushed the Stranger from his head. But like a greasy hand on a refrigerator handle, the Stranger's oily words remained. Bolt looked down at his own hand, where he gripped the silver tooth. He had clutched it so hard that when he opened his hand, it left an indentation in his palm.

The day passed, the sun set, and eventually the full moon rose again. Grom hadn't stirred, but Bolt knew he would soon. As midnight approached, Bolt's blood churned and splashed. He went below deck and entered Grom's cabin.

"What time is it?" Grom murmured. He sat up, wiping the tired from his eyes with the back of his hand. His gashes and bruises were completely gone now.

"Almost time to turn."

"So it wasn't a dream? I wasn't sure if you bit me or if I had imagined the whole thing. But I was like, 'Bite me,' and you were all, 'I don't think so.' What changed your mind?"

"I'm not sure," said Bolt. *I just hope I haven't made a terrible mistake,* he thought. "But midnight is here."

Bolt didn't get a good look at Grom's entire transformation, as he was too busy transforming himself. Bolt felt his nose grow and saw Grom's nose growing, too. Bolt quickly removed his clothes but forgot to tell Grom to do the same, and Grom ripped through his shirt and pants as if they were made of paper. Fortunately, Zemya had packed a few changes of clothes for him.

Grom barked, and so did Bolt.

How do you feel? Bolt asked, reaching into Grom's mind.

Rubbery. Feathery. Beak-ish.

Bolt knew the feeling, but he worried about what other things Grom might be feeling. *Do you feel like conquering the world, taking people prisoner, and eating lots of raw fish?*

I wouldn't mind eating fish right now. But doing the other things? Not so much.

Bolt gave Grom a thumbs-up—or rather, a wing-tip-up. Maybe Annika had been right—maybe Grom would be free of hate and violence. Or maybe those feelings would soon follow. Only time would tell.

They both rushed up the stairs and dove into the frigid water. There, they hunted fish, always keeping the ship within an easy swim. They sang to a walrus. They played catch with an octopus. They played peekaboo with a baby tuna.

They saw penguins, a small group of them. Bolt was surprised, as penguins didn't normally swim so far from shore. Bolt felt their underlying viciousness. He was worried how Grom might react when he felt that core rottenness, but the boy didn't even seem to notice it, happily devouring fish as he waved to them. "Hi, I'm Grom! This is my first time feeding!"

Bolt tried to remove the hatred from the birds—it had become a habit for him, sending out soothing thoughts of love and family. *Penguins are not meant to rule*, he thought. *And I like your feathers!* Penguins love being complimented about their feathers.

"We *are* meant to rule," a penguin yapped to Bolt. "But do you really like my feathers?"

Bolt and Grom fed through the night. It felt good to

have a fellow werepenguin near. It felt *right.*

Maybe I should bite more people, Bolt thought to himself, and was immediately appalled for thinking it.

But, despite the fun, Bolt remained worried about Grom's potential evil, although Grom showed no signs of any. The next morning, they returned to the boat, their stomachs bloated with fish and with no plans to take over the world. That was promising.

When Bolt had first been bitten, he had had no one to teach him his werepenguin powers. He promised himself he'd help Grom. Besides, maybe he could help Grom keep the Stranger's hateful influence away. So, that next morning, they sat cross-legged on the deck.

"Do I really need to do this?" asked Grom. "I'm a werepenguin. Doesn't this all come, you know, naturally?"

"If I don't train you, you could . . ." Bolt's voice trailed off. He hadn't warned Grom about the Stranger's mind control. He didn't want to worry him.

"I could what?"

"You could . . . miss dinner."

That quieted Grom. No penguin wants to miss dinner.

"Now, open your mind and close your eyes," Bolt told him. "Feel the penguin inside you and the penguin in me."

"This is stupid," said Grom, his eyes wide open.

"Just try it," pleaded Bolt. Grom growled but closed

his eyes. "Now, feel your penguin," Bolt urged. "And try to block me." Bolt's mind slipped inside Grom's head. *Pick your nose,* he commanded Grom, and Grom plunged a digit into a nostril.

"Hey!" complained Grom. "Did you make me do that?" He wiped his finger on his pants.

"Try to stop me," said Bolt, insistent. Frowning. "That was too easy. Fight back!"

This time, Bolt thought, *Raise your right hand.* Grom's brow furrowed and his fists clenched as he fought the control. *Raise it! Raise it!*

Grom raised his left hand.

"Are you raising your left hand because you get your left and right hands confused?" Bolt asked.

"Yeah," Grom admitted.

"Well, it's an improvement anyway," said Bolt. *Make a fist!* Grom made a fist. *Scratch your neck.* Grom scratched his neck. *Speak with a British accent.*

"Blimey, mate. Got some bangers and mash?" asked Grom.

Bolt sighed, stood, and walked over to the railing. If Grom couldn't even stop Bolt from forcing him to talk like he was from England, how could he stand up to the Stranger's more twisted commands?

Bolt only hoped he could control Grom because he'd

been the one to turn him into a werepenguin and so now they had a special bond. Regardless, Grom needed practice. A lot more practice.

Bolt's stomach growled. He'd worry about Grom after he ate.

Bolt sent his thoughts over the waves to the fish in the sea near him. Penguins eat fish, and fish eat algae; it's the circle of life. All penguins feel connected to the fish they eat, although distantly, and Bolt could sense their wiggling fins and blinking fish eyes. They were linked in the penguin-verse somehow, melded into one, distant relations formed from swimming together for millions and millions of years. Although Bolt still had the overwhelming desire to eat them.

I need lunch! Bolt thought, holding his hand over the rail. A silvery trout leapt from the ocean and landed right in Bolt's hand. "Wow. It worked!" exclaimed Bolt. "Um, is it OK if I eat you?" He didn't have to ask, but it felt rude not to.

"Sure!" the fish squeaked in a quiet fish voice. Trout are always eager to please.

This would make getting dinner a lot easier, Bolt thought. Unfortunately, defeating the Stranger would not be that easy. If only the Stranger were a trout!

The calm waters helped Annika write in her bandit code notebook without getting seasick. She brought her quill to the page.

THE CODE OF THE BANDIT, CHAPTER 7, SUBSECTION 2

ON HONESTY

~~A bandit should always be honest with his clan, although he can lie to anyone else; you're a bandit, not a Boy Scout. Fib! Cheat! But don't cheat anyone in your clan unless you're playing a card game and losing, then it's OK.~~

~~Let's look at a couple of examples. First, let's say you are caught stealing a pineapple from a fresh fruit stand. The farmer threatens to take you to jail—but if you confess, he will let you go with only a warning. Should you admit to your crime? Of course not. You should tell the farmer a giant bullfrog is about to eat you both, and run away.~~

~~Next, let's say you've inherited a million dollars from a rich uncle and all you need to do to claim the money is to give a banker your name and address. Should you give the banker your name and address? Of course not. You're a bandit! You should grab the money, hit the banker over the head with the pineapple you just stole, and throw him in the path of the giant bullfrog that's chasing you.~~

After crossing out the passage on honesty from her book, Annika wrote her addendum on a fresh piece of paper.

THE CODE OF THE BANDIT, CHAPTER 7, SUBSECTION 2

ON HONESTY—*amended by Annika Lambda*

Bandits should be honest at all times, just like everyone else. Sure, we're ruthless and cunning, but you can be honest and be those things, too. For example, if you say you're going to help free the world of evil penguins, you don't just quit to live with a group of moles. You stick with it! And if you tell your best friend you will travel to the South Pole to fight an evil were-penguin, then you do exactly that, even if you're sort of scared and very homesick. That's called being a good friend, and good friends are honest to each other.

Lying never pays anyway. Like if you tell someone a giant bullfrog is chasing you, but it's not, they might ignore your pleas for help if a large amphibian runs after you later. If you tell one lie, pretty soon you have to tell another lie to protect the first lie, and then another, and you end up in some web of lies and you can't even keep track of them, and then you're still eaten by the stupid bullfrog.

Annika Lambda

Annika put down her paper and came back up on deck, where Bolt and Grom were sitting, their eyes closed. The two boys were speaking to the penguin cosmos or something. Bolt was still her best friend, but he was spending most of his time by himself or training Grom. Annika felt left out. She had asked Bolt if she could be his assistant trainer, but Bolt had said, "No. Not unless you can feel the penguin-verse. It's a werepenguin thing." She didn't quite

understand it. Bolt also seemed to be changing, growing more spiritual and distant. But underneath Bolt's bushy eyebrows—were they growing bushier?—were the same eyes she had known for . . . How long? Months? Was that all? It seemed like she and Bolt had been best friends forever.

She watched as Bolt stuck out his hand and a fish jumped into it. Next, Grom held out his hand and waited, but nothing happened. He stood there, arms outstretched. "This is a waste of time," Grom grumbled.

Annika sensed some sort of aura around Bolt, too. He seemed to radiate heat, and also the faint smell of fish. It wasn't a pungent stink, but it did mean Annika needed to scrunch up her nose when he came near her, just a little.

Bolt wasn't a warrior, but he was powerful now, and becoming more so. It made Annika nervous. Was she scared of him? No, that wasn't it. How could she be frightened of her best friend?

Was she sad? Yes, exactly. She felt sad because she feared that if Bolt spent all of his time in the penguinverse, she would lose him as a friend. She had already lost Blackburn. She couldn't lose Bolt, too!

No. That would never happen.

But she was lying to herself. And lying, even to yourself, was against her new bandit code.

Bolt wandered to the other side of the boat, probably to think penguin things, and Grom stood by the railing

alone, still holding his hand out over the waves. Nothing happened. After about a minute of this, Grom growled, turned, and bumped into Annika. "Sorry, didn't see you," he mumbled.

Annika didn't step out of the way. "Do you miss them?"

Grom blinked, looking back at Annika. "What?"

"You left your family. Do you miss them? Do you think you'll ever see your sister again?"

"Why would you think I'd miss them?" asked Grom, eyes narrowing, as if he were suspicious of the question. Grom was guarded, even more so than Annika. As a bandit, you learned quickly to hide your feelings. Grom reminded her of herself, just a little, even if he insisted he was not a bandit.

Annika frowned. "Because I miss my papa and the other bandits back home. I miss Blackburn, too. But maybe it's not so bad for you. You've got a new family now, right?" She had once been skeptical of anyone calling a group of penguins *family*, but those feelings were in the past.

Grom grumbled. "It's not really the same, but I guess. I miss Zemya. We were close. But then again, I couldn't catch worms for her forever. I was always like, 'Maybe I should go,' and Zemya would be all, 'Have some more borscht,' and that would be that."

"She seemed very nice. I wish I had gotten to know her better."

Grom smiled, which was not something Annika had seen him do before. It looked a bit awkward—it was obvious Grom didn't have much practice smiling—but it was genuine. Then he scowled, as if realizing he was smiling and finding it distasteful. "Whatever. She was nice and all. Sure."

"You must have felt lonely, huh? You were an outsider. That's why you wanted Bolt to bite you, isn't it? So you would belong to something?"

"I wanted him to bite me so I wouldn't die," said Grom, rolling his eyes.

"I mean before that. Bolt told me you wanted him to bite you, back when you were in the mole hole."

Grom looked away and grumbled. "Look, I should practice being a penguin or whatever." He hurried away from Annika and down the ladder, toward his cabin.

Grom hadn't said much, but he had said enough. She understood what Grom must have felt like, living in Pingvingrad, always feeling like you didn't completely belong. All Brugarian bandits felt that way, hated by everyone, living in a forest away from society.

She glanced over to Bolt, who was quietly barking like a penguin, his eyes closed, his mind drifting somewhere else. At that moment, Annika felt more like an outsider than she ever had before.

36. A Song of Ice and Ice

The ship bumped against the icy shore as arctic winds swirled across a vast, cold land. Large crests of snow filled the vista as far as the eye could see.

"Are you s-sure this is it?" asked Annika, shivering.

Bolt was certain, although he couldn't quite explain why. It was just a feeling.

"And p-people live here?" Annika was too cold to speak without stuttering.

"Penguins live here. And a werepenguin." Bolt should have been scared, so close to the Stranger. But, strangely, he wasn't. It felt penguin-y here. It felt like home.

Except.

Or maybe *accept*? Odd that *accept* popped into his head just then. He couldn't explain why.

Bolt felt a hostile and violent aura coming from the glaciers, creeping toward them like a giant spider approaching its kill. That was something that did scare him. "Do you feel that?" Bolt asked Grom. "Do you feel the hate?"

"What are you talking about?" asked Grom, who clearly did not feel the hate, much to Bolt's relief.

Born from love, Bolt thought, clinging to the hope that it mattered.

Annika swung a rope ladder from the boat, and they climbed down it, first Bolt, then Grom, and lastly Annika. She had brought a heavy coat lined with sheepskin, but she still trembled. "I thought this would k-keep me warm."

"There's a reason sheep don't live in the South Pole," said Bolt, who wore only a T-shirt and jeans, as did Grom. Werepenguins did not feel cold.

"I feel a bit toasty, actually," admitted Grom.

"You d-don't have to b-brag about it," snapped Annika between chattering teeth.

At first, all Bolt saw was white: white snow tossed by the wind, white snowcapped mountains in the distance, and ice and snow at their feet. But as his eyes adjusted to the glare, he also saw penguins. They stood far up in the mountains, gathered in circles on the icy plains. They peeked out from holes in the ground. Thousands of them, everywhere.

"They're watching us," said Bolt.

"A b-bit unsettling," said Annika.

"Whazzup, penguins?" asked Grom, waving.

They walked farther inland, upon more ice and snow, lots and lots of snow, and as they did the penguins grew more numerous, emerging from wherever they hid to gawk at the newcomers, curious.

But these penguins did not stare with friendly expressions. Bolt felt their hate like a gelatinous mass of anger. It was almost as if they had expected him. They probably had. Bolt would not catch the Stranger by surprise.

In fact, Bolt could feel the Stranger's thoughts. *Come to me, come to me.* Bolt did his best to ignore the words, but he couldn't tune all of them out. The hate in the air was thick.

"So much violence," moaned Bolt. "The very air is coated with it, like an evil chill."

"Don't start c-complaining about the ch-chill," snapped Annika amid her shivering.

"I like it here!" said Grom, happily whistling.

They continued walking. Bolt let the hate blow by him with the breeze as he warmed himself with happier thoughts. *Charity. Goodwill.*

But those happy thoughts merely bounced off the dense wall of misery filling the island and fell, unheard, at Bolt's feet. He tried again. *Friends. Caring for one another.*

None of those thoughts traveled more than a foot before dissipating into the wind.

It felt different than Pingvingrad had, where all of Bolt's thoughts had bounced off silver. There was no fuzziness here, only so much evil that it seemed to suffocate everything that was good.

Welcome to my home. I have looked forward to this day! Bolt curled his hands into fists as the Stranger's voice filled his head, and his shoulders, and his legs, and other places he didn't want to think about.

Bolt forced the thoughts out of his ears, and his nose, but like a bad cold, they merely refilled inside him. He breathed slowly, expelling each feeling of rottenness as it flooded into him, like trying to empty a bathtub with the faucet still running.

You were chosen to be with me, thought the Stranger.

No! I was chosen to fight you.

You don't really believe that, do you? You are one of us now.

"Leave me alone!" Bolt screamed.

Annika and Grom stared at Bolt.

"Why w-would we l-leave you alone? I thought you w-wanted us here," said Annika.

Bolt was sweating, but his head was clear. "Sorry. I wasn't talking to you."

"Then who were you t-talking to?" Annika asked, brow furrowed.

"No one," mumbled Bolt, stomping past her. He snuck a peek at Grom, wondering if he had heard the Stranger, too. Apparently not. Grom walked forward with a hop in his step.

Did the Stranger even know Grom was here? Or because Grom was born from love, could the Stranger not sense him at all?

The penguins—tens of thousands of them probably, although Bolt didn't have time to count—continued to stare as Bolt, Annika, and Grom walked down a path dug into the snow, a narrow trough that wound through glaciers, up ice slopes, and around fissures.

"Will they attack us?" asked Annika, eyeing the birds.

Bolt shook his head. The Stranger wanted Bolt to arrive. He was waiting.

In front of them were mountains, icy crags that were so tall they seemed to reach up forever. The mountain range looked close by, but they walked for over an hour, although it was impossible to say for how long, exactly, before reaching its edge. They could no longer see their ship or even the water where they had left it.

Up ahead, the winding path began to rise up, leading into the mouth of an ice cave. Although they were still a good half mile from its entrance, an incredible amount of hate energy emanated from it, more hate and more pulsating evil than Bolt had ever felt before, and he had felt

plenty of similar pulses over the last few weeks.

The Stranger was waiting.

Yes, I'm waiting!

"Go away!" Bolt wailed.

Annika and Grom stopped. "Why are you t-telling us to go away?" snapped Annika, annoyed.

"No reason," Bolt mumbled.

They continued onward along the path. Bolt dug one of his hands into his pants pocket, feeling the smooth tooth inside. One plunge of the dagger would end the Stranger's life.

But Bolt couldn't kill. He wouldn't kill.

He had to, to save all the penguins.

No!

Yes!

No!

"Argh!" Bolt screamed, and he didn't even care that Annika and Grom shot him confused glances once again.

Grom hopped along, seemingly oblivious to the heavy despair around them. If only Grom wasn't so inexperienced as a penguin! He hadn't even been able to keep Bolt's thoughts out of his head during their practice sessions. Not once. Could he hope to stop the Stranger's?

Bolt halted. He looked at the cave, then back at Grom. And then at Annika.

This was the moment he had been planning for,

dreading, since their adventure began. But *why* he had been picked for this monumental task, *why* fate had given him a penguin birthmark, still remained a mystery to him.

It didn't matter. Bolt was the chosen one, and he needed to fight the Stranger alone. How, exactly, he didn't know—how could a boy who refused to kill defeat the world's mightiest monster, even with a tooth? And he still had no idea what all of the seer's chant meant.

"You guys stay here," said Bolt.

Annika turned around sharply. "What are you talking about?" she asked, her mouth falling open along with Grom's.

"I appreciate you both coming with me. I really do," said Bolt. "But this fight needs to end with me."

"Face it, Bolt. You're no warrior," said Annika.

"I know," said Bolt. "I'm just an orphan who never wanted anything but a family. But maybe that's enough. You have to fight for your family. You taught me that, Annika. And, Grom, you sacrificed so much for your sister and for me. I can't have you guys risk your lives for nothing. I need to do this."

Bolt strode forward, almost surprised when Annika and Grom stayed behind.

He wished he were as brave as he pretended to be.

37.
The Lair of the Stranger

As Bolt entered the ice cave, he bit his lips—until he remembered that biting his lips was just a bad habit and he was doing way too much of it lately, and so he stopped, but then immediately began to bite them again. How could he not? He'd try to break this habit when he was not in grave danger. *If* he was, one day, not in grave danger. It had been a long time since he had felt anything other than encroaching dread.

Despite the danger, Bolt admired the cave's beauty. It glittered with ice so pure and blue Bolt had to look away and blink a few times.

The ceiling of the cave was impossibly high and glistened like glass. If it weren't for the long icicle stalactites hanging from the ceiling—or were those stalagmites?

Bolt never could remember which was which—looking as sharp as knives, Bolt might have called the ceiling beautiful. Dead fish littered the ground.

In the back of the cave, on a raised shelf lined with stalagmites that reminded Bolt of whale fangs—or were the ones on the ground stalactites?—was an elaborately carved ice throne. Next to the throne stood a female penguin in a suit of armor. Sitting on the throne was a man.

The Stranger.

Power seemed to ooze from him. Bolt couldn't feel cold, but he felt the man's coldness all the same. It crept up Bolt's back like a cockroach.

And Bolt knew creeping cockroaches well. The orphanage back home had been filled with them.

Bolt continued walking inside the cave, and the Stranger stood up and waved. Bolt paused in surprise. He had expected a giant man, one who seemed larger than life.

The Stranger was tall and thin, bone thin. His face was lined with a dozen oddly shaped, long scars. But with his hair in a ponytail and a long, straggly beard, he looked more like an old hippie than a werepenguin ruler. He wore a gray pair of shorts, a tie-dye T-shirt, and Birkenstock sandals with socks pulled up mid-calf. His first words were, "You made it. Outta sight, man!" His eyebrows were so thick and his nose so long they reminded Bolt of someone wearing funny Halloween glasses. His thin lips smiled

crookedly, revealing blackened teeth underneath. "How was the trip?"

"Long."

"Yeah, and what a long, strange trip it's been, huh? Sorry about living so far out, though." The Stranger waddled toward Bolt, a slow and shifting waddle. He weaved around a few piles of dead fish, careful not to step on one. "But we're finally together! Can you dig it?" When he reached Bolt, he put his hand up for a high five. Bolt ignored it. The man shrugged, lowered his hand, and turned to the armored penguin. "Saytana, don't be a drag. Get over here. Say hello to our honored amigo." To Bolt he added, "It's not easy to find suits of armor that fit penguins, you know."

The penguin waddled over, her metal clanging, her visor up and revealing a sneering beak with a long scar across it. The penguin snarled.

"Nice to meet you, too," said Bolt. He tried to dip into her mind. *I am here to help free you!*

The words bounced off her. "The armor is made of silver," said the Stranger. "Pretty groovy, huh? Even I can't penetrate the stuff. But Saytana is naturally evil anyway. She doesn't need much help from me." He did a small, happy hop and then put his arm around Bolt's shoulders. Bolt shivered at the man's touch. The crawling-cockroach feeling returned. "It's been a bummer waiting for you, man. But here we are! I must admit, I'm totally stoked. First, you defeat my Baron. Not easy to do! Then my Earl! And then my dentist! You're the man! Or the boy, really. Age is relative, you know? I mean, I'm 328 years old, but really, do I look it? High five!" Again he held up his hand, and again Bolt ignored it. "Get with the program, man. We'll have a gas together, I know it. What a team we'll make! Two cool cats! Or rather, two cats, since we don't feel cool or cold, right? Ha!"

Bolt stepped back, so the Stranger's arm no longer hung around his shoulders. "A team? You're out of your mind. I'm here to stop you."

The Stranger didn't look worried at all. "Relax, my man. You have me all wrong. I'm the good guy in this story."

"The *good guy*?" Bolt might have laughed at the words, but this didn't seem like an appropriate time for laughter. "You're a monster who wants to rule the world's penguins, take all people prisoner, and force them to fry fish sticks for you. How does that make you a *good guy*?"

"I'll give everyone Sundays off!"

"I'm here to end this," hissed Bolt. He plunged his hand into his pocket and felt the smooth surface of the tooth. This was the moment he had fought for, planned for. He needed to grab the tooth and attack the Stranger. Now.

Bolt took his hand out of his pocket, nothing in his grip.

He couldn't. He wouldn't.

"You're here to end this?" asked the Stranger, repeating Bolt's last words, and then giggled. It wasn't a cackle—Bolt would have expected the Stranger to cackle—but instead it was a high-pitched snicker. "He-he-he. No, no, no," said the Stranger, wagging his finger at Bolt. "Get it together, friend. Not happening. I'll tell you what will happen, though." The Stranger paced back and forth, his hands gesturing wildly. "First, you'll join my army. Then the penguins will rise up and fight *the man.* And the woman. All of them. Why do you think I've spent the last hundred years dropping hate nuggets into every penguin in the world? Just for kicks? Well, sort of. But now, we will fight the penguin war to end all penguin wars. Not that there have been other penguin wars. You know what they say. Make war, not love!"

"The expression is the other way around," said Bolt. "Make love, not war."

"I like my way better. But either way, we will rule the world. Is that outta sight or what?"

"None of that is going to happen," growled Bolt.

"Don't freak out, man. Of course it will." The Stranger stopped pacing and stood in front of Bolt, his mouth twisted into a grin. With his black, decaying teeth, the man looked maniacal. Then again, he sort of was. "You just got to my pad, so we'll hang loose and start tomorrow.

Today, we'll make the penguins in the ravine tickle one another. It'll be a blast!"

"I won't do that," declared Bolt, horrified at the thought, knowing how much penguins hate being tickled despite being very ticklish. Few people know that penguins are the second most ticklish birds in all of the South Pole, right after yellow-billed pintail ducks. "Your reign ends today."

If only Bolt believed his own words! His mind raced. How could he defeat the Stranger without killing him? Maybe something from the seer's chant?

Nothing came to him.

The Stranger giggled again. Even Saytana, the armored penguin, let out a chuckle. Penguin laughter, which is a mixture of snorting and blubbering, is very disturbing. But Saytana's laugh was even more disturbing than most; it sounded wetter. Bolt hissed, baring his teeth.

"You really need to mellow," said the Stranger. He snapped his fingers.

Bolt's legs grew weak. He couldn't stand. It was as if he were a car tire and someone had slashed all the air out of him. The Stranger stared at him, one of his bushy eyebrows raised inquisitively. Bolt felt an enormous weight in his body and a voice commanding him, *Kneel, boy!*

Bolt found himself collapsing onto his knees, and despite his struggles against it, his head bowed.

"If I can control the world's penguins, I can control you. Don't forget who I am!"

"And who are you?" asked Bolt, forcing the words through his mostly frozen mouth.

"Well, honestly, I forgot my name long ago. It's a bummer. Just think of me as your worst nightmare come to life." The Stranger may have sounded friendly before, but there was no mistaking the evil inside him now, his voice dark and ominous. His eyes flashed red, and his face twisted into a malicious grin.

38. Born from Hate

Bolt could move his eyes and his mouth, but nothing else. The Stranger paced in front of him. “Do you think I was always a penguin creature, Bolt?” The Stranger picked up a dead fish from the ground, swallowed it bones and all, and then continued without waiting for an answer. “I wasn’t, although I can’t remember much about my life before.”

“I don’t care,” Bolt said, snarling. “Let me go.”

The Stranger ignored him, continuing to pace, talking as much to himself as to Bolt. “I remember a shipwreck. It was a real downer, man. Why was I on the ship? Why was it wrecked? I have no clue. I recall lying injured in the sand on a small deserted island and thinking that was the end for me. Sayonara, world. But that night a dying penguin bit me with its final bite. And you know what they say about penguins who die while biting you."

"I don't, actually," said Bolt.

"They say a penguin that bites you with its dying breath passes its soul on to you. Pretty heavy, huh? That night I changed. I was healed! And I could control all the penguins on the island. I told them, *Build me a ship, pronto.* This was a hairy task for penguins without any tools, or thumbs, or any idea what a ship was. So it took a while. I slowly went about growing my empire, spreading the power of hate across the penguin-verse. Nothing is more powerful than hate! Right on!"

"Love is greater."

The Stranger shook his head. "You sound like a hippie from the 1960s."

Bolt began to point out that it was the Stranger who sounded like a hippie, but then decided to let it go.

"You were all I needed, man," said the Stranger. "The final piece of my earth-sized jigsaw puzzle. Isn't that the grooviest?"

"No, it's the un-grooviest. But why conquer the world? Penguins are about love and family, not hate!"

Saytana snorted, and so did the Stranger. "I don't remember much about my pre-penguin years, but I recall someone swiping my kite when I was, like, eight years old. Man, I was so bummed! I swore if I was ever given

supernatural powers such as turning into a penguin, I would get revenge by ruling the world!" He spat on the ground and grinned, revealing small, short fangs in the back of his mouth.

Bolt's jaw dropped. Some dribble fell down his chin. "You want to destroy the world because you lost a kite?"

"It was a very nice kite."

"But isn't that sort of a ridiculous reason to want to rule the world?"

"Who are you to judge?"

Bolt gritted his teeth. He'd had much worse things happen to him than losing a kite, and *he* didn't want to rule the world, or at least not usually. He had always assumed the Stranger wanted to rule because he was a werepenguin, and werepenguins were naturally evil.

But could Bolt have been wrong? Maybe being a werepenguin didn't make you evil at all. Maybe the Stranger had been foolish and twisted long before he had become a monster, and it was the Stranger's powerful mind control, and that alone, that infused evil everywhere.

Maybe werepenguins could be good inside. *Were* good inside.

Bolt moved a finger. Then an arm. He felt the Stranger's control lifting.

Bolt knew what he had to do next. He would get to his

feet, leap at the Stranger, and use the tooth to put a stop to this madness. He had to push aside the whole *I cannot kill* thing, for the good of humanity and penguin-dom! Bolt felt hate—hate for the Stranger—starting to rise up inside him. He crouched to jump. Well, he *tried* to crouch, but the Stranger's mind was all around him again, clogging Bolt's ears and his mouth, the wickedness tickling his throat. It was so thick, he could practically hear coughing.

Was someone coughing? There was no one else here. He had just imagined it.

"Bolt, I can control you as easily as a mouse can wag its tail! As easily as a fly can flap its wings, or as a zebra can change its stripes!"

"Zebras can't change their stripes," said Bolt.

"I think you're wrong about that," said the Stranger. "They just don't like to talk about it. Anyway, you get the idea."

Bolt clenched his teeth. He was stronger than this! He needed to break these invisible chains! The penguin-verse was everywhere. *Love* was everywhere.

He felt his legs tingle. Somehow, he was doing it. He shook a hand. An entire hand! It wasn't much, but it was something. He wiggled his fingers.

The Stranger had his back to Bolt, pacing, still thinking of his past, or his kite, or zebras. It didn't matter, as long as he wasn't looking as Bolt raised a leg. Bolt was fully standing now. No time to waste. He plowed forward, and—

CRACK.

Saytana slapped a silver wing at Bolt, smashing into his shoulder. Bolt had completely forgotten about the armored penguin! Bolt hoped the loud crack wasn't a bone breaking. He didn't think it was, but it really, really hurt.

Bolt crumbled to the ground as pain shot up his arm.

"You think you stand a chance?" said the Stranger, looking down at Bolt, yawning. "You can barely stand at all!"

Just then, a voice popped inside Bolt's head. *Face it, Bolt. You want to rule!*

No, Bolt didn't want that! Or did he? He felt the Stranger plucking parts of his brain like a puppet master pulling strings or, Bolt mused, like a zebra controlling its stripes.

No! I must stop the Stranger! Bolt said to himself, his anger growing. *I must attack!*

But even as these thoughts saturated his brain, Bolt couldn't deny that he didn't actually *want* to fight the Stranger. The Stranger was right about wanting to rule, wasn't he? Bolt raised his hand and tapped his forehead in a military salute. His pain was gone. He stood up straight.

"Don't fight it, Bolt," said the Stranger. "This is your destiny."

Those words were the last thing Bolt remembered before he heard a SNAP, like a rubber band breaking.

"This is what you were chosen for, Bolt!"

"Sounds good to me," said Bolt, his voice monotone. "I accept who I am."

"Wait. *Except* or *accept*?" asked the Stranger.

"Accept," Bolt said. "Let's take over the world." And he meant every word of it.

Bolt stared blankly, thinking: *I am a werepenguin; penguins are my servants; people are my servants. I will spread misery and woe and, maybe, have a small snack.*

"Hey, man," the Stranger said, sidling up to Bolt. "Thinking of misery and woe and having a small snack?" Bolt nodded. "I thought I recognized that look. The best part of ruling is the misery and woe, although the snacking is a gas, too." He laughed. "You won't think of doing much else, actually. And you'll obey me, like the nice dog you are."

"Arf!" said Bolt. He briefly thought of Pygo, the penguin he knew from Sphen who had thought he was a puppy.

The Stranger clapped Bolt on the back. "You were always the key. You and I will rule the world nicely. Or rather, evilly. There won't be much niceness about it."

Bolt rubbed his hands together, enjoying the evil buzzing inside him. Even his birthmark tingled, but in a warm, happy way. He cackled. He actually cackled! And he sort of liked it. Maybe he should cackle more often.

"Someone is on his way to help us, too," said the Stranger.

"Who?" Bolt asked.

"We are penguins, not owls," said the Stranger. "You'll see. Now, come. I want to show you something." He gestured toward the back entrance to the ice cave. "I think you'll dig it."

Bolt followed the Stranger through a back door. The Stranger knew best. The Stranger was wise.

Bolt's brain felt as calm as a tranquil pond. He had fought the feelings of hate for so long that it felt good to finally give in to them. He felt a peacefulness and fullness he had not felt since he had turned into a midnight bird.

This was who he was meant to be. A ruthless penguin! A leader! A king! Why had he ever thought of being anything else?

All should fear Bolt the Terrible!

He liked the sound of that. Bolt the Truly Terrible!

Ooh, that was even better.

Bolt the Truly Terrible and Vicious! . . . Nice.

Bolt the Truly Terrible and Vicious and Savage Who Also Enjoyed Snacking! . . . A bit long, but accurate.

They walked along the edge of the cave, Saytana clanking behind them. They stood on a ridge that overlooked a wide, long ravine where thousands of penguins stood, waiting. Bolt wondered if these penguins had been standing there for hours or if they had congregated from some mind control that Bolt had not detected. No matter. They stood there for him! His army!

"Command them!" the Stranger encouraged Bolt.

Bolt stared. Command them to do what? For a moment he was at a loss. Then he guffawed, which was even more fun than cackling. "Poke your neighbor in the eye!"

A hundred penguins, those closest to the edge of the ravine, turned and shot out their wings, poking their neighbors in the eyes. A few yaps of pain rang out.

"That's my second favorite command," said the Stranger. "Must be a werepenguin thing. My fave is tickling, though."

"Great idea. Tickle each other!" Bolt cried out. He clapped as penguin wings reached under underwings, tickling wing-pits. The nearby penguins, many still blinking from being eye-poked, chortled miserably.

Bolt had always thought the one thing in life he was missing was a family, and that finding a family would make him complete.

He was wrong. The one thing he had been missing was forcing penguins to tickle one another. This was, indeed, what he was chosen to do!

Annika shook her head after Bolt had left her and Grom to enter the ice cave. Bolt may have thought he was being brave or noble by going alone, but she thought he was just being stupid. Bandits didn't rob carriages without backup, and it was a lot easier to rob a carriage than to fight the world's greatest werepenguin. Plus, it wasn't like Bolt was some mighty warrior, either.

She turned to Grom and reached into her jacket pocket, from which she removed a book. Her hands shook from the cold, but she breathed on her fingers to warm them. "This is the Code of the Bandit. It's not perfect, not by a long shot, but I'm making it better. It says I don't abandon my friends, among many other things. Bolt is my friend. And I'm going into that cave to help him. You don't have to if you don't want. I'll understand if you're afraid."

Grom bristled. He looked insulted. He folded his hands into fists. "Afraid? I stole worms for my sister and her mole friends every day, having to avoid rotten penguin dentists with giant toothbrushes. My sister was all, 'You can eat some worms, too?' and I was all, 'Um, I'm not a mole, so no thank you.' But I went and got them anyway. If you're going into that cave, I'm going in, too."

So she and Grom followed Bolt, watching from near the cave entrance as the Stranger talked about his demented past and hopes for world domination. Bolt was kneeling—Annika could tell he was straining against the Stranger's control but failing, and failing badly. She peeked at Grom next to her. Once the Stranger realized another were-penguin was here, could Grom keep the monster's commands at bay?

Grom was born from love and so could not be controlled by hate. That's what she had told Bolt. But deep down, did she believe it? Maybe. But maybe not . . .

Annika nudged Grom and made a variety of silent hand gestures—twirling her hand, pointing to the sides of the cave, and then making her fingers bounce up and down. "Got it?"

"You'll take the Stranger, I'll face the armored penguin, we'll grab Bolt, and then you'll sing 'Little Bunny Foo Foo'?"

"Exactly."

It wasn't much of a plan. Annika didn't really know how she could defeat the Stranger, and Grom probably couldn't take down an armored penguin, but they couldn't just hide near the entrance of the cave all day. Back in Pingvingrad, Blackburn—oh, how she missed him!—had preferred to twiddle his thumbs than to fight. She had been wrong to wait then. She wouldn't make that same mistake again.

She straightened. They would just run in. Overpower the Stranger. Easy peasy.

She tensed, grabbed her knife from her back pocket, and then she did the unthinkable.

She coughed.

Bandits didn't cough! Bandits were stealthy. Boris the Brave had a farting problem, and that's why he had been kicked out of their bandit clan. Horace the Hiccupper had been tossed out of the clan, too.

She and Grom dove to the side, hugging the ice to avoid being seen. Annika waited a moment, not even daring to breathe. Had anyone heard her? She peeked around the corner.

No one was looking their way. They were still safe.

But the delay proved costly. Bolt was standing up and was now . . . Wait, was he saluting the Stranger?

"Oh, Bolt," Annika squeaked, her heart breaking at seeing her best friend so easily manipulated. It was warmer in the cave than it was outside, but a chill blew through her. Why hadn't she, the world's greatest bandit, seen this coming?

They couldn't just run in. Not now. They couldn't fight the Stranger, and that armored penguin, *and* Bolt. They needed a better plan.

She knew Bolt had been talking to the Stranger during their voyage, hearing his voice inside his head, even though he denied it. Yet she had said nothing, convincing herself that Bolt was in control, that he could ignore those voices when the time came to fight. She had been a fool.

"What do we do now?" Grom asked in a whisper.

"Beats me."

"Can the Stranger be defeated?"

"Don't know."

"Does he have a weakness?"

"I don't know that, either."

"What's the average life span of an albatross?"

"I have no idea!" Annika wailed. "I'm no help at all!"

Grom shrugged. "Well, the albatross question wasn't all that important."

Bolt, the Stranger, and the armored penguin walked

out a back entrance. Grom and Annika followed, moving as quietly as the night, or rather quieter, since nights are mostly filled with cricket sounds and the occasional toad.

They reached the end of the cave and inched down the side until they spotted Bolt and the Stranger. They stood near the edge of a ravine where thousands of penguins poked one another in the eye. Bolt and the Stranger giggled.

And then the penguins began to tickle one another. Penguin laughter, a mix of spitting and gargling, is a disturbing thing to witness. Annika shuddered.

Grom looked angry and pale. Well, he always looked pale because he was a werepenguin, but now he looked paler. "I feel so much hate and despair," he whispered.

Annika's eyes widened. "Is that hate and despair taking over your mind in such a way that you want to attack me?"

"No," said Grom. "I feel like I hate the feeling of hate."

It took Annika a second to work that out, but she was satisfied.

"We could dig a hole, pop out, and take them by surprise," suggested Grom. "That's what we would have done back at Pingvingrad."

"But we don't have any were-moles with us. Or shovels. And the icy ground is rock-hard."

"Right." Grom scratched his head. They remained silent for a bit, Annika rubbing her finger up and down her knife.

"Well, whatever our plan," said Grom, "that Stranger guy has no chance."

Annika smiled. She knew that, underneath his hard edge, Grom was not nearly as confident as he pretended to be. That's because Annika felt the same way. She always acted like a tough bandit, but deep inside, she was often afraid. She still had so much about banditry to learn!

She glanced at the penguins and then back at Grom.

Born from love.

That better not be as silly as she feared it might be.

"I have an idea," she said.

A few minutes later, Annika and Grom inched closer to Bolt and the Stranger, ducking behind a snow mound. The penguins in the ravine had stopped their tickling, and now the Stranger and Bolt were throwing fish at each other.

Bolt tossed a fish in the air, and the Stranger caught it in his mouth, swallowing it in one gulp. Next it was the Stranger's turn to toss and Bolt's turn to swallow. After every toss they each took a step backward. They were now a good fifty feet apart, yet their aim and fish-catching were quite impressive. Annika noticed Grom was drooling.

"That sure looks tasty," murmured Grom.

The Stranger shouted, "Soon my guest will arrive. And then our real work will start. The world's penguins will fall to their knees!" Annika gasped. She hadn't even realized penguins had knees. "What should we have the penguins do next, mi amigo?" the Stranger asked Bolt. "Box each other on the ears? Twist their wings? Give wedgies, which is very hard for penguins since they don't wear underwear?"

Bolt smiled, nodding at each suggestion.

Annika felt sick. Grom looked furious.

The Stranger shrugged. "Righty, then." He snapped his fingers. The penguins began to pull each other's tail feathers in what looked to be a bizarre attempt at giving each other wedgies.

Grom's fists were clenched. He stood and pointed his finger at the Stranger. "Stop!" he cried out. "Stop right now!"

Annika clung to the rock, not daring to move, staring up at Grom.

"Who's this?" the Stranger asked, his eyes narrowing, his expression morphing from surprise, to curiosity, to delight. His eyebrows rose, and his mouth spread into a wide grin. "A werepenguin? Another one? Bolt, you didn't tell me you had a compadre! I'm not sure how I didn't sense

him," he said, seeming genuinely concerned. But then he threw his hands up and shrugged. "Well, no sweat. We'll make room for another lieutenant in our army."

The Stranger giggled. Grom looked, well . . . strange. His eyes rolled back into his head. He stumbled forward. His face was a blank slate. "Yes. We are meant to rule."

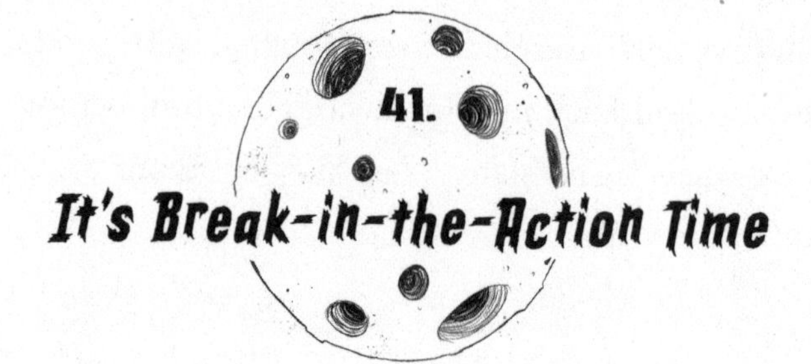

41. It's Break-in-the-Action Time

A cold wind slammed against my head, nearly knocking me backward with its force. The sun was setting, and the ocean winds howled.

"Perhaps we should head indoors," I suggested, always cautious of things that howl, including winds.

"I won't go inside until all the animals are loaded onto the ship," said the penguin caretaker. "The penguins may be my main concern, but all the animals need someone to look after them. Perhaps this is a good time to take a break from our story and venture one thousand miles away into the forests of Brugaria, where . . ."

"No! Stop!" I squeaked. "Let us not venture anywhere. I grow tiresome of your zigzagging in and out of stories, and I insist you stay in the polar ice cap."

The man whistled, a low, mourning sort of whistle, like one might hear at a funeral, or at least at the funeral of a former whistler. He sighed, deeply, as he often did. Somewhere on the boat, whooping cranes whooped. Elephants trumpeted. Possums made whatever sounds possums make.

"What could possibly be happening in the Brugarian forests that is relevant to our story anyway?" I asked.

"Nothing at all," the man admitted. "I just thought a slight break from despair and horror would be a welcome diversion. The bandits were throwing a tea party." He took a deep breath. "Never mind, then. Let's stay at the South Pole. The Stranger was happy. His plans for world domination, the plans he had made for so long, looked like they were finally coming to fruition. The penguin uprising would begin! And he had a brand-new werepenguin to help. He was practically giddy."

I shivered, thankful the winds only howled and did not bark like penguins. That would have been far more jarring. "So, what happened next?" I asked, squeezing the man's arm. "Tell me!"

"Do not worry. I will tell you everything, but I can't feel my arm. You're cutting off the circulation."

"Sorry." I stopped squeezing and stepped backward.

"Thank you," the man said, shaking his elbow. "As I was saying, the world was doomed."

42. The Annika Code

Grom marched toward Bolt and the Stranger. His eyes stared forward, his face emotionless. The Stranger inspected his new werepenguin pet with a look of total glee. Grom muttered something about ruling and maiming and rebuilding the large fish fryer.

Grom cackled, and so did the Stranger, and then Bolt. The Stranger snapped his fingers, and thousands of penguins began cackling behind him.

Annika had never heard a penguin cackle; she wasn't even aware they could. But the sound was so nauseating that she almost lost her lunch.

The Stranger could control them all so easily!

Annika felt the urge to run out with her knife and attack! Save her friends! She put her hand around its hilt.

But then she released her grip. The Stranger was about anger and hate. Fighting was also about anger and hate. And maybe Bolt had been right to try it a different way. Maybe it wouldn't take a warrior to defeat the Stranger, but love.

That had been the plan she had made with Grom.

She would have to trust it would still work.

She stood, revealing herself, and removed her bandit code book from her pocket. The Stranger didn't move to attack her but gazed at her cautiously. Annika opened to a page in her book and began to read, taking a step closer with every sentence.

"The Code of the Bandit, chapter 123, subsection 3. 'On Family,' amended by Annika Lambda." She cleared her throat. Her voice wobbled, but as she spoke, it gained strength. The words seemed to warm her. "A bandit clan is a family. Not because they are related by blood, but because they care about one another. And love one another, unconditionally. What is a family anyway? I think a family is anyone who makes you feel better when you're sad, and shares in your happiness. A family stands by your side, no matter what. Which means a mom and dad are a family, or just one of the two, or a grandma or an aunt or an uncle. A teacher can be family. And so can a best friend. And you know what? A giant bullfrog could even be part of your family, although that seems unlikely."

Bolt stared at Annika, his fingers twitching.

Annika kept reading, louder now as she walked along the edge of the ravine. "Nothing is more important than family, I truly believe that. Sure, I can't say every penguin in the world is part of my family, like some others can, but that's OK. I have a big family anyway, one filled with bandits, and I will always stand by them. But a werepenguin is also part of my family now. And so is a pirate, even if I never see him again. And, maybe, even another werepenguin I just met a week ago. Who would have thought that?"

Bolt wobbled. He took a step toward Annika, but then tried to take a step back and nearly fell. His eyes began to blink rapidly.

"This is ridiculous!" the Stranger scoffed, rolling his eyes. Bolt continued blinking his.

"I will stand by my friends and family," said Annika, no longer reading from her book but making a note to add a little more to the section on family later. "And I know, deep down in their hearts, my family will always stand by me. Because I love them, every one, and I'm pretty sure my family loves me, too."

Bolt smiled at Annika, and not an evil smile. He reached out his hand to her. She reached out to touch his.

"Are you OK now?" asked Annika, smiling.

Bolt smiled back. "Yes, thank you. I just needed to hear

your voice, I guess. To feel love instead of hate. Hate just makes everything worse."

Annika felt a blow on the back of her shoulders, and her legs gave way. It felt like she had been hit by a battering ram, although since Annika had never been hit by a battering ram, she could only guess that's what it felt like. She had been focusing so hard on Bolt she had completely forgotten about that penguin bodyguard. The bird stood over her, shining silver reflecting off the ice. The penguin raised up her metal wing to strike Annika again.

And then didn't.

Bolt flung his body into the penguin, knocking her away. "Don't hurt my friend!" he yelled. Annika was impressed. *Maybe he's braver than I give him credit for,* she thought.

Bolt backed away from the penguin and now stood side by side with Annika, the ravine directly behind them. She could sense the army of penguins watching from below.

The silver-armored penguin stood in front of them, hissing.

"Get them, my pet!" the Stranger ordered Grom. Grom nodded. Was that another cackle from his lips? He marched forward, his arms outstretched, his eyes glazed. Annika crouched—her foot was dangerously close to the edge of the ravine and the penguins below—ready for a fight.

And then Grom stopped and winked at Annika. He turned to face the Stranger. "You're all, 'Get them,' and I'm all, 'Why would I do that?' "

The Stranger scratched the top of his head, confused.

Annika shook the surprise off her face and grinned. "He's not born from hate," she said, "not like you. You can't control him." To Grom, she whispered, "Nice acting. You even fooled me for a moment."

"Interesting," mused the Stranger. He glared at Bolt, and Bolt glared right back. Something was going on between them, some sort of invisible war. Bolt's mouth was formed into a grimace, sweat bubbling up on his forehead. Finally, the Stranger stepped back and his shoulders slumped. Whatever mind control he had tried had failed. "You are strong, Bolt. I guess the Fortune Teller did say *except*. What a drag."

Annika, Bolt, and Grom had been so focused on the Stranger and their impending victory that they didn't see the armored bird until it was too late. The penguin rammed into Annika first, sending her hurtling backward and down the steep, icy ravine. A moment later, Grom and Bolt were tumbling down behind her.

To Bolt, it seemed like he rolled forever, faster and faster, hitting hidden shards of ice and branches and other unpleasant things as he plummeted downward before finally coming to a stop at the bottom of the embankment. There were a few inches of snow, and it helped cushion his fall.

Bolt blinked a few times to clear his head. Annika and Grom were splayed on the ground next to him.

"Are you g-guys OK?" Bolt asked, his voice wobbly.

"I think so," said Annika. "A little dizzy from all that rolling."

"Me too," said Grom, standing up and then spinning back to the ground.

Behind them, the ravine continued endlessly, a deep

gorge that zigzagged through ice mountains. But in front of them thousands of penguins glowered, eyes exuding hate.

"What should we do now?" Grom asked, getting to his feet.

"Umm, get out of here?" suggested Annika. Bolt thought that was an excellent idea.

They sped down the ravine, the horde of penguins stampeding behind them. Penguins are fast in the water but slower on land. That was fortunate, as Bolt was already slow and Grom didn't appear to be any faster. The snow was thick, which further slowed them down.

They only had one way to go—down the ravine. Its walls reached far up into the sky alongside them, creating a steep, icy wall they could never hope to climb.

Behind them, penguins charged. Fortunately, these penguins did not wear silver head mirrors or armor. Although the air was dense with thick hostility, Bolt could feel one or two birds getting nearer. He thought, *Trip!* and he could hear a penguin fall face-first into the snow, and a couple of penguins grunt as they fell in a heap atop it.

Bolt continued shooting out orders like *Veer right!* and *Turn left!* which made penguins stumble off course and collide into one another. He even instructed a few penguins to tickle a neighbor, which he hated to do, but it was better than being captured.

But there were so many penguins! Thousands upon thousands, so many that they seemed to cover the entire landscape in their wake. Bolt projected more thoughts at the penguins, but the layer of hate was too thick to order more than a few at a time. Not only that, his orders struggled to penetrate some penguin heads, clanging against their buried nuggets of hate.

Up ahead, the ravine narrowed, two mountains pinching together, although it opened up immediately after that. They would reach that narrow gap soon, but then what? Just more running? The penguins would never tire and never stop chasing them.

Annika, quick as lightning, had sped ahead of them but kept having to slow her pace, shouting, "Can't you two run any faster?"

"Not really," said Bolt.

"Doing the best I can," grunted Grom.

"Well, try harder!" Her voice echoed, disturbing some snow on the steep mountain slope, and a small snowball rolled down and landed by Bolt's running feet.

The snow was untouched and so pristine. A few more crumbs of white fell onto his shoes.

Bolt surveyed his surroundings. Falling snow. A narrow opening ahead. Thousands of penguins chasing them, filling the ravine in a sea of black and white. Bolt had an idea, and if he was going to try it, it had to be now.

Bolt sent out a wave of thought to the penguins behind him. These were not orders to *veer left* or *tickle one another.* These orders weren't to stop running, because he knew those thoughts, good thoughts, probably wouldn't penetrate their hate. So, instead, he encouraged the hate, sending thoughts that made the rottenness stronger, flooding into thousands of penguins with such fury they could do nothing but obey. *Bark! Show your anger! Cry out!*

A few penguins barked raspy, guttural cries of anger.

No! All of you! Bark!

There must have been half a mile of penguins behind them. But Bolt tapped into their collective hate, filling the entire cavern with his orders.

Thousands of penguins barked, their voices joining together into a deafening cry that might have awakened the heavens, if heavens slept (and they do not). But, more important, the sudden sound jarred the snow on the mountain cliffs, the serene blanket of white that had sat peacefully for decades, if not centuries.

Bark! Bolt ordered.

And again, the penguins joined into an angry rapture of noise.

The snow began to fall, first a few clumps at the very top of the mountains alongside the gorge, and then more. Snow fell in bunches, thicker and heavier than even Bolt

had anticipated. The roar of the snow drowned out any remaining barking.

"Avalanche!" cried Annika.

"That was the idea," Bolt said.

They had reached the narrow slit in the ravine. Annika raced through it. And then Grom.

Bolt was behind them both. He turned and saw a world turned white, filled with the screaming rumble of snow chunks and ice boulders filling the ravine, penguins vanishing as snow fell over them in waves.

There was nothing but winds of white—the entire world had turned into a powdery cloud—and a gush of wind enveloped Bolt and blew him off his feet, just as he reached the narrow passage in the gorge. The gust blew him forward and through the gap.

Behind him the roaring snow buried the ravine, and with it, thousands of barking penguins.

44. The Almost Toothless

Annika, Grom and Bolt soon reached a section of the ravine that was easier to scale, then wound around a gorge, through a clump of frozen trees, and finally stopped at a clearing next to a flowing stream of water. They needed to catch their breath, tend to their wounds, and plan their next move. Fortunately, Annika didn't have a scratch on her, and Bolt had only a few small cuts. Grom had slightly twisted his ankle, but it was a small nuisance. Penguins, and people with penguin blood, heal faster than most.

Annika sat on a small ice mound, thumbing through her bandit code, the narrow rolling stream below her feet. The frigid water crashed across rocks and around fallen branches, alit by the still-rising moon above. It was a big moon, a magical moon. An always full sort of moon.

Bolt stood behind Annika, holding the silver tooth in his hands, while Grom sat farther behind them, eyes closed, trying to feel the penguin-verse. He was improving his penguin skills—he said he could detect penguins hundreds of yards away. Bolt was thankful that *born from love* protected Grom from the Stranger's evil influence, but the teenager needed more time to perfect his powers if he was going to help Bolt fight.

As Bolt sat down next to Annika, she jerked up; she had not heard him approach. "Sorry. Didn't mean to scare you," said Bolt.

"Not bad," she said, slipping her bandit book back inside her jacket. "If you could slink noiselessly like that all the time, you could almost be a bandit." She scooted over to give him room.

"It's hard enough being a werepenguin," said Bolt. Annika smiled and then pointed to the silver tooth in his hands. Bolt held it up for her to see better. "You know, I thought maybe, if I came face-to-face with the Stranger, I could just impale him with this." Bolt looked away, feeling lost. "And I thought about it, of course. But in the end, I just couldn't. It's not because I'm not brave enough . . ."

"I know," Annika interjected.

". . . but I don't want to kill him." He smiled at Annika, a brotherly smile. They were family, after all. "I won't kill

anyone. I've vowed not to spill blood. It's evil, and I won't be evil. That's the key. To embrace love."

"Then give me the tooth. I haven't made any vows."

Bolt shook his head. "The seer gave it to me. There must be a reason. It just hasn't come to me yet."

"It better come to you soon. We're going to have to face the Stranger again."

Bolt wished he had answers he didn't have, just like he wished he had strength he never felt. But mostly, he had questions: *How can we win? Will we survive? I'm hungry—anyone want to make me some dinner?*

He passed the tooth from one hand to the other, as if feeling the weight not just in his hands but in his entire body.

"It's OK," said Annika, putting an arm around his shoulders. Bolt twitched, surprised, and the tooth slipped from his fingers and bounced off their tips. He swiped at the tooth but ended up knocking it farther away.

The tooth tumbled down, down, down, bounced off a rock, and then right before it splashed in the water a large gray fish leapt up and swallowed the tooth in one gulp.

"Did that really just happen?" Annika asked with a yelp.

Bolt sprung to his feet. Could he jump into the water and catch the fish? No, the stream was moving too fast! The fish would be gone in a heartbeat, too.

Annika was about to dive in, preparing to plunge into the cold water, where she was far more likely to catch hypothermia than a fish, when Bolt held out his hand. "No. I got this."

Bolt closed his eyes and reached his arm out over the water. He furrowed his brow and scrunched his nose. The water below began to bubble and froth. Bolt's face twisted, his brows furrowing even more. Down below, the rolling water seemed to flow a little faster.

SPLISH! Instantly, the gray fish jumped out of the water, against the stream's current, tail flopping. In an impressive arc, the fish flew up a good four feet in the air and—*THIMP!*—landed straight onto Bolt's hand.

"Hi!" the fish squeaked to Bolt.

"How did you do that?" Annika gasped.

"The penguin-verse is strong," he said. Then, to the fish, "Can I have my tooth back?"

"It's sort of stuck in there, bud," answered the fish.

"Do you mind if I put you in my backpack, then?"

"Go for it."

Bolt still had his trusty unicorn-and-rainbow backpack strapped across his shoulders. He removed the backpack, unzipped it, and thanked the fish before tossing it inside. He'd worry about extracting that tooth later.

He inhaled, a breath that was longer and deeper than your run-of-the-mill deep breath. They needed to go back

to face the Stranger. Or really, Bolt needed to go back. He wished he could stay here, by this calming stream, but that was not his destiny. His destiny was to free the world.

But what of Annika and Grom?

Annika's code meant she fought for her friends. Bolt understood that. She was a hero, and even if she said she would stay behind, she wouldn't. She'd sneak up behind him like she did in the throne room and the fish fryer. Grom would probably do the same. He was also heroic.

But was Bolt a hero, like them? He needed a code, just like the bandits had, and the pirates. The Code of Bolt. He would need a better title for it, but he would start living it now. And his code was simple: you don't have to be a bandit or a pirate or a mole to stand up for what's right. You merely have to be you, and do your best. Because what else can you do?

Bolt wasn't ready for the Stranger before, but he was now. He would not be controlled—not anymore—as long as he held on to love. That's how Grom had kept the Stranger's voice out. Because he was *born from love.*

And if Grom was *born from love,* that love came from Bolt. Which meant Bolt had love inside him. Bolt could win; he just had to be himself.

"I'm going to take a walk and think," said Bolt.

Annika gave him an inquisitive look. "But you'll be back."

"Of course. In a few minutes."

He would be back, too. As soon as he defeated the Stranger.

If he defeated the Stranger. That was still a pretty big *if*, no matter how hard Bolt tried to pretend it wasn't.

45. The Battle of the Werepenguins

Bolt's blood simmered, which it would do until midnight, when it would bubble and boil before he transformed. Should Bolt wait until morning to fight? Or would he have a better chance battling the Stranger as a werepenguin?

Who knew?

Might as well face him now.

Although Bolt saw a penguin glaring at him, he barely flinched. *Smile!* The dense hatred in the air seemed to part, and the penguin's beak slid up, just a little. It was hard to say. Beaks are rigid.

Bolt was getting stronger. Was the approaching moon giving him that power, or was he just learning to harness his potential better? He had no idea.

More penguins stood nearby, though none attacked. To some, Bolt sent thoughts like *Be happy!* and *Hug your family!* A little of that penguin hate melted away, but not much. A speck, really. But it fueled Bolt with hope.

Bolt walked along the edge of the ravine where the avalanche had fallen earlier and saw no sign of penguins anywhere. He hung his head, hit with a tremendous wave of guilt. So many penguins may have died, and all because of him. Sure, the penguins wanted to destroy Bolt and his friends, but every penguin life was important.

Besides, they couldn't be blamed for their evil ways. It was all the Stranger's fault. The thought angered Bolt, but he knew anger would not defeat the Stranger. He couldn't let the anger simmer.

Bolt crossed a bridge, a natural span of ice that connected one ridge to another. One hundred, maybe two hundred penguins stood on it, and Bolt tensed as he approached them. But the penguins gave no sign of attacking. They let Bolt pass.

The Stranger was expecting Bolt. Bolt could sense it. Maybe that meant the Stranger was overconfident, and perhaps that would be the Stranger's downfall. Or maybe the Stranger would win, in which case he was not *over*confident just *properly* confident.

Bolt dipped his thoughts into the minds of the nearby penguins. Some thought, *You can save us.* Others thought,

You're a goner, you know. While a few penguins mused, *I don't care who wins as long as we can eat fish sticks soon.*

Bolt crossed the bridge, and the hundreds of penguins on the other side also made way to let him pass. Bolt's blood was bubbling quicker as midnight grew closer. Nearing the Stranger's ice cave, Bolt felt his enemy's energy, like a radiator blasting, or like a furnace in an ice rink.

And there the Stranger stood, outside the cave, tossing fish to Saytana. She tossed a fish back to him. Bolt tensed, thinking of the silver-tooth-engorged fish in his backpack. He thought, *Give me the strength to use the weapon—but not out of anger.* Was such a thing possible?

The Stranger burped and turned to Bolt, smiling. He did not even seem the least bit perturbed. "Welcome back! Have you changed your mind about joining me? Do you accept your fate?"

Bolt shook his head. "Never." He gritted his teeth.

"Why do you fight it, man? Why do you fight the feelings of ruling and hate that are inside you? I know they're there. When I visited you in your dreams, I felt them, just under the surface, trying to come out. You're as evil as I am."

"No, I'm not," Bolt said forcefully. "I'm good."

"Are you sure?"

Bolt didn't know. He *wanted* to be good, but being something and wanting something were hardly the same thing.

The Stranger smiled, and it chilled Bolt to his core. "I feel your doubt. Stop freaking out about it, though. Being a werepenguin means never having to say you're sorry. Embrace the hate."

Bolt narrowed his eyes and curled his toes, feeling harsh thoughts flowing from the Stranger and churning in the air around them. "I won't. I can't," Bolt said through clenched teeth.

"I think you will." The Stranger winked, and it felt like a giant boulder had been dropped inside Bolt's head, one filled with vicious thoughts of mayhem and dominance.

No! Bolt resisted. *Decency! Generosity! Honesty!* He pushed back the boulder of evil, but it was so heavy. So large. Bolt's knees almost buckled under the weight of it.

He closed his eyes, trying to gain strength from the penguin mist around him. He just needed to find a hint of love somewhere, anywhere, but it was like trying to grab a strand of wind. His mind drifted, across the snow, over the ice bridge, along a ravine, and then back. The penguin-verse was such a dark, desolate place, cluttered with hate nuggets like a wall of hail.

But he felt something else, too. Something far purer than hate. Right behind him.

Annika had come, and she stood behind Bolt. Of

course she had followed him; he was not surprised at all. She smiled at Bolt, and the smile warmed him. He could feel her love for him. Like a sister. Like family. She wasn't a penguin, but her friendship mattered. Every friend mattered.

He could feel Grom, too, although he was not there with Annika. Still, Grom was sending his own thoughts into the penguin-verse, thoughts of his own sister and moles, thoughts of gratitude for Bolt's help, his own thoughts of love. And it was Grom's thoughts, just as much as Annika's, that tingled inside Bolt.

A calm came over Bolt, a calm carried on the whispers of the penguin-verse. He had grown stronger, but that strength was nothing like the power of love he felt now: his own love, boosted by the love of his friends.

When Bolt opened his eyes, it was as if the world had gone from black and white to full color. Or since penguins are mostly black and white, it was as if the world were now a more vivid black and white.

A soft squeal, like the sound of a balloon emitting helium, blew from Bolt's lips and through his ears as a small, crusty nugget of hate, one buried inside Bolt's head long ago, flitted out.

Pffft!

The Stranger glared at Bolt. And Bolt now felt another

giant block of evil crashing onto him, but this time Bolt deflected it easily, and it bounced away. More virtual hate flew, followed by more effortless deflections. Bolt stood tall, chest out. "You can't control me." He brushed aside the hate as if it were dust. "Is that all you got?"

The Stranger's face turned beet red. "Feel my power, boy!" he yelled as he whipped another hate block in Bolt's direction. This one Bolt felt, and he staggered back.

"I guess that's what I get for being a little overconfident in myself," Bolt muttered.

Bolt held out his hand at the Stranger, fingers spread apart. It was a meaningless gesture, since his powers lay in his head, but it felt cool to hold out a hand like they did in the movies when someone was conjuring spells and such. He sent a shock wave of force toward the Stranger, a vibrating, furry, mind-controlled energy blob of love and kindness. At the same time, the Stranger threw his own hate boulder at Bolt. They collided, blue love energy against reddish hate rock, sizzling in the air. Neither seemed to have an advantage, energy against stone.

Bolt's arm grew tired. He took a deep breath, then lowered one arm and raised the other. It still felt cool to have one arm raised.

Behind him, Annika gasped. He sensed her surprise at his power. Frankly, Bolt was a little surprised, too. He

had never done anything like this before! He wanted to sit back and congratulate himself for his awesomeness. But he couldn't let up, not for a moment.

Bolt took one step toward the Stranger, and the Stranger matched him. Their energy bursts remained in the air, crackling above them. Both Bolt and the Stranger moved closer to one another. Closer. They were now so close, Bolt could smell the Stranger's rancid fish breath.

"This is so uncool, Bolt. Perhaps you weren't chosen to rule. Instead, you were chosen to fail!" The Stranger sent another boulder at Bolt, so big and strong that it shattered both the love blob and hate rock above them. The Stranger lunged at Bolt, closing his hands around Bolt's neck. "This ends the only way it ever could!"

And then the Stranger was no longer on top of Bolt. Annika had flung herself at him, and they were rolling on the ground, Annika scratching and kicking. And then Saytana—Bolt had forgotten about her—was on top of Annika, biting and slapping.

Bolt was about to jump on Saytana, although jumping on someone who had jumped on someone who had jumped on someone felt a bit unsteady. So he hiccupped instead.

There were no clocks anywhere near, but Bolt heard a chime in his head anyway, a chime that always sounded in his head at midnight during a full moon.

His skin tingled and bubbled like boiling water in a

teapot. Steam spritzed from his ears. His skin stretched, and his bones reshaped. His arms curled into semi-pretzel shapes before feathers popped out, forming wings. His legs shrank, and his belly ripped through his pants.

The backpack's straps that had been around his arms snapped, and the bag fell to the ground. Bolt cursed himself for forgetting to take it off; he had really liked that backpack. He would also need new pants in the morning, if he survived. Frankly, new pants were not at the top of his concerns, although he did think of it.

Bolt's nose was the last thing to turn—the order of his transformation was always different—and he opened his beak and roared.

There was a time that whenever Bolt turned into a penguin, he thought mostly like a penguin; he would forget he was part human. But he had taught himself how to remember who he was—he was still Bolt, just a penguin version of himself.

And, now, a master of the penguin-verse.

The force of the transmutation had thrown Annika off of the Stranger, and Saytana off of Annika. But the Stranger had not transformed like other werepenguins did. He was a werepenguin, but a far worse one. He stood ten feet tall and was as wide as a tank. The Stranger-penguin was pure white, from the tips of his feathers to the top of his head. His beak was twisted, like a soft-serve ice cream cone. And when he opened it, a long, snakelike tongue slashed out. His eyes flashed orange.

"You should have fought me as a human, silly boy," he said in a deep rasp that sounded like doom personified. "You cannot defeat me as I am now. For I am not just a werepenguin, but the GOAT. The greatest of all time!"

The Stranger-penguin swatted his wing, impossibly long, and it smashed into Annika, sending her flying off her feet. When she landed, her foot bent back awkwardly, and she lay on the ground whimpering. "You broke it," she cried, tears in her eyes.

"I'm hardly done breaking things," the monster roared, staring down at Bolt, who felt very small next to him.

The Stranger slapped his wing at Bolt, but Bolt sensed it coming and hopped out of the way. They were linked, both part of the same penguin cosmos. Again the Stranger swung his wing at Bolt, but Bolt had anticipated the move and jumped back to avoid it.

Meanwhile, Saytana faced the fallen Annika. Bolt

aimed his thoughts at the armored penguin. He didn't expect much to happen. Silver was impenetrable, wasn't it?

Maybe not . . .

When they were trying to enter PEWD, Annika had been picking a lock when penguins were coming. Bolt made one hesitate just enough for Annika to scurry away. Later, Kiki the silver-fanged penguin was about to hurt Annika inside the fish fryer dome. Bolt had made Kiki pause then. Just for a second.

Why had he pushed through silver those times but not other times? The answer rushed inside Bolt as fast as a penguin mother waddling toward her egg. It was because both of those times Bolt hadn't thought of saving himself. He had thought only of saving Annika.

Love had been the key, even then.

Bolt narrowed his eyes as he stared at Saytana. He gripped the love in the penguin-verse, the love of his friends, and his thoughts penetrated her silver plating as if it were as thin as paper.

He flicked his wing, and Saytana flew into the air and landed with a thud twenty feet away.

The Stranger stared in surprise. "How did you do that?" And then a snowball smashed into the Stranger's head.

Another ball of snow hit him. Annika wiped away

her tears with one hand while scooping up a ball of snow and throwing it with the other. She had good aim. Unfortunately, snowballs can't do much damage to ten-foot tank-sized werepenguin monsters.

The Stranger stomped toward Bolt, ignoring the snowballs pelting his head. He was upon Bolt in an instant—faster than Bolt had imagined he could be—and kicked him.

Before he could crawl away, Bolt felt a sudden burning sensation in his head. He was slowly being lifted. A surge of energy surrounded him, levitating him off the ground! He couldn't move his wings or legs, couldn't break out of the crackling energy globe that encompassed him. The Stranger-penguin stared at Bolt with glowing orange eyes.

"Didn't know I could do that, huh?" the creature snarled. "This is your last chance to join me. Your last chance to accept your fate. *Accept!* Not *except!*"

As Bolt hovered in the air, he could feel the Stranger's attempts to force evil into his head. But Bolt was not the scared boy looking for beds to hide under. Not anymore. He was strong. Powerful. Bolt *was* the penguin-verse.

Unfortunately, he still couldn't move. The large energy blob of hate and cruelty swirled around him, crackling with viciousness.

"The hunger for power is in you, Bolt!" cried the Stranger-penguin. "The hunger is inside all of us! It's real, man! And it will consume you!" And then he rammed his beak through the energy blob and straight into Bolt's stomach.

The pain! Bolt's insides burned. He peered down. Blood trickled down his belly.

He gasped for breath, but it was hard to suck any in.

"Take that!" Annika cried, firing another round of snowballs at the Stranger. It was all she could do on a broken foot. One snowball bounced harmlessly off the Stranger's wing.

"Would you quit it with the snowballs already?" the Stranger moaned, peeking over his shoulder. But then he smirked, shifting his attention back to Bolt, seeming to be

deciding where he should plunge his beak next. In Bolt's neck and end the fight forever? Or smaller pecks to prolong the torture?

Bolt's mind was growing fuzzy as his wound continued to bleed. He glanced at Annika again, noticing his backpack on the ground next to her.

What was it the Stranger had said just moments ago? *The hunger is inside all of us! It's real!*

The seer had chanted almost those exact words: *The hunger inside, it's so strong and so real!*

Bolt could not speak in a human voice as a werepenguin, at least not well, so it took all his concentration to shout at Annika: "Throw him the fish!"

Annika blinked. "Huh?"

"Inside the backpack. Do it!"

Out of the corner of his eye, Bolt could see Annika opening the discarded unicorn-and-rainbow backpack and reaching inside. A smile crossed her face as her hand landed on something slimy and wet. "Hey! Mr. Stranger!" she called. "Care for some dinner?" She tossed the fish in a wide arc, toward the Stranger. She was a talented thrower of things. It sailed high, shimmering in the air.

The fish somersaulted once, twice, three times. It seemed to fly in slow motion. The Stranger, without even thinking, opened his mouth to swallow it whole. It was

instinctual, really. Habit. Bolt knew a lot about habits, like biting his lips.

They say old habits die hard, and that's true. They can die *very* hard.

The Stranger caught the fish in his mouth, swallowing it in one gulp. For a moment, nothing happened. But then the Stranger's face turned green. His stomach rumbled loudly. He coughed, and a trickle of blood dripped from his beak. He looked at Bolt in panic. Then he glanced down at his stomach.

The energy holding Bolt in the air shattered, and Bolt fell back to the ground. The Stranger's orange eyes blinked wide, and then he let loose an enormous belch.

The tooth that had been sitting inside the fish flew out of the Stranger's mouth, coated with red phlegm and maybe a kidney.

Seconds later, the Stranger stumbled to the ground, gurgling. Until suddenly, he was still.

Bolt felt the dense hatred in the air dissolving around them. He hadn't realized how truly thick it was until it was gone.

Annika hobbled onto her foot and limped over to Bolt. She would be fine, the foot would heal, but what about the Stranger? Was he dead? Were the penguins free?

No. Bolt sensed a small, almost invisible current of

hate left in the atmosphere. The Stranger might be horribly wounded, but he wasn't dead yet. He was weakened, though, and so was his mind control.

Still, Bolt could feel his thoughts now unrestrained, his aura of goodness spreading. Until—*clomp!*—it rammed into something at the end of the ridge. Or rather, someone.

A familiar, high-pitched, half-penguin, half-human voice rang out. "I'm here! Did I miss anything? Because if I missed something, I'll be very angry. And you don't want to see me very angry."

A burly and powerful werepenguin stomped forward, his eyes flashing red. The monster wore a cape made of scallops. Bolt recognized him at once.

Baron Chordata.

"But . . . but you're dead!" yelped Bolt.

"Obviously not," said the Baron.

47. The Return of the Baron

Grom sat in the snow, eyes closed, trying to sense the penguin energy around him, but it was hard to do. In the middle of his trancelike efforts he felt something horrible, a massive disturbance in the penguin-verse. A stabbing pain in his stomach. But then the pain subsided, replaced by something warm and hopeful. Grom found himself drawn to the warmth, like someone stepping outside a nice underground mole hole and onto a hot, sandy beach.

And then he opened his eyes.

How long had he been sitting here? An hour? Two? He stood up to stretch his legs—they had started to cramp—and went to join Bolt and Annika.

“Bolt? Annika? Hello?”

No one answered.

"Guys? Stop fooling around."

He was met with silence.

"Guys?"

They had left.

Without Grom.

Maybe they ran off because they didn't like him. Grom knew he scowled a lot. He wasn't a people person. He wasn't really a mole person either, and he was barely a penguin person, at least not yet. If Grom thought about it, he wasn't really much of anything.

He had felt that way for a while but kept it inside. What good would it do to complain or feel sorry for himself? But those feelings returned now. He didn't belong here. He didn't belong anywhere.

Annika suggested that Grom wanted to be a werepenguin so he wouldn't feel like an outsider anymore. He didn't say anything back to her then, but he knew she had been exactly right. Every midnight, Zemya and the others had transformed into mole creatures, but not Grom. They ate grubs and worms while Grom sat by himself eating hot dogs. The moles had fleas, and their whiskers got tangled, and of course they couldn't see all that well. Grom sometimes pretended he had fleas to fit in, and grew his hair long, and partook in the occasional

grub or two—but all those things made him feel more alone. Also, grubs sometimes stuck in his teeth.

And now here he was: alone. Again. He kicked a small ice stone by his feet.

Grom stood, stewing and heating up so much that the ground under him began to melt. He would leave the island. He would swim far away, find a rookery that would take him in, and live with penguins. This whole adventure was way harder than he thought it would be anyway. Only an idiot would fight the world's mightiest werepenguin with nothing but a tooth for a weapon.

Let Bolt and Annika be killed or whatever. Let the world's penguins remain evil. What did it matter to Grom?

Unfortunately, Grom didn't believe anything he was telling himself.

He didn't regret risking his life for years to dig up worms. He did it for his family, and nothing was more important than family. Penguins were his family now. Bolt and Annika were his family. What sort of person would Grom be if he just left them high and dry?

He loved them. Odd, that word. Sappy. But it was the truth.

Bolt's and Annika's footprints in the snow were easy to follow. Actually, Bolt's footprints were easy to follow; Annika had left none. Grom didn't need to follow their path anyway; penguins have an excellent sense of direction. They sometimes travel a hundred miles just to breed, without needing a map or street signs or anything.

As Grom walked, he passed clusters of penguins. He sent out thoughts to distract them, thoughts like *Look away!* and *Your shoelaces are untied!* as he had been taught. Penguins don't even wear shoes, so it was amazing that they always fell for that trick.

Then, along the way, Grom felt like his head was swimming, and his legs buckled. He glanced up at the full moon. It was midnight. He hadn't turned into a were-penguin many times, but he knew the feeling.

He gasped for air, although his lungs cleared almost instantly. They had changed into penguin lungs, and his spleen changed into a penguin spleen, although Grom wasn't sure if penguins even had spleens, or even what spleens did, but the point was that all his internal organs changed, and it was both painful and uncomfortable although it happened very, very fast.

And then he was standing there. A full-fledged penguin. His clothing shredded on the ground beneath him.

His mind was fuzzy. He knew he was both penguin and human but had a hard time remembering his name or why he was here.

He knew he had to follow the footprints in front of him but wasn't completely sure why. And he knew he wanted to eat fish, lots and lots of raw fish. Were these footsteps leading to a fishery? He didn't think so.

He followed the prints anyway.

Penguins saw him and quivered in fright. He felt their confusion—*Who are you? Don't hurt us!*—but he also sensed a change in them. It was as if some giant bowl of evil stew had been tipped, and their hostility spilled out.

They were still hostile, but less so.

When he approached the next ridge, he saw a puzzling scene.

There was a werepenguin. Grom recognized him. Yes, he was a friend, although Grom couldn't quite place his name. Blot?

A girl lay on the ground clutching her foot and grimacing. She was familiar, too. Hanukkah was her name. No, Annika. Grom was proud he remembered that.

On the ground, a short distance away, lay something else. An armored penguin. Grom looked at her enviously. He would have liked his own armor. The penguin was dazed, but certainly not dead or even badly injured.

One more figure lay on the ground, unmoving. Something large and ferocious, some werepenguin beast, and Grom was glad it was still.

What was this thing? The Stranger? Yes, that was his name. He was alive, but the rottenness that emanated from him was now more of a trickle than a spray.

While Grom walked closer, he felt a new horror. Another werepenguin. This one wore a cape. Rottenness filled the air around him with such tightly packed cruelty that Grom had to catch his breath.

Baron Chordata? I thought you were dead! Blot said. No, it was *Bolt*, not *Blot*. And he didn't say those words, he thought them. Grom could hear them in his head.

I'm not dead, nope. Sorry to disappoint, the creature answered silently. *I wasn't comfortable living inside the belly of an orca. It was extremely cramped. But what could I do? I was weak. Nearly dead. So I sat there until, eventually, the whale burped me out. I hid for a while, regaining my strength. But every fish I ate I imagined was you, Bolt. Every fish bone that I snapped I pretended was your neck. The Stranger sensed I was alive and invited me here. He told me that the three of us would raise our army of penguins. But I knew he was a fool. I knew the only way you'd help us is if you were dead.*

How would I help you if I were dead? Bolt asked.

It was a bad plan, the Baron admitted. *But I see you've defeated the Stranger. A shame. I didn't see that coming. But you are mine, Bolt! You were born from my hate! Nothing can help you!*

Not true, thought Grom. *I can.* He strode forward, his wings clenched at his sides. He squawked.

The Baron glared at him, and Grom felt a *thump, thump, thump* in his mind, like someone was banging against

it with foam blocks. It didn't really hurt, but if someone hits you repeatedly with a foam block, you'll eventually get pretty annoyed, and that's what happened here as the thumping continued. With each thump echoed the words: *You are mine to control, you are mine, you are mine . . .*

Stop that, Grom thought. *I'm getting really annoyed now . . . Stop . . . Annoyed . . . Yes, master.*

That last thought jarred Grom enough that he staggered. He couldn't make out everything that was happening through his penguin-addled mind, but he understood he was not a creature born from hate, and that was all he really needed to know. *I am not a monster. I am not a monster.*

He continued to stride forward, shaking his head to clear it. *You can't touch me.* The Baron looked frightened even as thoughts continued to bounce off Grom's head. *Destruction. Chaos. Rule.*

The Baron stood between them, Grom nearing the Baron, and Bolt a little farther away. This would have been a perfect time for a game of Monkey in the Middle.

You are all making me angry, thought the Baron. *Very, very angry. And you don't want to see me very, very angry.*

And then the ground shook and the Baron's head vibrated from side to side, so fast his features blurred. His head did three complete turns on his neck. Steam erupted from his ears. His beak expanded, and razor-sharp twin

fangs sprouted from them. His body stretched, and so did his legs. His eyes blazed red.

The Baron had been short, about the same height as Bolt, but the Baron-penguin now stood seven feet tall.

Grom didn't know much about this creature, but he knew it was bad news. Grom needed to fight this monstrosity. He waddled forward—Grom could waddle quickly, quicker than ordinary penguins, anyway. Grom thrust out his beak, but the Baron slapped it away and rammed his shoulder into Grom's head. Grom fell backward, and everything felt even more jumbled than before.

He thought he saw Blot, or rather Bolt, rushing toward the Baron-penguin. *I will protect my friends! I will protect the world!* Bolt thought—it was amazing how Grom could hear his thoughts so clearly—until *smack!*—the Baron's wing smashed against Bolt's head, and Bolt flew into the air. *Odd,* thought Grom. *Penguins don't fly.*

Then Bolt crashed to the ground. *Oh, that's more like it,* thought Grom.

48. Born from Love

Bolt got to his feet, woozy from the Baron's blow. He regretted rushing at the monster; Bolt had been so surprised to see Grom and the Baron that he had acted impulsively. But being part of the penguin-verse was intuition, not impulse. He would never beat this monster with his muscles. So, although he stood only a few feet from the Baron, Bolt stayed where he was. Holding out his wing (just to look cool), Bolt bent his mind forward, sending blue shockwaves of love hurtling through the frigid air.

The Baron ducked, and the energy blob grazed his shoulder. *Ooh, my shoulder feels all lovey-dovey*, he mocked. But they were so close that he simply took a step forward and kicked Bolt in the shin. Bolt slipped on the ice and fell.

You cannot defeat me, Bolt, thought the Baron. *You are a part of me and my hate. You don't have an orca to save you this time. I should have beaten you then. Now I'll hurt you twice as badly. Yes, that'll be nice. For me, at least.*

Bolt tried to form another ice-blue love blob, but the Baron slammed into him with his massive belly, sending Bolt rolling down the slippery slope, where he landed on Grom's blubbery penguin body, which was splayed across the snow.

"Watch it," Grom muttered.

But Bolt was too distracted by the Baron's last words: *Twice as badly. Yes, that'll be nice.*

Bolt still remembered every word of the seer's chant. For example, the chant had sixty-seven syllables; the meter had been off by one. And there was still one couplet that Bolt thought he had deciphered but wasn't completely sure:

But you won't win unless you take this advice—
Born from love may entice, but a bite's twice as nice.

He looked over at Grom, *born from love.* That was the answer! Bolt needed to be born from love, too.

Bite me, Bolt ordered Grom.

Grom was blinking, regaining his senses. *What'd you just say to me?*

Bite me! Literally, I mean. I wasn't insulting you or anything.

Bolt held his neck toward Grom's beak. *Just do it quick, OK?*

Why would I bite you?

I can get rid of most of the hate inside the penguins of the world, but I'll never be able to remove it entirely. And I won't be able to fight the Baron. Not the way I am now. Because I was born from the Baron's hate. But if I'm reborn from love, from the goodness inside you, I think I'll have a chance.

He needed to be bitten twice—once by the Baron, and now again by Grom. Bolt really didn't know if that would work. Had a werepenguin ever been bitten twice?

I don't want to bite you, thought Grom.

Meanwhile, the Baron was stomping toward them, his thoughts hammering into them like an overactive woodpecker. *I will destroy you!*

Come on, Grom. I need your help. This could be the only way. Bolt could have forced Grom to do it, controlling Grom's mind and making him lower his fangs. But that would have sort of defeated the purpose of being bitten by love. *Please? What's the worst that could happen?*

Then, without another word (spoken or otherwise), Grom opened his beak, leaned over, and sunk his teeth into Bolt's neck.

The pain was incredible, and Bolt's eyes blinked violet and red. He thought he might pass out. But just as soon as the pain arrived, it was gone. As the first drop of Grom's

saliva penetrated Bolt's veins, he felt his body grow numb, like it was being pumped with antifreeze. The feeling surged down his shoulders and up his wings and then down into the rest of his body. He quaked as if he were having a fit. For a brief moment he thought he was going to explode and that his last words would be, "What's the worst that could happen?" which was sort of funny.

But he didn't explode. Instead, he grew. His neck stretched, his legs extended, his feathers elongated, and so did the rest of him. Even his head expanded. It was as if he were being inflated with air. The world spun around him, and he heard someone gasp, and he also heard someone belch, but the gasping was louder.

And when the world cleared, Bolt looked down at Grom, and down at the Baron, and down at everything. He must have stood twenty feet tall. He opened his beak, and the bark that rang out could probably be heard clear across the South Pole.

"Wow, Bolt," said Grom. "You're big."

The Baron smiled, and it was the broadest penguin smile Bolt had ever imagined. It distorted his entire face so he looked less like a werepenguin and more like some sort of were-demon. "Yes, Bolt!" he cried. "Look at you! You can rule the world!"

"Uh, yeah. About that? No thanks." Bolt now had twice the capacity for love, twice as much as anyone ever

had before, and that love filled the penguin-verse like an expanding balloon, crowding out the evil, actually devouring the hate cells that floated inside it like a penguin at an all-you-can-eat seafood buffet.

Mmm. Bolt could really go for a meal right now. He was so big he could eat a lot, too.

But dining would need to wait for later. Saytana, the armored penguin, had recovered her wits and waddled up to face him. He peered down at her, her silver not even a nuisance anymore. *You can stop fighting now. You are good. You are family.*

"Sure," Saytana yapped happily. Her hate nugget was instantly gone, dissolved with the remaining negativity in the air.

Bolt grabbed the Baron between his wings, lifted him up to eye level, and roared in his face. The Baron winced as the hot air breezed through his penguin feathers. Maybe Bolt had bad breath? Well, it hardly mattered. Bolt was so big he could do anything. Conquer all! Rule the world!

But neither sounded fun. Bolt had thought such things before and always had to tamp down those emotions, reminding himself that ruling the world was very bad. But now the thought of hurting and controlling people, or fighting and battling, disgusted him.

He was big enough to hurt anyone but had no desire to. Not even the Baron.

He put the evil werepenguin gently back on the ground. *Stay there.*

The Baron stood in place, unable to move, as if he were a mannequin in a department store window.

Bolt looked behind him, where Annika and Grom were now huddling together, watching. Both seemed nearly petrified with fear as they gazed at the giant Bolt. Annika's eyes were teary. Was she crying? Well, her eyes were wet, anyway. Bandits didn't cry. "You're my best friend," she said quietly. "You won't hurt us, right?"

Grom stood in front of her, as if to protect her. From Bolt? But Bolt wouldn't harm them! He loved them!

Bolt looked down at his webbed feet. Being twenty feet tall was a problem. Monsters were twenty feet tall, and Bolt wasn't a monster. He was just an orphan boy with a birthmark who was sent to Brugaria and became best friends with a bandit.

I'm just Bolt.

That was his code now. The Code of Bolt. The first line of the seer's chant had been: *Discover your code—and embrace it you must.* In a way, it was the most important line.

Because it was a code not only for Bolt but for everyone: regular people, pirates, bandits, and penguins. Be yourself, because it's the only thing you can be. Everyone is chosen for something, whether it's being a werepenguin fighter or being a good friend or member of a family or part of a community. What's important is to be the best you that you can be.

For Bolt, that meant to love, and to allow himself to be loved. That was why he could defeat monsters. That's why he was chosen.

It was like someone punctured a tire just then, and the tire was Bolt. Air seemed to leak out in one sudden breath. He grew thinner so he looked almost flat, and then shorter, one after another, thinner, shorter, thinner, and then he was his normal werepenguin height and his normal werepenguin width. He looked at Annika, blinking.

He looked at Grom, too. Grom's werepenguin body pulsed with feelings of caring and of family. *Born from love.* Just like Bolt.

But while Bolt's physical size was that of a normal werepenguin again, his mind felt twice as big: twice as smart and twice as aware. He glanced across the snow to the Baron, who was still frozen in place. Bolt flicked a wingtip at him, just slightly, and the air curdled around his hand. The Baron fell to his knees but was no longer immobilized. "We will rule . . ." he began, but Bolt pinched his fingers and the Baron's beak snapped shut.

He was so easy to control now, although controlling the Baron brought Bolt no pleasure.

Whatever hate the Stranger had stuffed inside Bolt

once and whatever claim the Baron had on Bolt's brain were gone. Bolt waved his hand across the snow. There were penguins nearby, and their minds were cleared instantly, freed of all their crusty nuggets of hate. With time, he would do the same for every penguin in the world.

He turned back to look at the Baron, who was standing and trying to speak through his clamped beak, and the Stranger, who was now twitching a little, injured but not dead. Their time was over. Bolt would not kill them. He was not a killer and never had been. Besides, Bolt was far more powerful than both of them put together. *Get him out of here*, he thought, jabbing his wing toward the Baron. It was the last time Bolt would ever order the penguins to do anything for anyone. But something told him they'd be happy to carry out this particular task.

A hundred happy, mind-freed penguins dashed toward the Baron. The Baron attempted to implant evil into their heads—Bolt could sense it—but those efforts failed as quickly as they started. Those thoughts could not survive in the new penguin-verse. Not anymore.

The Baron whimpered to Bolt in a penguin squeal, "But I thought we were BFFs?"

As the penguins raced toward the Baron, he turned tail, literally, and ran, penguins trailing after him, eager to get their wings on him and tackle him in a big hug. A few moments later they had all disappeared over the ridge.

"What about him?" Annika asked, jabbing a thumb at the Stranger, who was slowly getting to his feet.

Bolt eyed the werepenguin, still massively huge but also powerless. *You will live here, ruling no one and nothing.*

Not even a couple of penguins? the Stranger asked, wings clasped.

Nope.

Pretty please?

Never again. Penguins will live as penguins should, with families and love. So will you.

Just as the Stranger had implanted a crusty nugget of hate into the world's penguins, Bolt planted a fluffy crumb of love into the Stranger's head. It would grow and blossom, and while it wouldn't take hold overnight, it would eventually. *You will find a family. You will finally be a true penguin.*

"I can make you a new kite," said Annika. "It won't be so bad."

The Stranger brightened, just a tiny little bit. One day the Stranger might even be happy.

49. The Forest Bandits

Annika beamed when the *Bobbing Borscht* landed off the shores of Volgelplatz. Bolt was glad Annika was home, but he also felt the distance between them. His mind wandered constantly. How could it not? He was in continual communication with the entire world of penguins. Some of them called him *Master,* but he quickly corrected them. *No. I am your brother.* He would not rule them. Mostly, he would leave them alone, but occasionally check in to make sure he hadn't missed any crusty nuggets of hate hidden away.

He almost felt like a ghost now. Here, but not here. Annika said he seemed sort of semitranslucent at times. He wondered if, given enough time, he might disappear into the penguin-verse entirely.

They advanced through the Brugarian forest. Annika had no way of telling the bandits they were coming, which made their entrance awkward. Her father appeared, cloaked by the dark of the forest, dressed in tattered lederhosen and a penguin hat. "Stop. I am Vigi Lambda, the bandit. You are trespassing on our land. Since everyone knows this is bandit country, that makes you very stupid, very ignorant, or perhaps a friend who's come for dessert?"

"Papa? It's me."

Their embrace was long, each clasping the other tightly, gentle sobs rising from the older bandit, soft purrs of contentment from Annika. Soon, other bandits emerged from the forest and hugged them both, a giant hugging ball that only broke up when someone in the middle farted.

"Sorry, I ate too many beans at lunch," said one of the bandits, but Bolt couldn't tell whom.

"And Bolt! What an honor!" Felipe, Vigi's left-handed right-hand man rushed to Bolt and hugged him. From his faint smell, Bolt guessed it had been Felipe who had eaten too many beans. "What a delight to see you! You're practically one of us, after all."

"Thank you." After Bolt had defeated the Earl and freed Vigi and Felipe from the Earl's dungeons, they had sworn a lifetime of bandit loyalty to him, an unexpected and rare honor.

"Don't forget we also promised you twenty percent off

any item bought during our annual Forest Bandit Bake Sale, which starts next week," Felipe added.

Vigi joined Felipe in welcoming Bolt, and then he noticed Grom, who had remained quiet, off to the side, looking uncomfortable, as if he didn't belong here. "And who is this? Another person who becomes a werepenguin during the full moon?"

"Is it that obvious?" asked Grom, rubbing his bushy eyebrows.

"Sort of," said Vigi. "Still, any werepenguin friend of my daughter's is a friend of mine, as long as you don't peck any of us to death."

"Nah, I'm not that sort of werepenguin. I'm more of the 'hey, why can't we all just get along' sort of werepenguin."

"Even better." Vigi smiled and clasped Grom on the shoulder. Grom smiled back.

That evening, a great feast was prepared. The pungent smell of burnt iguana permeated the air like a thousand stink bombs. If it weren't for the competing scent of 276 vanilla-scented air fresheners hanging from the nearby trees, the stench would have been unbearable.

Raw fish had been offered to Bolt and Grom, and they thanked the bandits for their thoughtfulness. Dancing soon broke out, and Grom proved himself a marvelous dancer, first doing an Irish jig and then wiggling on the ground and performing something he called "the worm."

Apparently, it was a very popular mole dance.

Bolt wasn't a dancer. So he found himself sitting alone near the great bonfire, its embers floating into the night as he felt the penguin-verse. Bolt enjoyed being alone now. The penguin-verse was so big! Being with people almost felt claustrophobic.

"May I join you?" asked a woman, her voice raspy and ancient. "I know I am but a lowly former housekeeper, not deserving of sitting next to such a hero as you."

Bolt had not seen Frau Farfenugen since he had left Volgelplatz, and he eagerly motioned for her to sit. "How are you?" he asked. "And the Fish Man?"

"He is well, at least as well as anyone can be who is married to a lowly former housekeeper like me, which is not as well as otherwise. He is not here tonight. He is in a bowling league with a group of penguins." Bolt gasped. Bowling penguins? Had evil returned? He needed to get back to work! Save the world! "Lawn bowling," Frau Farfenugen added.

"Oh, that's fine, then."

The former housekeeper soon excused herself and joined the dancing in the middle of the clearing. Bolt watched for a while but soon found himself wandering alone through the forest. The sounds of a party, mixed with the continuous penguin buzzing in his ears from the penguin-verse, was a bit much. As he walked, he came across three penguins, a mother and father and their chick. Bolt nodded to them.

"That's him! That's him, Mommy!" squawked the chick.

"Are you the one who saved us?" asked the mother penguin, eyes wide. "Are you *the chosen one*?" Bolt wondered if this was how celebrities felt.

No, not anymore, Bolt thought back, bowing his head and continuing his stroll. He wasn't who he used to be—not a penguin, not even really human, either. He was something else. Something new.

That realization saddened Bolt. He had never wanted anything but to fit in. But it seemed like he never would, not anywhere.

"Bolt?" It was Annika. She jogged up to him and rested her hand on his shoulder. "I saw you walk away. You've been so quiet. Is everything OK?"

"I just have a lot on my mind."

"You're one with the penguin-verse, aren't you? We haven't talked about it, but I can tell." Bolt nodded and took Annika's hand. "But it's over now. The Stranger is defeated. The world's werepenguins are surrendering. Which means you'll stay with us, right? In the forest?"

Bolt shook his head. "I'm leaving in the morning."

Annika squeezed his hand. "Why? You still need a family. Everyone needs a family. You know that more than

anyone. And you can have one now. Here. As a bandit. My father wants you to stay. So does Felipe. So does everyone. I know we're not a penguin colony, but you can have a good life here. We can be like brother and sister."

"We already are." It was tempting. After all, Bolt didn't really have anywhere to go. He could talk to penguins anytime, from anywhere. Could he make his home here?

No.

He would never belong here. He would just feel more alone than he did when he was actually alone, which didn't seem to make sense but it did to Bolt. "I can't stay."

There was another reason, too. Werepenguins never aged if they lived in places with magical, always full moons like Brugaria. But in other places they aged normally. Or at least Bolt was pretty sure that was true.

Some people might do almost anything to never grow old. But to Bolt, that thought revolted him. He wanted to grow up.

"I lost Blackburn, and now I'm losing you," said Annika, stifling a sob.

"You're not losing me. We'll always be best friends, in the penguin-verse."

"It's not exactly the same thing," said Annika. "Where will you go?"

Bolt hadn't thought that far ahead. He could find a

rookery somewhere and live with penguins. But that didn't seem right either.

No, he would travel the world, searching out the remaining evil in penguins and removing it. He wouldn't be part of a family necessarily, but he would live his code and just be the best he could be.

Tears ran down Annika's face. "Will I ever see you again?"

Bolt smiled. "Of course." But in his heart, he knew he was lying to Annika once again.

Epilogue
Off the Docks

The foghorn rang. It was evening now, and the last of the animals had been loaded. The penguin caretaker and I sat on the deck as the ship readied to leave port.

"What happened next?" I asked.

"All our heroes lived full lives. Blackburn grew old with his new mole family. Annika never saw Bolt again but became the greatest bandit that ever lived. She also became famous for killing a giant bullfrog, but I don't know the whole story. And Grom? He went with Bolt, eager for a fresh start. America seemed as good as any place to go. Grom couldn't really live underground with were-moles anymore, you see, and he didn't know the forest bandits well enough to want to stay with them, either, although he was invited to. So Bolt and Grom went to a pier in Volgelplatz the very next day, where they found a ship boarding animals to take to a zoo in America."

I smiled. My standing here on a ship that was headed for a zoo seemed like a big coincidence. No, not a coincidence. Fate. Destiny had brought me to the St. Aves Zoo all those months before so that I could save the animals now.

"The captain gave Bolt and Grom passage in exchange for their working as deckhands," added the penguin caretaker.

"And so Bolt came to America."

"Actually, he didn't, at least not then. Bolt jumped off the boat in the middle of the ocean. He told Grom he would come to America eventually. But he had penguins to heal, and needed to make sure they treated one another with decency and love."

"Penguins have always seemed pretty nice to me," I said. "So he must have succeeded."

"I think so. But it's a lot of work. I have to take care of the penguins in a single zoo, and that's difficult enough. I can't imagine how hard it must be to take care of all the penguins in the world."

"And what came of Grom?"

"He talked his way into a permanent job with the zoo, taking care of the penguins. He was like, 'I'm good with

penguins,' and they were like, 'You even look like one.'"
The man winked and said no more.

It was then that I noticed the ship was heading out into the great sea. Our own voyage had begun.

"And what then?" I asked.

The man clapped me on the back. "My story has ended, my friend. Our agreement is finished. I have told you the whole of my tale."

"And I will never forget any of it, not a word, as long as I shall live," I answered. "Um, what was the name of the boy werepenguin again?"

"Bolt?"

"Right. Now I will never forget a word of it. Thank you, sir. Or should I call you *Grom*?"

He did not respond, but perhaps that was an answer in itself.

"Did Grom ever see Bolt again?"

"Once. But that's another story. And what a story it is."

"If you tell me that story, I will give you—"

"My penguins now have a home, thanks to you," he said, interrupting me. "There is nothing else you can barter with." In the background we could hear penguins squawk. "I must be with them, to calm them during the voyage. Thank you again, my friend." He bowed. "You have saved us, and for that, the penguins of the world will always be your friend."

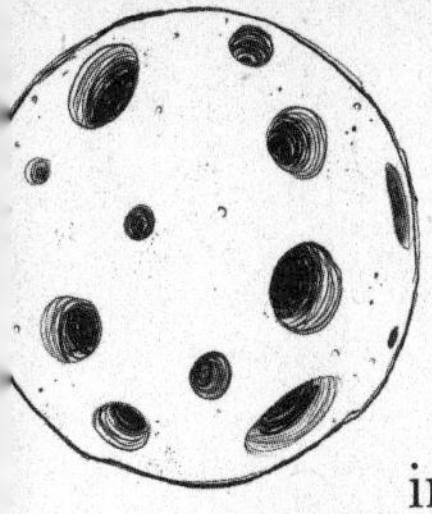

"As long as they don't expect to come over and stay for the weekend," I said with a chuckle, imagining trying to find bath towels for twelve million penguins. And where would I find all the dead fish to feed them? "Wait. One last question," I said as the man walked away from me. "Is it hard to be a werepenguin?"

"No harder than being a were-raccoon or a were-sloth, I suppose."

"Are there really such things?"

"Were-animals are everywhere. If you know where to look."

And with that, the man took his leave, and I stood there, thinking of his final words to me. I still do.

Have you ever been outside, after midnight, and seen a creature with red glowing eyes? Or just an animal that is wearing a nightgown?

If so, beware.

For when the moon is full, evil lurks in unsuspecting places, if not in penguins, then in many creatures, big and small.

Beware the penguins? Maybe not anymore.

But beware the unknown?

Always, always, always.

Acknowledgments

If you haven't written a book—and if you haven't, I highly recommend it—you might think the author writes a few things and then it gets magically printed and shows up on your doorstep or library or bookstore or even your eReader if you're into that sort of thing.

Oh, gentle reader (or the not-so-gentle reader to whom this book is dedicated), you would be as mistaken as a penguin thinking it can bowl, or at least bowl well. For books, and this book in particular, was created not just from my keyboard-weary fingers but with the assistance of a team of experts, pros, friends, supporters and zoologists (well, maybe not zoologists). They all have made me look good, unless there is a part of the book you didn't enjoy, in which case it's their fault. They failed us.

But, despite some of these people potentially messing up that one part of the book you didn't like, I'm going to thank them anyway. I sometimes get asked how I draw so well, and my reply is always "I don't" and point out that the wonderfully talented Scott Brown is responsible for the illustrations in this book and not me. That's good news for all of us, as this is an example of my drawing of a werepenguin:

Not great, huh? So, three cheers for Scott (please join me: Hip, hip hurray! Hip, hip hurray! Hip, hip hurray!... you know, I am quite aware you are not joining me in cheering, and I'm a little disappointed in you).

In addition to my lackluster drawing skills, my grammar is

not always perfect. I repeat words or use too, too, too many words or repeat words or misspell wrods and frankly, do all the sorts of things you probably do when you write. If you're in school, your teacher corrects you. If you're a published author, copy editors do all that, except they seldom star, circle, and underline things, or even draw smiley faces next to the really good parts. A shame, really. Still, I can't thank Abigail Powers and Kate Frentzel enough, although this one time will have to do.

If the book wasn't designed, you'd have words falling into the margins, pictures cropped poorly, pagination all mishandled and a book that looked like it was designed by, well, me.

For example, this sentence is upside down because no one designed it.

So, thank you to Kate Renner, who designed both the covers and everything inside them with superb skill, and right-side up.

I am also fortunate enough to work with not just one wonderful editor for this book, but two wonderful editors: the magnificent Dana Leydig and the marvelous Aneeka Kalia. If Dana got us off to a fast and successful start, Aneeka took the baton and led us to a rousing, crowd-cheering finish.

Books don't just need to be written, designed, illustrated and edited but marketed, so people know where and when they can buy them. Otherwise, books just sort of vanish into the vast netherworld of never-read things. So, if you're reading this, our publicist probably had something to do with it. Thank you to Tessa Meischeid, who has been a vital part of Team Werepenguin since the beginning.

Thank you also to Kendra Levin; to my agent, Hannah Mann; to Lauren, Emmy, and Madelyn (as always); to my friends and family, interested others, and that guy who gave me his parking space during holiday shopping season. You're the best!